Garden

of

Last Hope

Emma Shelford

*To Laura,
Back to the Otherworld...
— Emma Shelford*

This is a work of fiction. Names, characters, places, and incidents either are the product of the author's imagination or are used factitiously, and any resemblance to any persons, living or dead, business establishments, events, or locales is entirely coincidental.

GARDEN OF LAST HOPE

www.emmashelford.com

First edition: April 2016
ISBN: 978-1530439355

For Dad,
for all the bedtime stories

Chapter 1

He walked swiftly through the woods. The trees pressed close to the path, long tendrils of hanging vine softly brushing his shoulders. He swept them off unconsciously and peered behind him as if looking for someone following. His feet never broke pace.

The sound of cracking twigs stopped him abruptly. His hair glinted fiery copper in a ray of sunlight as he frantically scanned the forest around him. Distant voices began to murmur.

He leaped to a nearby tree and scrambled up using rough grooves of bark as handholds with the ease and grace of an experienced tree climber. The first branch was high in the air. He clung to it and quieted his breath to listen.

"Seriously, Crevan, I don't know why we're bothering." A voice drifted clearly up the tree, deep but with a touch of childish petulance. "You know he's just run off again on one of his *adventures*." The last word almost glistened with sarcasm.

A different voice answered the first, its tone curt.

"Father wants him close to home ever since that business at the marking ceremony." A brief silence was followed by the appearance of two men. Crevan had short copper hair to match the watcher in the tree, and he wore a resigned expression. His brother Owen trailed behind sullenly. He swung a long sword at nearby ferns in a desultory manner, his strawberry-blond hair pulled into a low ponytail. Both wore loose shirts of a fine silken fabric and long slim pants of a muddy green.

The young man in the tree held his breath in an effort to avoid detection. His eyes crinkled with contained laughter as he gazed down from his perch at his two brothers. Quietly, he stroked the bark of the tree and narrowed his eyes in concentration.

"And now you want to find him to show Father that you don't fumble every task he gives you?" Owen gave a derisive snort. "Good luck with that. You know our dear brother is too slippery to be caught, and he's the favorite. It'll take more than finding him today to win Father's approval."

"Come on, we have a lot of ground to cover." Crevan strode off through the forest, clearly eager to put distance between himself and his surly brother.

The young man in the tree waited until his eldest brother had left Owen behind. He continued to stroke the bark. Owen heaved a sigh and gave the trunk of the tree a solid whack with his sword before he turned to follow Crevan. The watcher stared intently at the ground in front of Owen's feet.

Soil stirred and a large root emerged unnoticed from the forest floor, a sinuous arc shedding dirt and needles on its ascent. It rose higher and higher until Owen unwittingly slipped his foot into the arc. The watcher stopped stroking the bark as Owen attempted another step. The root entrapped his foot perfectly and he sprawled to the ground, his entire body stretched across the dirt.

He cursed loudly, and the watcher clutched a hand to his mouth to stifle explosive laughter, eyes watering in mirth and face scrunched up with glee. Owen cursed again and dusted himself off. He stomped after Crevan, never once looking at the offending obstacle. The root sunk quietly back into the ground.

The young man waited until the stomping noises disappeared into the silence of the forest before he clambered down the tree. He chortled quietly as his feet picked out crevasses in the bark. On the ground, he leaned against the tree and grinned broadly. Then he reached into the pocket of his pants to draw out two objects.

One was a shiny copper penny, the facing side engraved with a blooming rose. On other side was the profile of a young woman with long hair and sharp features, softened by a smile.

He grinned at the coin and held it up to look at the engraving. Then he dropped it back into his pocket and focused his attention on the other object.

A golden locket lay across his palm, its surface covered with a finely wrought design of leaves and vines highlighted by the darkness of dried blood within the crack of the pattern. The warm metal shone softly in the dim light of the dense forest, a glimmer of sunlight in shadows. He pried open the locket with eager fingers. It yielded with a soft click to reveal two miniature portraits and a curl of baby-fine black hair. Carefully, he moved the lock of hair onto the tiny portrait of a dark-haired beauty with a knowing smile, to uncover a picture of a man with laughing eyes.

He walked to the other side of the tree. Almost entirely hidden in an overgrowth of ferns and moss were the remains of a stone archway. The keystone and upper arch had long since crumbled, leaving only ancient stones of the side pillars. He grinned and stared at the image of the man for a minute, then snapped the locket shut and hung it around his neck. Holding his hands aloft, he stepped forward and touched the uppermost stones of the pillars. His eyes slowly closed.

A light began to pulse in the doorway. First it outlined the stones, then it filled the emptiness between them. Ghostly shadows of the missing stones traced a clear arch above his head. Brighter and brighter the light grew. He held his position, eyes sealed tight and arms spread.

Just as the light grew to blinding proportions, he abruptly withdrew his hands. With eyes still closed against the light, he stepped through the doorway.

The light dimmed to dull daylight, and he emerged from the other side of the doorway and blinked rapidly. He stood in a tiny patch of scraggly grass surrounded by wild-looking hydrangeas and foxgloves which swayed gently under a leaden sky. The garden was enclosed on three sides by a chest-height wooden fence. Beyond lay other small garden plots in a long row, flanked by a continuous line of thin two-storey houses made of gray stone.

He turned to look behind him, eyes wide. On the blank wall of the house, a haphazard arrangement of stones in the approximate shape of a squat doorway was outlined in a faint glow that faded as he watched.

He blinked in astonishment. A slow grin spread over his features, and he threw his fist in the air.

"Yes! I did it!" He laughed wildly and turned on the spot to gaze around him with a rapturous look. On his second turn he swung toward the house and stopped short. A girl of about seventeen stood watching him warily. Her cut-off jeans were too tight and her hair was pulled into a severe ponytail, but her cautious eyes were large and pretty and her mouth fell in a full-lipped pout.

"Who're you, then?" The girl crossed her arms over her chest and shifted weight to her other leg. "What are you doing in our garden?"

The young man gave her a dazzling smile and swept into a deep bow. The girl's wariness melted with a small smile.

"Greetings, my lady." He stood upright again. Seeing his bow had not been acknowledged with a returning curtsy, he looked puzzled. Then his face brightened. He stuck his hand out in front of him stiffly, fingers outstretched. The girl raised an eyebrow, but grasped his hand and shook it briefly. The young man beamed at her.

"I'm glad to make your acquaintance." He brought her hand to his lips and kissed it with another small bow. She blushed. "Let me introduce myself. My name is Bran."

Chapter 2

Gwen Cooper surveyed the chaos of the suite before her. Light streamed in through the doorway behind her and cast her shadow over a nearby pile of boxes in the dim room. A tiny kitchen was tucked into a cubby on her left, its counters unseen under cardboard boxes and an old-fashioned birdcage. The cage's inhabitant, a yellow budgie with a fluffy white crest, chittered indignantly at her.

"Quiet, Pongo," Gwen said as she picked her way through the mess to deposit an armload of clothes beside the birdcage. "Or else I'll regret having you as a roommate."

"Here." Her friend Ellie Brown emerged from a hallway that was half-obscured by a squashy armchair salvaged from a thrift shop down the block. She tossed Gwen a brightly colored foil bag. "I found his treats. Pop one in—he should shut up."

Gwen ripped open the bag and slotted a treat through the bars. The budgie jumped to grab it from her fingers and scuttled back to his perch. He glared at Gwen with beady eyes when he bent to eat the treat. Gwen laughed.

"I don't think your new bird likes me much." She swept back her long black hair into a ponytail, a few strands of dyed blue bright in the dim light. She wore shorts in the late August heat and a low-cut tank top that did nothing to hide the green tattoo that stretched from her collarbone to her shoulder blade. Vines and leaves swirled in an intricate pattern, a constant reminder of her journey through the Otherworld. A parallel world, the Otherworld was only accessible through magical means and inhabited by a people known as the Breenan. Gwen and Ellie had stumbled into the Otherworld during a trip to England last May, along with a local boy named Aidan. Along the way, Gwen and Aidan had been forced to participate in an initiation ceremony where they had both received tattoos revealing their partial Breenan parentage.

Ellie rummaged through a cardboard box. She gasped and held up a bundle of light-blue fabric.

"Look what I found." Her round cheeks, pink with exertion, lifted in a smile. She shook out the bundle until it became a dress, a floor-length gown that would not have looked out of place in the Middle Ages.

"No!" Gwen shook her head incredulously. "You kept that? I thought it would bring back too many bad memories." Ellie had worn the blue dress during her enslavement in the Otherworld, three months before. She had been kidnapped and forced to dance to the brink of madness by Queen Isolde, Gwen's Breenan mother. Gwen, along with Aidan and a friendly Breenan prince named Bran, had saved Ellie in the nick of time. Ellie looked at the dress thoughtfully.

"I guess it does. But I spent so much time making it, it seemed a shame to get rid of it." She draped it carefully over the armchair. "Besides, it's a great costume for my medieval dance troupe."

"I can't believe you started dancing again. I thought you swore off dancing forever."

"Yeah, well, dancing is what I do." Ellie shrugged with a wry smile. "And hey, I finally got you out as well." Gwen, to Ellie's astonishment and delight, had joined Ellie in her Latin dance classes over the summer. Gwen was enjoying them far more than she had expected.

"You'll have to get Aidan to come along to class. We're always in need of more leads, and you two would make a cute dance pair." Ellie beamed at Gwen. Gwen and Aidan had grown close over their trials in the Otherworld. She had left England expecting to not see Aidan again. But when he had expressed interest in going to university, she had sent him information on schools in her hometown of Vancouver, Canada, and had been elated when he had decided to move there.

Now, however, she felt a twisting, gnawing sensation in her stomach whenever Ellie mentioned Aidan—which was often. She didn't understand why, but she felt anxious and grumpy when she thought about Aidan moving halfway across the world to be with her.

Ellie must have noticed her silence, because she said, "What's up? Aren't you excited he's coming out?"

"Yeah, of course," Gwen said automatically, hiding her face by putting away cans from her box on a shelf behind her. She turned back to see Ellie staring at her with a half-exasperated, half-sympathetic look on her face, hands on her hips.

"Spill. What's eating you?"

"Nothing," Gwen said. Ellie raised an eyebrow in

disbelief. Gwen sighed and rubbed her eyes. "It—it's just that—" She paused, trying to formulate her confused thoughts into something articulate. "I mean, he's moving so far—and we've only known each other a few weeks." She swallowed. "What if it doesn't work out?"

Ellie waded across the box-filled room. She gave Gwen a hug and then stood back, hands on Gwen's arms.

"It's going to be great. I could see how well you guys fit together. You'll see." She gave Gwen an encouraging smile and squeezed her arms. "Now stop worrying so much."

Gwen watched Ellie pick her way back to the hallway. She did not feel reassured, and her teeth gnawed at her bottom lip. A copper ring, given to her by Bran so he could track her location, was warm on her thumb. She fidgeted with it, lost in her thoughts.

***

Bran sauntered down the busy road. Occasionally, he stepped off the sidewalk and into traffic. Cars honked and swerved to avoid him and he waved back, all smiles.

"Where are you off to, fancy boy?"

A trio of girls were perched on a short stone wall in front of a boarded-up house. Bran whirled around. He grinned when he saw them and moved nimbly to their side.

"Greetings, ladies."

"Oh, we're ladies now, are we?" The speaker, a girl with heavy eyeliner and artfully ripped stockings under a black miniskirt, laughed and tossed her dyed black hair out of her face. "That's a first."

"And what else would I call you? I'm nothing if not

truthful." Bran reached down to pluck a blade of grass that grew valiantly in a crack at the base of the wall. He held it behind his back and twisted his fingers. Unseen by the girls, the blade of grass wriggled and expanded, pushing upward, sprouting thorns, budding a black blossom. Bran frowned slightly when the magic sputtered briefly, but after a moment he pulled out his creation.

"For you, lady of the shadows. A midnight rose to complement your dark beauty."

The girl stared at the blossom. Her cheeks colored slightly.

"Are you taking the mickey?"

Bran looked puzzled.

"Would you like me to? I'm not sure where this 'mickey' is."

One of the other girls laughed.

"Go on, take the flower. He's mad, but he's got class. You've done worse."

The first girl hesitantly took the rose.

"Thanks, I suppose. Why the costume?"

"These clothes don't belong here, do they?" Bran looked down at his slim green pants in consideration. "Where can I find better?"

"There's shops down the road. Go on, find something normal. Perhaps then you'll be fit to be seen."

Bran bowed with a flourish.

"Farewell, my lady. May the stars dwell in your midnight tresses."

The girls laughed, but the first girl patted her hair self-consciously. Bran winked at her and turned on his heel in the direction of the shops.

***

"Would you bring the pepper while you're up?" Aidan's mother, Deirdre, said.

Aidan grabbed a pepper shaker from a cupboard in the little kitchen. His vivid copper hair caught the late-afternoon light when he passed by a nearby window to squeeze into an alcove with a small table. There was just enough room left over for two wooden chairs. Deirdre sat in one, a steaming casserole dish in the center of the table before her. Her eyes were tired and her dark hair liberally streaked with gray, but she smiled when Aidan flopped into his chair.

"Thanks, love." She took the proffered pepper shaker and started to dish out the casserole. "Did you find that suitcase you were looking for upstairs?"

"Yeah, thanks. I put it in the hall. It's a great big one. Are you sure you don't want it?" Aidan took a bite of food and then fanned his mouth, blowing out. "Hot!"

Deirdre tutted with a smile. Then she said, "No, it's fine. I have that other small suitcase. You're welcome to carry around that beast of a bag."

"Fanks," Aidan said, his mouth full. He swallowed. "Mum, I'll miss your shepherd's pie."

Deirdre looked down at her plate.

"Are you sure you want to do this?" she said. Aidan sighed and put down his fork. "What will you do with a degree in music? What sort of jobs are out there?"

"Mum, we've been through this." They looked at each other across the table. Aidan's jaw was set and Deirdre's lips were tight. "Music is the one thing I'm really good at. I know you don't believe in me, but I do."

"Oh love, it's not that. I know you're talented. But it's such an unreliable career. Why don't you enroll in a more practical course? Something you can get a job in when you're finished? You remember Mary, her husband is looking for an apprentice—"

Aidan heaved an exasperated sigh.

"Mum, no. We've been through this. I want to do this." He resolutely picked up his fork and dug into his food with deliberate motions. Deirdre worried her lip as she looked at her son, who avoided her gaze.

"If you really want to pursue your music, I'm sure there are good schools in Britain. Why Canada?"

Aidan kept his gaze averted from his mother's, and looked out the window into the busy street beyond.

"I told you, I want to live somewhere new. I've hardly ever traveled, except for that trip to France with you when I was ten. I want to explore and see new things."

"Why don't you save up and take a vacation sometime? You don't have to move."

Aidan took another bite of his food. When he had swallowed, he looked at her and said, "Look, Mum. Can we drop this? I won't change my mind, and you won't approve. Can we just enjoy our meal?"

Deirdre looked at Aidan for a moment, and nodded slowly. Aidan turned his focus back to his plate. Deirdre picked up her fork and toyed with her casserole for a minute.

"I spoke to Mary at work today," she said with an attempt at a light, conversational tone. "She said that she was visiting her cousin who lives east of Thetford. It's on their local news—there's a young man who's wandering about town. He's acting very oddly, and they wonder if

16

he's a patient from the care facility up the way. He's quite sane at first glance, but then the questions he asks, and the strange things he does," she paused for a sip of water. "Well, everyone's a bit concerned."

"What sort of things?" Aidan raised his eyebrow.

"Oh, trying to take things from the shop by trading his shirt, almost getting run over on the motorway. No one's called the police yet, mainly because he tends to approach pretty girls and flatter them with lovely little speeches."

"Ha. What a nutter." Aidan sprinkled pepper on the remainder of his casserole.

"Mary had a glimpse of him as he was leaving town. She was asking questions about you after she told me the story. Apparently the young man looks remarkably like you. I set her straight at once, of course. She should know better, but the resemblance is supposedly very strong."

"What? She thought I was running around stopping cars and ripping off my shirt for the girls?" Aidan laughed incredulously. "Honestly, she's known me forever. That's a bit rich."

"Well, quite. I told her I didn't appreciate the insinuations." Deirdre cut a green bean and speared it with her fork. "Anyhow, keep your eyes open for your doppelganger. He was headed in this direction, last Mary heard."

Aidan looked at her curiously.

"I wonder why…" Confusion was followed by a flash understanding. Deirdre, focused on her food, didn't notice Aidan's shifting expression. He sat stunned for a minute, then scraped back his chair.

"Sorry Mum, I just realized I've got to go."

"But you haven't finished your dinner." She looked up,

concern and disappointment on her face.

"I know, I'm really, really sorry. Look, I'll come by tomorrow, I promise." He kissed her on the forehead and snatched up his plate on the way to the kitchen, then ran out the door. Deirdre sat in stunned silence as the door slammed shut.

***

Bran stood at an intersection of two highways, surrounded by farmland. He stared down one road, then the other, puzzled, until he pulled the tracker penny from his pocket and rubbed it with a thumb. It glowed briefly, and he nodded in satisfaction. A cow mooed in a nearby field and Bran chuckled with delight.

He continued his slow progress down the road, the midday sun warm on his head. Cars zoomed by, filled with curious passengers who eyed the walking Bran doubtfully. He took no notice, but focused on the inhabitant of the next paddock, a piebald horse who grazed the dry grass with single-minded purpose.

"Perfect," Bran said, and leaped the dividing ditch to land in the paddock. The horse paid him no mind until Bran softly stroked the animal's side then vaulted onto its back. Astonished, the horse whipped its head around, but calmed after a few soft words from Bran. A gentle dig to the horse's side brought the animal to a walk, then a trot.

The ditch approached. Bran eyed the distance and kicked his heels. The horse broke into a reluctant canter. Closer and closer the ditch grew. The horse tossed its head nervously, but Bran laid a gentle hand on its mane.

They flew over the ditch toward the highway, and

Bran's expression of concentration gave way to jubilation. The horse must have felt the joy of its freedom, because it continued to canter down the shoulder of the highway. Drivers gawked at the copper-haired figure astride the piebald horse as the pair passed under a sign that read *Amberlaine, 5 mi.*

***

Aidan slowed to a walk, panting. The main street of Amberlaine was quiet in the heavy air of the summer evening. He stopped and looked around as if searching, but the exasperated resignation on his face spoke to the futility of his hunt. He leaned against a lamppost to stare at the blank window of a closed shop, deep in thought.

Shaking his head as if to clear it, he looked at his watch and crossed the street to a nearby corner store. A bell tinkled as he pushed the door open.

Two chatting girls beside a magazine rack looked around listlessly as the door shut. They spied Aidan and immediately gasped and elbowed each other.

Aidan stopped in his tracks and stared at them in bewilderment. A second later, the girls' faces flushed pink with embarrassment, and one giggled nervously.

"What's going on?" Aidan asked the giggling girl. She looked at her friend and they both laughed.

"Sorry, we thought you were someone else." Her friend elbowed her again and they smirked at each other.

"Who did you think I was?" he asked carefully.

"Oh, just this boy. He was in here a minute ago. He was very—nice," she added lamely as her friend giggled again. Aidan let out a very quiet sigh.

"Did his name happen to be Bran, by any chance?"

Both girls stared at him, wide-eyed.

"Yeah. Do you know him?"

Aidan sighed again, a little louder this time.

"He's—he's my cousin. Do you know which way he went? I'm trying to find him."

"Yeah—you're Aidan, right? I used to see you at school, before you graduated." She looked him up and down appraisingly. "So, Bran's your cousin? Where've you been hiding him all these years?"

Aidan ignored her comment.

"Which way did he go? I really need to find him."

"He headed out toward the old mill. Try that way." The girl pointed out the door.

"Thanks."

The girl called out to his retreating back, "Say hello to him for me!" Aidan rolled his eyes as the door slammed behind him to the sound of laughter.

He paced down the road with purposeful strides. He glanced from side to side as he walked, and frowned in disappointment at every person who was not Bran. The road quieted and the sun dropped lower in the sky and still he searched, his face growing more and more despondent.

A hand clapped down on his shoulder and he whirled around. A beaming Bran stood before him, sharp features and copper hair a close match to Aidan's own. He was dressed in baggy blue jeans and an oversized t-shirt depicting a grinning shark.

"Hello." Bran's face was smug. "I finally found you."

"Bran." Aidan gaped at him. "What the hell are you doing here?" He visibly collected himself and gave Bran a small shove. "You stole the locket from Gwen, you prat.

We were supposed to destroy it."

"I know! What a waste that would have been. Lucky I saved it." Bran turned on the spot, arms spread. "And now I'm actually in the human world! It's amazing here. Those wild metal wagons, and the food, and the clothes," he indicated his own. "It's brilliant."

Aidan looked flabbergasted.

"How long have you been wandering about? And how did you get those clothes? You can't have any money…" Bran continued to beam at him, unperturbed. "You stole them, didn't you?"

"I tried to trade my favorite dagger, but the girl at the clothing room started to scream," Bran said cheerfully. "So I left. If she doesn't know a good trade when she sees one, well."

Aidan passed a hand over his eyes.

"All right, just—let's go back to my place and figure out what to do." He turned Bran in the right direction with a firm hand on his shoulder.

A truck rolled by, engine rumbling in the quiet summer evening. Its sides advertised a local business. Bran jumped when the truck passed them with a whoosh.

"Wow! That was a big one." Bran laughed at himself, and Aidan's mouth twitched. Bran peered after the departing truck and said, "Oh, I wanted to ask you. What do the squiggles on the truck mean? I've been seeing them all over the place."

"You mean the writing? It says 'Smith Contracting.' You know, the name of the bloke who owns the lorry."

Comprehension flooded Bran's face. "That makes so much more sense. Can you really read the squiggles?" Aidan nodded. "I forgot you don't have the usual plant inscriptions. It also explains some of the really odd messages in people's gardens."

"What do you mean?"

Bran pointed to a stone wall in front of a two-storey brick house. Wisteria and roses twisted together in an attractive mass of vines and flowers.

"Like that one. It says, 'All meat shoe valley running tree lord.'"

Aidan let out an explosive laugh.

"You must have been confused." He looked around, then pointed to the neighboring garden where a neat row of petunias and alyssum lined the walk. "What does that one say?"

"Mmm—piglet pennant piglet pennant pignant pellant..." Bran tripped over his words as he spoke faster and faster, and both he and Aidan cackled.

Aidan finally pulled himself together.

"Come on, let's get back to my flat."

"Why? The night is just starting! What do you do for fun in your world?"

"We should probably lie low. The police might be looking for you."

Bran, who clearly wasn't listening, grabbed Aidan's sleeve and pointed down the road. Light spilled out from an open doorway, and strains of a fiddle and guitar floated on the air.

"Let's go there. It's too early to go to your home."

Aidan shifted his weight from foot to foot. He glanced up the dark road in the direction of his flat, then toward the welcoming busyness of the pub. Bran pushed him toward the open door and Aidan didn't resist.

"Come on! Is it so exciting at your house? Do you have

a feast to get to?"

Aidan laughed.

"Hardly. It's only me."

"Well! We'll have some music, chat with the humans, eat some human food." Bran licked his lips. "Do you have anything to trade with?"

Aidan smiled, a genuine one that spread across his face.

"I can cover it. We do things differently here."

"Oh, I know." Bran smiled blissfully. "It's superb."

"By the way, you said you were looking for me. How did you know where to go?"

Bran dug into the pocket of his jeans in response. He triumphantly held up a copper penny. Aidan glanced at it, one eyebrow raised.

"It's the penny you made! The tracking one I showed you how to make in the forest, months ago. It can work both ways if you know what you're doing. Since you made it with a bit of your own hair it has a connection to you." Bran let a rare frown crease his brow. "I tried to find Gwen first using the tracker ring I gave her, but the signal was too weak, like she was far away."

Aidan let out a mirthless laugh.

"That's because she is. She's in Canada." Noticing Bran's confusion, he tried to clarify. "North America? Across the Atlantic Ocean? A long way west?"

"Is there land beyond the sea?" Bran's eyes popped with astonishment.

"Of course. Gwen's far away, and you're certainly not walking there."

"That's too bad." Bran gave a little sigh and grinned at Aidan. "It'd be fun if she were here too."

***

Gwen jumped when her pocket vibrated. She slid out her phone.

"I just got a text from Aidan," she said to Ellie.

"What'd he say?" Ellie adjusted her backpack onto one shoulder as they walked on the sidewalk down a busy boulevard lined with tall, graceful trees.

"Hold on a sec." Gwen tapped her phone. Aidan's message appeared on the screen.

I have a visitor. Name starts with B and ends in ran. Now what?

Gwen let out a gasp of laughter in disbelief.

"What?" Ellie asked impatiently.

"Bran's come into our world. Remember how he stole my mother's locket from me, the one that makes portals between the worlds? I guess he used it to make a portal. Now he's found Aidan." Gwen's shock was mixed with another emotion she had a hard time placing—was it jealousy? She wanted to see Bran, to interact with a part of the Breenan world. The feelings surprised her. Her time spent in the Otherworld had been anything but fun. They had hiked through endless forest, been chased by wild animals, and been involved in a precarious case of mistaken identities. At the end Gwen had even had to face her mother who had left her as a baby. Why did she feel a strange longing to be a part of that world once more? It didn't make sense.

Ellie was bug-eyed.

"Oh wow. So, now what?"

Gwen shook her head.

"I have no idea. Aidan will have to convince him to go

24

back, I suppose. And hopefully get the locket off him in the process. There's nothing I can do from over here." She laughed incredulously. "Poor Aidan. Bran won't be easy to convince."

"Well, check your phone and keep me updated. Curious minds want to know."

Gwen's phone beeped again. Curious, she checked the screen.

"Aidan wants to chat. Here, stop for a sec." She held up the phone so Ellie could see as well. Aidan's face appeared on the screen, accompanied by loud chatter in the background.

"Hi, Gwen." He looked sheepish. "Hope we're not bothering you. Bran wanted to say hello."

The screen blurred with motion before it stopped on a familiar face.

"Hi, Gwen, Ellie!" Bran beamed at them. "The magic in your world is amazing. I never want to leave."

"Bran! I can't believe you came here. What are you two doing?"

"Aidan is showing me how humans spend their evenings." He took a gulp of beer and smacked his lips in appreciation.

"Not so loud! What if someone hears you talking about 'humans' like you're not one?"

"Oh, Gwen. Always worrying. I wish you were here. I tried to find you, but Aidan says you're over the ocean."

"Shall we go outside?" Aidan's disembodied voice emanated from the phone. "It's hard to hear."

The screen blurred, chattering voices came and went, and footsteps thumped. Ellie elbowed Gwen.

"Maybe we should go visit England again. I forgot how

cute Bran is."

Finally, the phone went quiet and stabilized.

"You know," Bran said in an uncharacteristically thoughtful manner. "I wonder…"

"Uh oh," Gwen said. "I don't like the sound of that. What are you up to?"

"Give me a moment." His eyes narrowed in concentration.

"What are you doing?" said Aidan's voice. Bran waved him away.

A jolt in Gwen's abdomen made her gasp. Not in her stomach, precisely—if she had had to describe it she would have said her center had shifted an inch to the left and back again. She looked at her hands quickly, expecting to see fire, but smooth skin and short fingernails greeted her eyes, unadorned by the flames she had sometimes seen before she could control her magic.

"Quick, check me over," she said to Ellie. "Did I do any magic just now? Does anything look out of the ordinary?"

"No, you look fine. What's up?"

"I felt really strange for a moment." Gwen had her magic under control these days—what was going on? Why had her core reacted so strongly to nothing at all? She wasn't feeling any particularly strong emotions that might trigger her magic. A second jolt hit her and she inhaled swiftly.

"There it is again. I don't understand—"

She looked into Ellie's wary face, and everything went dark.

Chapter 3

One moment, everything was darkness and confusion around Gwen. The next, she was suspended in a bright, featureless space, with nothing supporting her. She had a momentary feeling of weightlessness, and then collapsed onto solid ground where she hit her bottom hard against stone. Her eyes wouldn't focus properly. She sat still, trying to reconcile her body to her new surroundings, feeling very strange.

"Gwen!" a strangled voice croaked close by. There was a scrambling and a blurry face swam in her vision. She blinked in confusion, too disoriented to be nervous or jumpy.

"Ellie?" she murmured. "Where are you?"

Her eyes cleared and she recognized the pale, wide-eyed face in front of her.

"Aidan?" She stared at him for a minute, her foggy brain whirling. How was this possible? Had she been hit by a passing car, and was now unconscious? "Am I dreaming?" She looked around. The setting sun cast shadows of houses on a narrow lane lined with cobblestones.

"Uh—" Aidan sat back on his heels. "No, you're not asleep. You're in Britain."

Gwen looked at him, uncomprehending.

"That's not possible," she said slowly, her voice thick and difficult to push out. She cleared her throat. "I was in Vancouver a minute ago."

"Yeah, about that…" Aidan glanced behind Gwen.

Gwen carefully turned to look behind her. Sprawled on the ground as if he had fallen where he stood lay Bran, his features calm and unruffled. She stared for a moment, and glanced down at her hand where Bran's ring cooled on her thumb. Where the ring touched her skin, red burn marks were forming.

"I think he tried to summon you from Canada with the ring. We were talking before, and he said it was theoretically possible, but that he'd never tried it. He collapsed and you appeared out of nowhere." Aidan ran his hands through his hair, making it stand on end.

Gwen got to her hands and knees with deliberate care. Her stomach started to turn and grumble. She tried to ignore it as she shuffled over to Bran.

"Is he okay?" She put her fingers on his neck to check for a pulse. Bran's heartbeat throbbed under her fingers. She could hear his breathing, deep and even. She shook his shoulders gently, then more forcefully. Bran's head flopped back and forth, but his expression remained serene and his breathing unchanged. She sat back on her feet and looked at Aidan.

"I think he's just asleep."

Aidan glanced around. No one stood in the lane, so he bent down and heaved Bran onto his shoulders in a

28

fireman's carry, staggering under the weight.

"It's not far," he said, his breath coming in short gusts. "Can you walk? Let's go to my flat."

Gwen wobbled to her feet and followed Aidan's weaving footsteps. She felt disoriented, and her surroundings appeared remote, unreal. Her feet hardly seemed attached to her body as they stepped one after the other down the lane.

Aidan was panting by the time they arrived at a two-storey brick house on the corner. Gwen gripped the handrail tightly as she navigated a set of rickety stairs inside the main door. Aidan jiggled the doorknob of the first door on their left, then kicked it open.

"The lock doesn't work anymore. Sticky."

Gwen entered the small apartment, half-open boxes scattered haphazardly on the floor. A single lamp kept the darkness beyond the window at bay.

Her stomach gave a nasty flop, and she was suddenly sure she was going to be sick. She must have turned green, because Aidan looked at her warily. "Where's your bathroom?" she forced out.

He pointed to a door across from her and she stumbled to her feet. She reached the toilet just in time to deposit her breakfast there. She sat shaking on the floor to let her stomach slowly calm. What had happened? How had she been transported halfway around the world? And what was she going to do now?

When she came out, Aidan was waiting for her with a mug of water. She sank onto the couch gratefully. Aidan pulled a box over and perched nearby, searching her face with a worried expression. She sighed.

"So, Bran brought me across the world and helpfully

fell unconscious so he can't undo it. Now I'm stuck in England with no plane ticket home, and—oh no, no passport. How am I going to get home?" She looked at Aidan, panic filling her mind. "And Ellie—she must be worried out of her mind." She pulled her phone out of her pocket, and saw with dismay that she had no signal. "Dammit, my phone doesn't work here."

Aidan dug into his own pocket.

"Here, use mine."

Gwen quickly dialed Ellie's number. Ellie picked up halfway through the first ring.

"Hello?"

"Ellie? It's Gwen."

"Gwen? Thank goodness! Where did you go? One second we were talking, and the next you blipped out of existence!"

"I know. Bran pulled me to England using magic."

"What? You mean you're in England right now? No way!"

"Way. Just when I thought I'd figured out this magic thing, something else bites me in the butt."

"What are you going to do?"

Gwen sighed.

"I don't know yet. I'll call my dad in a bit and figure it out. I'll get him to let you know what's happening." Gwen paused, then said, "Sorry about missing dance class tonight."

"Yeah, you'd better be sorry." Ellie gave a tiny laugh which didn't hide the worry in her voice. "Call your dad soon, okay? And be careful."

"Okay. I'll see you soon."

"You too."

She leaned back into the couch, her worries temporarily alleviated by hearing Ellie's voice. Gwen and Aidan were quiet for a moment. Gwen let her head rest against the couch.

"It's really good to see you." Aidan's voice broke the silence. Gwen turned her head to look at him. His expressive face was equal parts hopeful, nervous, and happy. Her heart squeezed a little. She hadn't realized how much she had missed him. They'd talked at odd hours, the delay in the video both funny and frustrating, and they'd texted back and forth, but it was different seeing him in front of her—solid and reassuring and so real. She felt her cheeks lift as her smile grew wider and wider.

"I missed you too."

He leaned forward to tentatively brush her hair back from her face, letting his hand linger on her cheek. She brought her arms up and wrapped them around him in a hug which he quickly reciprocated. Her face nestled into the crook of his neck where she breathed in his warmth and relaxed into him. She was enjoying the sensation so much that she was shocked into cold wakefulness when a dart of anxiety pierced through the euphoria.

She pulled back, the good feelings wormed through with anxiousness. Was it right to lead him on, to let him put all his faith in their blossoming relationship? Dread and guilt weighed her down at the thought of him moving all the way to Vancouver to be with her.

Aidan seemed to sense none of this as he smiled into her eyes. She tried to smile back convincingly. To cover her confusion she glanced at Bran, and remembered how she had arrived.

"What are we going to do with him?"

Aidan tightened his lips as he looked at Bran's unconscious form. He frowned.

"Wait. Did he move?"

Gwen dropped to her knees and scuttled over to Bran on the floor. Bran was unmistakably twitching. His face contorted with spasms and his limbs shook.

"Oh no, oh no," Gwen said frantically as she put a hand on Bran's shoulder to stop the twitching, without effect. "What's happening to him?"

"Should I call an ambulance?" Aidan's face was white. He reached for his phone on the table. Gwen thought quickly.

"I don't know—what if it's some sort of Breenan sickness? Can the doctors even do anything?"

"We can't let him die on us."

They stared at Bran's spasming form, paralyzed with indecision. Before Gwen could reach any conclusions, Bran's eyes flew open.

"Bran!" Gwen said. "Are you okay?"

Bran breathed heavily for a moment and stared at the ceiling. His face was white with an unusually serious expression. Eventually, he turned his head to focus on Gwen.

"Hi, Gwen." He tried for a smile, but it was strained and only a ghost of his usual flippant grin. "The spell worked."

"Yes, it did, you meddling Breenan." Gwen squeezed his shoulder lightly. "How are you feeling?"

Bran closed his eyes as if the effort of keeping them open was too much.

"I've been better." His face twisted and his chest shook with unreleased coughs. He struggled to sit and Aidan

32

swooped down to prop up Bran's torso. Bran finally opened his mouth. Instead of a barking cough, sparks flew out from between Bran's lips. Flashes of blue and green shot out as far as Bran's knees before they sizzled into nothing. When the fit was over, Bran leaned back into Gwen's and Aidan's arms.

Gwen looked at Aidan. He was as pale as Bran.

"Okay, that was weird," she said shakily.

"I suppose calling the ambulance isn't the brightest idea."

"Bran, do you know what's wrong? How can we help?"

"I think I did too much magic."

"You don't say," Aidan said under his breath.

"It doesn't happen very often, back in my world. Our training—they warn us about it. It's not easy to overextend yourself, so it's not usually a problem." Bran gave a weak smile. "What can I say? I'm an extraordinary person." His body shook and sparks flew out of his mouth. Gwen flinched. Bran leaned back again. "It's not good. I need to get back to my father. He might be able to heal me."

"Might?" Gwen said. "What do you mean, might?"

"I haven't heard of anyone who's actually recovered from overuse of magic. It interferes with your core, and everything in your body is connected to your core. Your body starts going out of control, until…"

"Until what?" Gwen said, her jaw clenched unpleasantly in anticipation of his answer.

"Like I said, I haven't heard of anyone recovering." Bran closed his eyes and rested his head on Gwen's shoulder. "But I'm sure someone somewhere has. And if anyone can heal me, my father can. He has a lot of power."

Gwen sighed.

"Oh, Bran. You couldn't have let the locket be." She looked at Aidan. He shrugged in resignation.

"I suppose we have to take him back to the Otherworld. To his father. Maybe he'll know what to do."

Gwen's heart leaped unexpectedly. Back to the Otherworld—fear filled her, but a thread of something else wove through the fear. Could it be excitement?

"Okay," Gwen said, hiding her conflicting feelings. "I guess we're going back."

***

"Ugh, this bag is about to burst like a piñata." Aidan hoisted his backpack more securely onto his shoulders. They had left Bran tucked up in Aidan's bed in order to stock up on food and supplies for their journey to the Otherworld, or as much "stocking up" as could be done at the local corner store. Gwen thought nervously of their packets of chips and day-old buns, and felt woefully underprepared for the perils of the Otherworld. She pulled the oversized raincoat she'd borrowed from Aidan more closely to herself over her tank top and shorts, wondering how she could find some Breenan-style clothes once they passed through a portal.

"You're sure your mum won't mind us borrowing her backpack and sleeping bags?" Gwen bit her lip as she thought of meeting Aidan's mother for the first time. Aidan hadn't said much about her, beyond her disapproval of his musical aspirations. What was she like? What would she think of Gwen?

"Yeah, it'll be fine. But, I wanted to remind you—I haven't told her about what happened in May. About the

Otherworld, my father, or anything."

"Why not?" Gwen was astounded. She had poured out the whole story to her father as soon as she had arrived home.

"She's not interested in that part of me," Aidan said dismissively. "She's always told me to hide my magic, and never wanted to hear about it. So it's better if she doesn't know." He kept his eyes straight ahead. Gwen wondered what it would have been like to grow up without her father's support of her strangeness. She decided it would be incredibly lonely. Her hand slipped into Aidan's, fingers interlocking. He glanced down, startled, then grinned shyly at her.

They walked that way for a minute, Aidan's hand warm in hers and the evening air cool against her bare legs. Gwen felt strangely calm and happy, despite her niggling undefined anxieties about Aidan, her worries about getting home again, and her fears about their future path. Aidan cleared his throat.

"Ah—there's something else I haven't told her." He snuck a glance at Gwen and quickly looked away. Gwen raised her eyebrows.

"What else is there to tell?" Surely their journey to the Otherworld was secret enough.

"I haven't told her about you," he said in a rush.

Gwen felt her stomach flop.

"What?" She dropped his hand immediately and he let it fall. "You mean I'm going to turn up on her doorstep without any warning?" She let out a breath in disbelief. "Why didn't you tell her?"

They stopped in the middle of the sidewalk. Gwen felt her hands rise to sit on her hips. It was clichéd but she was too annoyed to change her position. Aidan stuck his hands in his pockets defensively.

"I—I just…" he said to the ground, then squared his shoulders and looked into Gwen's eyes. "I didn't want her to think that I was going to university and Vancouver only for you."

"Well, you are coming to Vancouver for me."

"Well, yes, but the music." His breath whooshed out. "That's my decision, that's what I want to do, and I was afraid she'd—I don't know, blame you for making me choose an impractical career." He hunched his shoulders and looked at the ground again. "I was going to tell her eventually. Once I'd moved."

Gwen looked at his miserable form and sighed. It was hard to stay angry at him when she heard why he'd done it. She hoped she wasn't making a mistake dragging him to Canada.

"Come on, then. Let's get this over with." She tucked her arm through his and they started to walk again. Aidan continued to sneak nervous peeks at her face.

Finally, he said, "We're here, at the great estate of Amberlaine. I call it Mum's Manor." They stopped in front of a tiny cottage, steps from the main road. The cottage's miniscule front garden put on a valiant show of flowers and foliage despite limpness from lack of watering and seedpods in need of deadheading. Checkered curtains covered the windows against the fading daylight.

Aidan knocked briefly and pushed open the door.

"Mum?" he said, poking his head through the gap.

"Aidan? You're back!" a voice called from another room. Gwen could hear the scraping of a chair and soft footfalls. She tensed and tried to compose her face into a pleasant, upstanding-citizen expression. She felt unequal to the task, and pulled Aidan's raincoat higher up her neck to cover her tattoo. There was little she could do about the blue stripe in her hair, and she nervously patted it smooth.

"I brought someone with me," Aidan said. His mother padded through an entryway at the end of the corridor, her smile bright at the sight of Aidan. Gwen could immediately see their resemblance in her smile and in the shape of her eyes, but there the similarities ended. Aidan's mother had chestnut-brown hair liberally salted with gray, and her features were soft and rounded. Age and worry had taken their toll, but Gwen could see the pretty, apple-cheeked young woman she must have been when Declan had met her.

His mother's smile turned quizzical at Aidan's words and her gaze fell upon Gwen. Her eyes widened. Gwen tried for a friendly smile.

"Hello. I'm Gwen." She stepped forward and stuck out her hand. "It's nice to meet you."

Aidan's mother blinked a few times, then slowly shook Gwen's outstretched hand. "Hello, Gwen. I'm Aidan's mother, Deirdre."

"Gwen's in town for a few days and I thought I'd show her around the countryside a bit, can we borrow your rucksack and sleeping bag for a few days, are they in the shed still?" Aidan rushed his words out one after the other.

Deirdre looked flustered at this barrage of words.

"Ye—yes, they're in the shed. Wait," as Aidan started to move past her. "Just a minute. You're leaving soon. You have to finish packing up your flat."

"It's only for a few days. I'm not leaving for another two weeks. There's lots of time."

"I had hoped to see you more before you left." Deirdre's lips tightened and Gwen felt a stab of pity.

Aidan must have sensed his mother's distress, because he swooped down and planted a kiss on her cheek. "Only a few days, I promise, Mum. Then I'll come visit you loads before my flight." He moved down the corridor, calling, "I'll only be a minute, Gwen!"

Gwen felt an irrational panic at being left alone with Deirdre. She cast around for something to say, anything, but Deirdre beat her to it.

"So, Gwen, judging from your accent, I suppose you're from North America. Judging from where Aidan is moving to at the end of the month, I suppose you're from Vancouver."

Gwen swallowed, noting the coolness in Deirdre's voice.

"Yes, that's right." She wondered what to say, and decided on the truth. "I was on an exchange program here with my university in the spring. That's when I met Aidan."

"I see." Deirdre looked at Gwen, her lips tight and her gaze considering. "And now you're back, for a visit?" She left Gwen a pause in which Gwen nodded mutely, feeling flustered. "It's a long way from Vancouver."

Deirdre suddenly looked out the door, as if realizing the import of her words. Gwen bit her lip, feeling wretched. Deirdre's obvious distress at her son's imminent departure was one more worry to add to her anxieties over Aidan's move. Now, more than ever, Gwen fervently hoped that she and Aidan had made a good decision. Was there any way to make this right?

"Deirdre," she said, feeling awkward at the use of her

name. "I know meeting me is a bit of a shock for you. Honestly, I didn't know that you didn't know about me—but that's beside the point." She took a deep breath as Deirdre looked at her again. "I know you must be worried about Aidan, moving to another country, and now you're meeting some girl you don't know. I know that he and I haven't known each other for very long, but..." Gwen gave a tiny sigh, frustrated that she couldn't tell Deirdre about their trials in the Otherworld. "I know he's going to be amazing in the music program—he's so talented, and it really is his dream—anyway, I guess what I'm trying to say is, I'm sorry it's so far away. I really don't want to be the cause of separating you two."

She found herself wringing her hands and shoved them in her pockets to keep them occupied. Deirdre was still, watching Gwen's face as she continued.

"I never knew my mother, growing up. I used to long for her, until I physically ached. I just—I don't want this move to come between you two, that's all." She bent over and rustled in the full backpack that Aidan had dropped by the door with the careless comfort of home. She extracted a pen and the corner store receipt and scribbled her name, phone number, address, and email.

"I know it's not much, but here's how you can get a hold of me. Please—if you need anything, ask. I don't want you to feel out of touch."

Gwen offered the receipt to Deirdre. Deirdre looked down at the little scrap of paper without moving for a moment. Gwen wondered if her overture had not been taken well. Finally, Deirdre reached forward to take the paper, and Gwen saw with shock that her eyes were full of tears.

"Thank you, Gwen." Deirdre hesitated, then enveloped Gwen in a soft embrace. Gwen was stiff with surprise for a moment, but then returned the hug with gratitude.

Aidan clomped into the corridor, two sleeping bags under one arm and a backpack hanging off the other shoulder. His mouth dropped open.

"Uh—hello?"

Gwen and Deirdre parted. Deirdre briskly wiped her eyes and tucked the receipt into her pocket.

"You found them, then," she said, her competent-mother voice back on.

"Yeah," Aidan said, looking between Gwen and his mother, his expression wary.

"Look, why don't you say bye to your mum and I'll wait outside," Gwen said to Aidan. "Can I borrow your phone?"

"All right," he said, handing her his cell phone.

"Thanks for the loaners. It was really great to meet you," Gwen said to Deirdre.

Deirdre nodded and smiled, sadly but with warmth. "You too, Gwen. Take care."

Gwen closed the door behind her with a click and breathed in the evening air deeply. She felt relieved that Deirdre had taken her little speech well, but her anxieties about Aidan's move were only heightened, and now the consequences had a face and a name.

Talking to Deirdre had reminded her of her father, puttering around in his artist's studio and expecting a visit from her this afternoon. She dialed his number.

"Hi, Dad," she responded when he answered the ring.

"Hi, sweets. How's your day going?"

"I can't talk long. Ellie knows the whole story, so you

should give her a call after. But the short story is, I've been magically whisked away to England, and now I have to go to the Otherworld to take a very sick Bran back to his family."

There was silence on the other end of the line.

"Dad? Are you still there?"

A whoosh of released breath answered her.

"Are you sure that's wise?" His voice was restrained and cautious. She smiled wryly.

"Not really, but Aidan and I are the only ones who can help. Bran's really sick from his spell. He helped us out when we were stuck in his world, so now it's our turn."

"Is Aidan going with you? Good." Her father sounded a little more confident. "Still, I don't like the thought of you traipsing off to a parallel universe again. Are you sure it's necessary? There's no one else you could deliver Bran to on the other side, quickly?"

"No. It's just us."

"Be careful and take care of each other, all right? And call me as soon as you get back. How long will you be?"

"I don't know. Not long, I hope, but I don't know where Bran lives, exactly." She heard her father sigh on the other end of the line. She tried for an estimate to make him happy. "If I don't call in one week—"

"A week!"

"One week, then you can start worrying, okay? Not a moment before."

A pause, then her father gave a strained chuckle.

"I'll do my best."

"Thanks, Dad." Gwen felt her throat closing up. "Thanks for understanding." She tried to control her voice, and felt herself failing. "I love you."

"I love you too, Gwennie. You be careful, okay? I'll see you soon, lovie."

"Bye, Dad," she whispered, and hung up before he could hear her cry.

***

"I don't know what you said to my mum, but I didn't expect her to start hugging you." Aidan opened the cupboard to scout for more food. They were back at his half-packed flat, a sleeping Bran snoring gently on Aidan's bed. Gwen peered inside a nearby box while Aidan's back was turned, hoping to get a glimpse into his daily life. She felt like she knew him well, yet not at all. How he reacted under pressure, what he wanted in life, how he made her feel—she knew him perfectly. But what kind of music did he like? Was he into sci-fi or historical dramas or B-rated horrors? What was his favorite food? All the details that layer over the core of a person, all the quirks that round out a personality—Gwen had dived straight to Aidan's center and now had to work backward and outward to learn who he was.

The box contained nothing but plates and cutlery. She jumped guiltily as Aidan came back with a few cans of beans and tuna and a large plastic water bottle.

"What can I say? I'm very huggable." Gwen grinned at him. She stuffed her borrowed backpack with the cans and sleeping bag. Aidan laughed.

"Can't argue with that."

"Looks like that's everything." Gwen fastened her backpack and moved to Aidan's, but paused when Aidan leaped up.

"Wait." He bounded to the bed and grabbed a battered black case lying on the sheets. Gwen lifted an eyebrow, mystified. Aidan tucked it into his backpack and carefully clipped the pack closed. He caught her eye and colored slightly.

"What?"

"You think you're going to have time to play your flute?"

"You never know," he said defensively. "I had to play last time. Oh, and here's that infernal locket. Keep it away from Bran."

Gwen slipped the golden locket into her pocket, the metal cool on her skin. Aidan patted his backpack.

"All right, I think we're ready. Do you want to leave tonight, or wait until the morning?"

Gwen looked out the window at the early evening sun that streamed through the glass. She was wide awake and antsy. It was still mid-morning back in Vancouver. She was eager to open a portal to the Otherworld, to see the endless forest of her mother's realm, to breathe the air of a land where she didn't have to hide her magic and her past. Not that she was greatly oppressed, not anymore. Her father knew everything, of course, and now that Ellie knew her secrets the two of them had great fun inventing new tasks for her talents.

She looked more closely at Aidan and saw the same eagerness, half-heartedly masked behind his question. How much more must he want to visit the Otherworld, since he had no one else to share his experiences with? She felt a pang at his loneliness, and slipped a hand into his.

"Let's get started tonight. The sooner we get Bran back to his family, the better."

Aidan squeezed her hand tightly, and then leaned forward to press his lips to hers. She let herself sink into him, her fingers twining in his, her mind a boat adrift in a sea of bliss. A wave of unease flowed by, and she pulled back.

Aidan opened his eyes slowly, bliss smoothing his features.

"I didn't say hello properly, earlier. So, there you are."

Gwen couldn't help laughing aloud at this.

"Hello, yourself." She let go of his hand and shrugged into her backpack. "Okay, let's do this."

Aidan swung his own pack onto his back and strode over to Bran. He shook Bran's shoulder gently.

"Wake up, Bran. It's time to go."

Bran blinked himself awake and struggled out of the blanket. He pushed his legs over the side of the bed and paused, head in his hands, as if it pained him or he were overcome with dizziness. Gwen and Aidan exchanged concerned glances. Bran gave a cough and let out a few errant sparks, then looked up with a half-grin.

"Let's go for a walk, shall we?"

Aidan tucked his arm around Bran and hoisted him up. When Bran was steady, Aidan looked at Gwen expectantly.

'Why don't you do it this time?" Gwen said. "Have you tried before?"

"Yeah. It doesn't work. I think it's because I don't know who my father is. Who am I supposed to concentrate on?"

"Oh, I hadn't thought about that. Okay, give me a minute."

She took a deep breath and pictured her mother. She

wondered at her eagerness to return to the Otherworld when she thought of Isolde. They had separated on somewhat friendly terms before, but Gwen hadn't forgotten Isolde's enslavement of Ellie, or her role in luring talented humans to the Otherworld and to their eventual deaths. Isolde was a strange and dangerous woman, and Gwen had no desire to see her again.

And yet—her heart beat faster as she held out her arm and concentrated on Isolde to start the magic that would open a portal between human and Breenan worlds. She reached into herself, to her magical core that burned steady and warm within her chest. It was second nature now, instinctual, so different from when her core had been locked away, her magic suppressed through fear. Now she accessed it freely, drawing it through her arm and out before her.

The fabric of their world split apart, chiffon torn in two. A circular opening stood before her, its edges fluttering in a breeze that did not originate from the still apartment. Dim brown shapes touched by slanting sunlight shifting beyond the portal.

Gwen frowned in puzzlement. What was she looking at? Slowly, the truth dawned on her, and she started to laugh. Aidan poked his head through the portal and jerked back in shock.

"We're two storeys off the ground," she said.

The dim shapes resolved themselves into tree branches as Gwen's eyes adjusted, and she saw an owl peering at them with alarm. It spread its wings and launched itself with silent wingbeats. The portal wove itself closed with a slippery whisper of cloth sliding over cloth. Aidan wrinkled his nose.

45

"Now what?" He shifted Bran more securely against his shoulder and Bran winced.

"Let's go outside and find somewhere quiet," Gwen said. "At least we'll be on the right level there."

Gwen led the way and Aidan and Bran shuffled along behind, squeezing down the narrow stairwell with difficulty. Once outside, the street was dim and quiet and they slipped into a nearby lane without detection.

"You ready?" Gwen looked at Aidan, whose face was pale in the shade of the tree-lined lane. He looked nervous but excited. Gwen wondered if her own feelings were as clearly written on her face.

"Go for it, portal-maker," he said with determination.

Gwen brought her mother to mind, gathered her magic, and ripped open a portal.

Chapter 4

Autumn had come early to the Otherworld. Deirdre's garden had been full of flowers, overblown and dry yet still with a blousy sense of sunny days and sticky nights. The forest of the Otherworld had forgotten summer almost entirely. The ground was carpeted with a thick mat of fallen leaves, vibrant crimsons and golds blanketed over layers of crunchy brown debris. Great oaks and birches soared above in disheveled splendor, their naked branches stripped of leaves. Ragged wisps of mist curled and twined between tree trunks and passed through drifting leaves that descended in the still air.

Gwen shivered. The mists cooled the evening air to an uncomfortable degree. More than that, though, she felt the forest was infused with melancholy, as if a sad song had just finished playing and the forest was in an arrested state of quiet emotion before the spell was broken by applause.

But the applause never came, and the quiet sadness stretched on.

"Are you seeing this? All the mists, I mean?" Aidan's whisper barely pierced the thick blanket of quiet.

"Yeah. I've been trying to switch my vision, but it seems like this is all there is to see." In their previous visit to the Otherworld, she and Aidan had been taught to see beyond the enchanted veil that Isolde had put on the forest to make it appear forbidding and unwelcoming to strangers. Using their magical vision, they could pierce through the enchantments and see the bright, beautiful, and welcoming forest glades of Isolde's realm.

Now, however, Gwen could see only the mists of this forest, no matter how she strained and unfocused her eyes until they crossed. It was disconcerting to lose an ability.

"It's as if there's only one forest now." Aidan looked up at the tree trunks that disappeared into the misty canopy. "It's not frightening or lovely, it's only a forest."

"Do you think this is the true forest? Maybe both views before were enchantments. Isolde does seem to like things looking nice. She may have jazzed up the forest for her own amusement."

"So why isn't the enchantment on it now?" Aidan looked at Gwen in puzzlement. She frowned, disquieted by the implications of Aidan's question. Isolde had told her that the enchantments were a vital part of the realm's defenses. New human talent fueled the defensive spells in the past, but Gwen had assumed Isolde would find another way to protect her lands, with different enchantments or perhaps an army. Now Gwen wondered what giving up the locket had truly meant to Isolde.

"Do you think something happened to her?" She hardly knew Isolde, and didn't much like what she had seen, but Isolde was still her mother. What if she had died? Gwen didn't know what she would feel.

"Well, she's still alive." Bran's voice was weak, but his

words were reassuring. "You made a portal, didn't you? You couldn't have done that without your mother as your living anchor. It's probably something to do with the troubles at the borderlands."

"What troubles?"

"Father's been sending out a lot more border patrols lately. Something about refugees, an invasion—I don't know, I don't pay much attention to his politics."

"Invasion? What's going on?" Gwen glanced at Aidan, who shrugged. "When did this all start?"

"A few months ago. Perhaps in the spring sometime?" Bran yawned. "You worry too much, Gwen. I'm sure your mother is fine."

"Come on, then. Let's go." She quashed the unease in her mind and walked forward a pace, then stopped. "Which way?"

"I can't tell where we are, and these mists aren't helping." Bran peered around blearily. "We'll have to walk until we find someone to ask."

It was slow going through the forest despite a clearly visible path. The trees encroached on all sides, not nearly as welcoming as the pleasant glades of their last visit. Although Gwen didn't feel that the forest was actively trying to thwart them, still the undergrowth was thick and twisted, and bushes scratched Gwen's bare legs. She had expected a continuation of summer warmth, not this sudden immersion into the cool of autumn.

Gwen spotted an irregular shape lodged in the crack between two trees growing out of a single trunk. She bent down and grasped a long rod, feathers on the end stiff and unyielding.

"Look. An arrow." She ran her fingers down the shaft

to the arrowhead. Its copper point was sharp and barbed with two deadly prongs dipped in a viscous liquid, long since dried. Her fingers paused before they reached the tips.

"I guess they do more than dance, after all," Aidan said faintly.

"What's that supposed to mean?" Bran said. "I'd much rather hunt than dance."

Gwen thought about what the arrow meant. Isolde and her court needed to eat, and presumably they hunted whatever game lived in this forest. But Isolde ruled over a realm. Surely there were more people living in it than resided in her castle? Gwen hadn't thought about it before, and now wondered about the extent of her mother's influence.

"Look at this." Aidan bent to pick up a woven basket, its once-bright stripes of color now dull and moldering after clearly spending many weeks lying forgotten among the brush. They continued to walk amid more and more signs of habitation—notches blazed into trees, a cluster of bright leaves carefully gathered and then discarded to dry on a fallen tree trunk, a footprint in a splotch of mud.

Aidan's hushed voice breathed in her ear.

"I think we'd better prepare for an encounter with a local sooner rather than later."

A rustling ahead alerted Gwen to another presence.

"Shhh!" She threw her arm out and the back of her hand thumped against Aidan's chest. He paused immediately.

"What did you hear?" He looked around with the jerky motions of a hunted animal. Bran looked around with less intensity. Gwen tilted her head to the side, straining to catch the noise again.

"A crunching sound. Up ahead." She froze when she heard a voice, low but clear, murmuring in the distance. She and Aidan looked at each other and Gwen's heart pounded. Her earlier eagerness to explore the Otherworld evaporated, and fears emerged like a roaring beast. They had been in terror of their lives on their last trip. The constant threat of exposure as half-humans had hung over them, carried around like a strangling noose of fear. It was easy to forget in the calm reality of the human world. But now, faced with real Breenan once more, Gwen's memories of last May returned as sharp and alarming as when she had first experienced them. She looked at Aidan, her terror echoed in his face, his round eyes mirroring her own. Aidan swallowed audibly.

"We did want to find someone, to ask directions."

Gwen tried to take a deep breath, but found there was no room for it next to the fear lodged in her chest.

"I guess we did. Okay, we keep it simple, ask them what direction to go in to find the Wintertree realm, and then skedaddle. Good?" Aidan nodded. Gwen said, "Okay, let's do this. Carefully."

Bran frowned.

"Don't be so worried. It'll only be a band of villagers. Unless…" He left his sentence dangling.

"Unless what?" Gwen said, her heart pounding faster.

"Unless they're bandits. But I doubt it." Bran slumped against Aidan's side. "I need to rest for a moment. Only a moment." A small wisp of blue smoke puffed out of his left ear.

"Perhaps we should park Bran here." Aidan pointed to the shady cover of a nearby bush. "Until we find out what's happening. All right, Bran?"

"Yeah." Bran crawled his way to the bush. Gwen grabbed some fallen pine branches and carefully propped them against the bush to conceal Bran.

"Good idea," Aidan said.

With Bran taken care of, Gwen and Aidan paced forward, slowly and stealthily. The murmuring stopped, but occasional rustles and crunches continued. The path cut a meandering line through the undergrowth. Gwen slid around a tall tree trunk and looked forward.

At first, she saw nothing. More forest stretched out, endless tree trunks and green moss into the distance until the horizon was lost in brown woods. Aidan sidled up beside her, gazed for a moment, and then gasped. Gwen looked closer, puzzled.

The mounds she had taken for particularly thick undergrowth, piles of dry bracken, or dense ivy climbing up trees, were something else entirely. In front of her was a vast interconnected construct—*house* wasn't really the right word, although Gwen thought *warren* might be close—covered in an array of branches and leaves and evergreen needles until it blended into the forest. Most of the structure sprawled in a network of mounded heaps, but sections plunged below the ground and tunneled through hummocks of earth. There were even some parts that climbed up nearby trees, covered in a thick layer of glossy ivy vines. Small slits here and there among the branches acted as windows, and she saw one hole in a little hill carefully outlined by uncut stones.

Now that Gwen could see the warren in full, a more unsettling sight emerged. She clutched Aidan's arm convulsively. Standing behind hanging boughs and sturdy trunks and even perched in the trees were dozens of people. They silently watched Gwen and Aidan through listless eyes. An old woman leaned against the trunk of a tall fir tree, a mother with a baby standing behind her. All three were dressed in tunics that melted seamlessly into the greens and browns of the forest. All had the same indifferent and unresponsive expression on their faces, even the baby. Gwen shivered. They looked at her, but it was as if nothing Gwen did could really matter to them.

"Hello?" Aidan's voice disturbed the stillness of the Breenan silence and made Gwen jump. "Sorry to bother you. We're passing though, on the way to the Wintertree realm. Is this the right direction?"

The silence continued for a long uninterrupted moment. Sweat prickled on Gwen's scalp. Finally, a woman stepped forward to face them in the middle of the path. She was old, with deep lines etched in the tanned skin of her face. Gwen was reminded of the grain in weathered wood. Her silvery hair, tied back in a long braid, was tinged with a warmth that melded into the surrounding autumn leaves. Her tunic was similar to the other women's, a simple mid-length garment with a strip of leather gathering the waist. Her age had bent her over slightly, but she had about her an air of gravitas despite her posture.

"Greetings, travelers." Her voice was deep with age but surprisingly clear. "Not many pass through these woods of late. Not since the troubles began."

Gwen was relieved that they hadn't yet been skewered by an arrow.

"What troubles? We aren't from around here," Gwen said hastily as the woman gazed at her dispassionately.

"We have always been a prosperous realm. Enemies do

not cross our borders, and the land is generous. We have always had all we needed, until the troubles began.

"One moon before the longest day, game in these woods began to fail. The deer fled, and flowers blossomed without bearing fruit. The wolf and the lion stalked the forest once more, and when they found no suitable prey they hunted us, the forest people. Many folk left the woods, their homes, in search of better groves where the deer run and fruits grace the trees. Enemies of our realm raid within the forest's borders, stealing whatever they can carry. Our clan," here she gestured calmly to the camouflaged Breenan. "Have stayed clear of the invaders, gleaning what we can to survive."

Gwen listened with growing discomfort. One month before the summer solstice was when she and Aidan and Ellie had traveled into the Otherworld. Was that a coincidence? Had they somehow upset the balance in Isolde's realm?

"What of the queen? Doesn't she protect you from invaders? This is still Queen Isolde's realm, right?"

The old woman's eyes narrowed.

"The queen has failed us. When she accepted her role as ruler, she swore to protect her people, and ensure the land was pleasant and fruitful. In exchange, we feed her court and abide by her laws. But we are not protected, and there is little enough food for our own survival, let alone provisions for the queen. She has failed us." The woman repeated this last sentence with a heavy finality.

Gwen looked around the warren, and noticed the many unpatched holes in its walls. It had been kept up earlier in the year—a patch of drying branches in the wall had clearly been green in the spring—but nothing had been maintained since. A number of large hooks dangled from swaying ropes attached to branches above. Gwen guessed from their sharp points that they were intended to hang meat, but they swung empty.

"I'm sorry," Gwen said. "I hope things get better for you. Soon." She felt the inadequacy of her comment keenly.

The woman nodded once in answer. Aidan glanced at Gwen and said, "Is the queen's castle very far from here?"

Gwen slipped her hand into his, grateful for his understanding. Worry crept insidiously into her mind. What had happened to Isolde? And did it have something to do with Gwen? The sinking feeling in her stomach told her it did.

The old woman pointed back the way they had come.

"Fifty paces, take the trail east. It will lead you to the castle."

Gwen looked over her shoulder as they left. The old woman stared after them, her face expressionless. The rest of her clan were eerie in their unnatural stillness. Gwen shivered and followed Aidan.

***

"Well, that wasn't weird at all," Gwen said as Aidan peeked at Bran, asleep in the bush. She sighed when Bran's head flopped bonelessly against his shoulder. "I wish he'd just get better."

"I suppose that explains the lack of enchantments. Whatever these 'troubles' are caused by, they seem to affect everything in these woods. Even autumn's come early here."

"Do you think it had something to do with us?" Gwen asked, trying to be casual. She chewed her tongue and watched leaves drift to the ground, unseasonably early.

"Oh, I don't think..." Aidan's voice trailed off, his reassurance turned thoughtful. "Hmm. The timing is right. But how could we have done anything?"

"I don't know. It just seems like a strange coincidence. And not many humans—or half-humans—go through the portals."

Aidan shrugged and took away the branch that covered Bran.

"Let's go find your—Isolde, and get some answers."

Before Gwen could reply, a twig cracked to her right. She jumped and twirled on the spot, all her senses on overdrive.

Three children stood before her. They were clad in brown tunics similar to the villagers, but their bare feet were filthy and blistered and their cheeks were smeared with dust and tear tracks. The eldest, a girl about seven, held a sleeping toddler in her arms. A young boy stood behind her as if to shield himself from Gwen and Aidan. He sniffled quietly as the girl looked steadily at them.

Gwen's breath caught. Where had they come from? Were they children of the village? But if so, why were they so unkempt? The children at the warren had been listless, yet clean and cared for. These children had been on their own for days.

"Please, do you have any food to share?" The girl's voice was calm and measured, as if she had asked the question many times before. Gwen gulped and shot a glance at Aidan, whose wide, horrified eyes gave her an answer.

56

"Of course." Gwen set down her pack and unclipped the clasp to rummage through its contents. She pulled out a package of buns and shrugged helplessly at Aidan. He swung his own pack down and drew out some chunks of cheese. They offered it to the children, whose eyes locked on the food. The boy's little hands reached forward almost involuntarily. The girl was slightly more restrained, but took the buns quickly as if afraid that Gwen would snatch them back.

"Are you on your own? Where are your parents?" Gwen asked the girl, who kept steady eyes on Gwen's face as she ate. The girl swallowed before she answered.

"They're dead," she said. Gwen's heart clenched at her matter-of-fact tone. "Invaders came and killed people in our village who didn't give them food and furs. Our father didn't give in," here she lifted her chin a little, proudly. "And they killed him for it. Mother too. We ran away from the borderlands like mother told us. Perhaps when the troubles are over, we can go back. If the troubles are ever over."

The girl dusted off her hand tidily as she finished her portion. The little boy looked at her with a bun gripped in his dirty fist. The girl shifted the toddler's weight in her arms and gave him the bag of buns to carry.

"Thank you for the food. We need to go now. Our father's sister lives in a village beside the great river. We need to find her." The girl edged past them to continue down the path, the boy close on her heels.

Gwen said nothing as they left. She didn't know what to say. Her heart ached with the thought of the children wandering the forest on their own, but she couldn't think of anything else to do. Gwen and Aidan were useless enough in the forest, especially without Bran helping. She hoped fervently that the children found their aunt soon.

Aidan put an arm around her shoulder.

"Come on. There's nothing more we can do for them. They grew up in the forest. They'll find their way."

"I hope so." Gwen was unconvinced by Aidan's reassurances.

"We need to keep moving." Aidan jerked his head at the motionless Bran, and Gwen nodded. They had to keep on task. Bran's life might depend on it. Wordlessly, Gwen and Aidan went to either side of Bran and hauled him up by his arms.

"Oy," Bran said weakly. "I was enjoying myself." He coughed and purple sparks flew out of his mouth. They hadn't seen purple before. Were the colors random, or was purple a sign of progression of the illness?

"Time to go, lazybones," Aidan replied, hefting Bran's arm over his shoulder. "We can't have you relaxing while the rest of us work."

Gwen followed Aidan and Bran down the trail, lost in her thoughts. Aidan counted under his breath.

"Forty-six, forty-seven," Aidan paced forward and stopped. "Fifty."

There was a gap in the bushes between two conifers where a small path opened up in the undergrowth. Gwen went ahead to look.

"Hey, it gets wider over here."

When Aidan and Bran rejoined her, Gwen swung Bran's arm around her shoulder and grabbed his waist. They walked along the path, much slower now that they traveled three abreast. Bran's footsteps were getting more and more sluggish. Gwen silently willed him to keep going. They had no form of transport here—they needed Bran to stay on his feet. The forest was dim and cool, too cool for Gwen's shorts, but she had no other clothes.

After twenty minutes of their awkward amble through a particularly thick patch of bushy undergrowth, they rounded a bend in the path. A lone figure walked toward them. Gwen gasped as she recognized him and Aidan stopped short, jolting their procession and waking Bran out of his trance. The man narrowed his eyes and spoke.

"You." Corann, Isolde's second-in-command and Ellie's previous abductor, looked Gwen up and down. His mouth twisted as if he tasted something vastly unpleasant. "What are you doing here? Come to gloat over the destruction you've wrought? You weren't satisfied with leaving us to ruin?"

Gwen was aghast at Corann's reaction. His eyes were filled with bitter anger, directed at her. What made Corann blame Gwen so vehemently?

"What do you mean? How did I cause this? This, whatever is happening to the forest? What did I do?"

Corann spat on the ground at Gwen's feet and she sprang back. Aidan and Bran both stepped forward.

"Get away from her," Aidan snarled. Bran looked like he wanted to say something, but he swayed wildly and Aidan hastily wrapped his arm around Bran's shoulder to hold him up.

"What's the matter with him?" Corann asked, but his interest was fleeting. He turned back to Gwen. "You left us unprotected. You took away the source of my queen's power and left her unable to defend her realm, unable to feed her people, unable to keep the wild beasts from our doors." Corann clenched his fists and turned away as if he

59

couldn't stand the sight of her anymore.

"You mean the locket," Gwen whispered. She saw Bran fidget in front of her and Aidan hiss something indiscernible to him.

"Yes, of course I mean the locket." Corann swiveled his head to pierce Gwen with venomous eyes. "By taking away our wellspring of creativity, you condemned this realm to a slow, lingering death." He sucked in his breath and clenched his jaw tightly, looking away again. The muscles in his cheek worked.

Gwen bit her lip in distress. Taking the locket had seemed like the obvious, easy choice. Saving countless future humans from torturous madness and a slow, lingering death—well, it hadn't been a choice, really. Gwen knew she would do it again in a heartbeat.

But she hadn't considered that there might be serious consequences in the Otherworld. And as strange and different as the Breenan were, they were still people. Her people, partly. And it seemed that most of them were innocent of the queen's transgressions and had no real knowledge of the machinations of the court. Gwen found it difficult to sympathize with Corann after his prominent role in Ellie's kidnapping in the spring, but her heart ached for the villagers they had met.

"Where is Isolde?" Gwen asked, trying to keep her voice strong.

"What do you care?" Corann's voice practically dripped with bitterness.

"You know where she is," Gwen said, and Corann shifted his feet slightly. Gwen glanced at Aidan, still supporting Bran's drooping form. Aidan shrugged slightly and nodded as if to say, *it's your choice.*

"Corann, I need to see her. I need to speak to—my mother." Even now the word felt foreign and ungainly in her mouth. She squared her shoulders and stared at Corann. He looked at her with narrowed eyes for a moment, then turned with an exasperated sigh.

"Do what you will," he threw back over his shoulder, and he stepped quickly down a path to their right.

Gwen moved to Bran's other side.

"I'm fine," Bran muttered groggily.

"Of course you are," Gwen said automatically, making sure she had a firm hold around Bran's waist as they hurried to keep up to Corann. She glanced at Aidan, who looked back at her with a reassuring smile.

"Do you think this is the right move?" she asked.

"Yeah, I do. You need answers, and this way we'll get them right from the horse's mouth."

"S'not very nice," Bran mumbled. "Calling Gwen's mother a horse."

Gwen and Aidan grinned at each other despite everything.

"I forgive you, Aidan," Gwen said.

"Many thanks, my lady."

***

They had hardly walked for five minutes when Aidan spoke.

"Doesn't this look familiar?"

Gwen looked more closely at their surroundings. The path was usable, but hardly the well-maintained trail of their previous visit. Vines hung in spindly tendrils to brush their shoulders, and large tree branches lay on the ground

61

to catch unwary feet, as Gwen's feet so often were.

"Yeah, that bent tree over there—maybe we're near?"

Corann snorted but said nothing. He kicked a tree branch off the path as if the immobile wood had done him a great wrong.

They turned a corner into an open clearing. It must have been the site of some potent act of destruction in the past, from the evidence of blackened bark and jagged stumps. A thick carpet of dying grass, the first to colonize the stricken ground, lay draped over discarded branches and against the remains of trees. The devastation spread in a wide circle.

Gwen gulped.

"We're almost there. This is where I broke open my core."

Aidan whistled softly and even Bran looked up from his dragging feet with interest.

Everything looked dead, especially in the autumnal air, crisp with an undertone of chill dankness that warned of approaching winter. The dead grass rustled under falling leaves, its brittle brown forms making only the slightest sound in the stillness. Gwen listened carefully, but there was no birdsong or any sign of movement in the surrounding forest. In fact, she couldn't recall hearing any animals since the owl at the portal.

"Enjoying the view, Gwendolyn?" Corann spat out with venom. "This was just practice before your big debut."

Corann's vitriol was wearing thin.

"Just take me to Isolde," Gwen said shortly.

Corann glared at her, then turned on one heel and marched down the path once more. Gwen adjusted Bran's arm securely around her shoulder and the three of them hobbled after Corann.

Two bends in the path later, the trees parted just enough to allow a castle to emerge from the gloom.

Gwen gasped, and blinked a few times to make sure her vision was true. Now that only one forest was visible, without the enchantments of darkness and terror or the improvements of Isolde's magic, the castle appeared as its true self. Unfortunately, the reality was much closer to the terrible ruin of the enchanted forest than it was to the decorated bastion of Isolde's creation. Some of the crenelated towers had hardly any crenellations left to boast of. Three of the domed and spired peaks had disintegrated completely, their remains scattered over the front steps and around the castle walls. Large sections of wall were simply gone, and Gwen wondered queasily what supported the ruined towers above. The doors to the ballroom through which light and music used to spill were silent and dark now. They were open, the empty blackness inside ominous and forbidding.

Gwen swallowed. What was Isolde doing here in this deathtrap of a building? And was all this really Gwen's fault? Her stomach twisted into great ropy knots and she gripped Bran's waist tightly.

"Easy there, Gwen," Bran said with a reassuring smile in his voice. "You'll cut me in half."

Corann picked his way up the crumbling steps, skirting chunks of castle wall. Gwen glanced at Aidan, who reached up from his grip on Bran to squeeze her shoulder.

"Come on, let's see what all the fuss is about. Then we can be off and take Bran home."

Gwen nodded tightly. They followed Corann's retreating figure, avoiding the boulders with difficulty.

The ballroom was so dark that Corann's footsteps on the parquet floor echoed in Gwen's ears long before her eyes adjusted to the dimness. The only light came from the great double doors, streaming over and around their bodies which cast long shadows over the dusty floor. Tapestries swam into view before Gwen's blinking eyes. One to her left, which depicted a hunting scene with humans as prey, was riddled with moth holes so she could hardly make out the scene. It was an improvement, to Gwen's mind.

"Look," Aidan whispered. "There's the queen."

Gwen whipped her head around to look past Aidan's outstretched finger. On a dais at the far end of the ballroom was a carved wooden seat, almost a throne. And on the throne sat Isolde.

Gwen's heart squeezed painfully and unexpectedly at the sight of her mother. The last time Gwen had seen her, Isolde had been elegant, proud, beautiful, and larger-than-life. Now—Gwen swallowed as she dragged Bran forward, Aidan following after an initial surprised stumble—now Isolde sank low in her chair, her head bowed as if under a great weight. Her dress might have been an emerald green in the past, but its ragged hem and drooping sleeves were now no more than a faded and dusty brown. Even Isolde's raven tresses hung limply, covered in a layer of dust so thick that Gwen at first mistook it for graying hair.

Corann knelt beside Isolde. He took her hand and gently stroked the lifeless fingers.

"My lady? You have a visitor." There was no response from the queen's bowed head. "My lady? Will you not rouse yourself? Please, my love?" Gwen bit her lip at the tender anguish in Corann's words, and she and Aidan exchanged a glance. Corann tried again. "My love, your daughter has come. Your daughter, Gwendolyn."

These words stirred what Corann's tender pleading could not. Isolde's head rose—slowly, so slowly—until her half-closed eyes focused on Gwen. Corann's lips pressed in a thin line and he glared at Gwen. Isolde's mouth opened slightly to draw in a long, shuddering breath.

"Gwendolyn." Her voice was deep and raspy, obviously unused for some time. "You have come."

"What happened to you?" Gwen blurted without thinking, then pressed her lips shut tight. She hadn't meant to be so blunt, but the state of Isolde had rattled her.

Isolde raised her hand slowly, as if with great effort, and waved away Gwen's question.

"I am a little ill. It is nothing of consequence." Isolde put her hand on Corann's arm when he opened his mouth in protest and he subsided with a furrowed brow. Gwen was puzzled, but had more pressing concerns.

"What's the matter with the forest? Why has it changed so much?" Gwen followed this with the question that she dreaded, but needed to ask. "Was it my fault?"

Isolde gazed at her for a long while. The tightened knuckles of Aidan's hand pressed against Gwen's side where he clenched Bran. Finally, Isolde spoke into the stillness of Gwen's held breath.

"The lack of new creative talent for my ballroom resulted in an unraveling of the realm's magic. I cannot keep it together without the humans."

"So it was my doing," Gwen whispered. She closed her eyes briefly, remembering all too clearly the children on the path, their eyes large above too-thin cheeks. Isolde continued to gaze at her, her face emotionless.

"If we could go back," Gwen said. "And do it again, would you have given me the locket?"

Isolde considered her for a moment.

"I do not know," she said finally. "I expect I would not have given you the chance to ask for it. But the point is moot. The locket is gone," Bran squirmed briefly against Gwen's side. "And events have unfolded as they will. The realm is fading, and there is little I can do for it." She turned her head to one side and Corann stroked her arm in consolation. He glared at Gwen and reflexively twitched his fingers as if he itched to attack them.

"Is there anything I can do to help?" Gwen said. Aidan sighed almost indiscernibly and she bristled. This was all her fault—if there was something she could do to help, then she would. Aidan didn't have to join her. She wasn't forcing him to do anything.

Isolde tilted her head in consideration. Gwen wondered if the creak she heard was from Isolde's neck or from the trees outside.

"There is a place. An island that houses extraordinary magic, perhaps even the power to heal all ills."

"Are you referring to Isle Caengal?" Corann asked incredulously. "The isle is real, but the spells are only legend."

"Perhaps. And yet, if the isle does hold that legendary spell of restoration, the realm could be healed. There is a chance, however small. Likely it is the only chance."

The silence was so thick that Gwen could almost taste it. She chewed the inside of her cheek, her mind whirling. Another task was just what they didn't need right now. They still had to transport an ever-weakening Bran to his home, and Gwen had only a week before her father would start to get frantic. But people were starving and dying because of Gwen, and if there were something she could do to make amends, how could she in good conscience pass it up?

"I'll try," Gwen said aloud. That was the best she could offer—she didn't want to make promises she probably wouldn't be able to keep. "I'll try to get the restoration spell from this island and bring it to you. As soon as we take Bran back to his father."

Isolde tried to smile. It looked difficult on her dry and dusty skin.

"Thank you, Gwendolyn. You have a noble heart." She transferred her gaze to Bran, his body drooping between their arms. "What ails the young Wintertree prince?"

"He used too much magic and made himself very sick," Gwen said, shifting her aching arm to support Bran better. "We're taking him to his father to be healed."

"Oh. Well, I would say your goodbyes soon. He will not be long for this world." Isolde's head started to drop, as if its weight were too much for her neck to support any longer. "Faolan is particularly adept at magic, but I doubt even he can stop an illness such as this."

Gwen glanced at Aidan and saw her own distress mirrored in his eyes.

"Corann, tell them where to go. I am—I am too tired." Isolde's arms fell to her lap and her head sank fully to her chest. Corann's lips tightened, but he turned and spoke to Gwen in terse, clipped words.

"Go to the shores of the eastern sea, on the edge of the Longshore realm. There is an island within sight of the shore that is rumored to be Isle Caengal from legends, although no one has set foot on it in living memory. Take the eastern path leaving the castle—it will lead you to Faolan's realm. Now go. The queen is tired."

Corann turned his back to them deliberately and faced Isolde on his knees to reach for her ringed fingers. Isolde didn't stir.

Feeling dismissed, and not sure what more she would accomplish by forcing Isolde to speak to them further, Gwen looked at Aidan and twitched her head to leave. They hobbled out, and Gwen looked back just once at her motionless mother on the dusty carved throne.

***

The echoing footsteps, four strong and sure, two slow and hesitant, had long since faded into the empty stillness that settled over the ballroom as thick as dust by the time Corann spoke.

"You didn't tell her." His thumbs, hardly visible in the dim light from the open door, stroked the back of Isolde's hand with a gentle touch. "Why not?"

Without raising her head, Isolde answered Corann. Her whispered breath registered scarcely louder than the flutter of a bird's wingbeat.

"What would it have achieved? If she cares for me, the knowledge would be a burden. If she does not, knowing would make no difference." There was silence between them for a long moment before Corann spoke again.

"This can't go on. The realm and—well, it's all falling apart. I don't know how much longer we have."

"Perhaps Gwendolyn will be able to help. She is our only chance now."

Corann exhaled loudly in annoyance.

"I think Gwendolyn has done quite enough already." A pause, then, "There has to be something I can do. I can't watch this happen. Tell me what to do." Corann's eyes were intense, raking over Isolde's bowed head. Isolde's sigh passed through the air like wind rustling through dry grass.

"There is nothing. The magic and the realm were too closely intertwined. Unraveling the two is not possible."

Corann's jaw tightened and his eyes flashed.

"I don't accept that."

Isolde partially raised her head and slowly, so slowly, lifted her hand to touch Corann's cheek with light fingertips. She smiled sadly.

"But you must."

Corann looked away and did not answer. Isolde dropped her head with a sigh and allowed the silence to swallow them once more.

Chapter 5

Gwen stumbled alongside Aidan and the faltering Bran for some minutes, guilt and fear silencing her. Guilt, now that Isolde had confirmed that the destruction of the realm was all her fault. Fear, because saving the realm meant traveling through the Otherworld, the sometimes vicious, always unpredictable land of her mother's people. What was worse, to reach this legendary island they needed to pass through other realms. Gwen shivered. As unwelcoming and dangerous as Isolde's realm was, at least she felt some familiarity with it. Beyond these borders lay a treacherous unknown.

Bran made a valiant effort to shuffle from the castle in the direction of his realm, but after a short time he stumbled to his knees, dragging Gwen and Aidan's shoulders down with him.

"Bran!" Gwen knelt down beside him. He started to shake, then to cough uncontrollably, the air in front of his mouth filled with sparks of every color. Gwen held his shoulders steady and looked helplessly at Aidan. When the coughing fit finally subsided, Bran sagged against Gwen.

"All right. Let's take a little rest, shall we?" Aidan said. He hauled Bran up, grimacing at Bran's unresisting weight. Gwen ran to the side of the path and cleared branches from the base of a tree. Aidan carefully placed the limp Bran there and Gwen balled up her coat to tuck behind Bran's head.

"Just rest here for a minute, okay?" Gwen said, rubbing Bran's shoulder. He nodded without opening his eyes. Aidan dug out a water bottle from his pack and offered it to Gwen. She gratefully accepted it—the coolness of the night hadn't diminished the thirst their walk had generated.

"What are we going to do?" Aidan said, his voice neutral. Gwen passed the bottle back and looked at him. He avoided her gaze and took a swig.

"I need to fix this." Gwen gestured at the forest, where mists swirled around the darkening tree trunks. "The realm is failing, and it's my fault."

Aidan sighed.

"It's not your fault. Isolde set up this ridiculous magic defense system, and she gave you the locket. She knew exactly what would happen if she did. You can't blame yourself."

Gwen could, and she did—she had made Isolde give her the locket. People were starving and dying in consequence of an action she had wrought.

"If I don't fix it, people will continue to die."

"Is it really up to you? What about others in the realm? This world is dangerous, and we know hardly anything about it. There are raiders and wild animals and who knows what else. We don't know what we're doing."

Gwen stared at Aidan, uncertainty quickly overtaken by frustration. Why couldn't he see that there wasn't another option? That she had to do this, or at least try?

"You don't have to come," she said, annoyed. "It's not your responsibility."

Aidan frowned and closed his eyes briefly.

"I'm coming. I won't leave you here on your own. But—just think about it, all right? And try not to let guilt cloud your judgement." He bent down and shoved the water bottle into the pack with more force than necessary. "Come on, we should move, cover a little more distance before we stop for the night."

Gwen shouldered her own pack while Aidan helped Bran up. Her mind buzzed with irritation. Why didn't Aidan get it? Couldn't he see that the responsibility for these people had fallen to her shoulders with a few quiet words from Isolde? That her actions had huge and far-reaching consequences? That no white knight would come to save the day, that it was only her, shaking and afraid under the misty trees? Only her, feeling very alone in the face of Aidan's incomprehension?

She followed Bran and Aidan down the narrow path, dusk reducing the light until tree roots blended unhelpfully into the dirt of the trail. Every so often, a prickling sensation traveled down her spine and she whirled around to see nothing but trees. Leaves continued to drift disconsolately around her, floating through the mists in a melancholic mirror of Gwen's own mood.

"Ugh! I'm sick of this forest. It's so dark and creepy." Gwen kicked at a pile of leaves, her frustration with Aidan and the forest melding together into one bundle of annoyance and anxiety.

"We should stop for the night," Aidan said, his voice calm and measured. Gwen thought irritably that he spoke to her as if she were a wild animal, ready to bite him unless he calmed her down. Just because he was a little bit right didn't make the feeling any easier to swallow. He continued, "It's too dark to see, anyway. Let's get out the sleeping bags."

Gwen bent over her pack, but before her hand reached the zipper a tingling crawled up her spine. She turned her head to look for another presence, but the forest was still. The dimness swallowed up distant trees when she tried to peer beyond their immediate surroundings.

"What's the matter?" Bran asked. His half-open eyes were on her, sleepy but curious. She shrugged.

"It felt like someone was watching us. I'm just being silly, I guess." She zipped open her backpack with a defiant gesture, but froze when a deep rumbling growl reached her ears. She looked back at Bran, whose widened eyes stared past her. She jerked around to face the growl.

Pacing toward them through the gloom was a tremendous lion, just like the one they had seen on their first visit to the Otherworld. Its curly mane and odd, almost human face grew more distinct as it padded straight to them on silent footfalls. But there was a peculiar, almost translucent quality to the lion—the fur on its flanks rippled out of time with its steps, as if the lion was a reflection rippling in water, rather than the real thing. Gwen's terror did not agree and she remained frozen, panicked, with no idea what to do or any plan in her head. The lion growled again, its voice strangely distant and echoing.

When the lion had their attention it sprang forward, no longer content to pace quietly. Its mouth opened in a forceful snarl and powerful legs propelled it forward.

Gwen knew she was going to die. Too late, she

remembered her portal-making powers, but there was no time to use them in the split-second left to her. She didn't want to see her end, not like this, but she couldn't force her eyes closed. Instead, she crouched, useless and trembling, and waited for death.

Aidan stood and tried to shout but his voice only croaked feebly. The lion ignored him and tensed its mighty legs in one last spring. It soared toward them and Gwen gazed into its golden eyes. This was the last thing she would ever see.

Then, the eyes rippled. They undulated, and faded, until only inches from Gwen the lion disintegrated into thin air. Nothing was left but memory and the stillness of the darkening forest.

Gwen's breath, now that she wasn't holding it any longer, came in great heaving gulps. She crawled over to Aidan and clutched at him, pulling him down until he knelt with his arms around her. She gasped and clung to him, needing his presence, his warmth, his solid realness, the safety she felt in his arms.

Once she had enough breath to speak, she pulled away and scrutinized him, grabbing his forearms.

"You're okay?"

He looked dazed and a bit wild, but nodded his head. She turned to Bran, who lay in his former position against the tree trunk, eyes more alert than before but otherwise unaffected. When he saw her look at him, he gave a little laugh.

"Kitty has some teeth, hasn't he?" He readjusted himself with a wince. "Lucky the enchantment is still partly up. The forest hasn't reverted completely to its wildest self."

"Is that what happened?" Gwen asked, sitting on her bottom. She wasn't sure whether her legs would hold her upright, even while kneeling. "Is that why it was so—insubstantial?"

"Looks like. We'll be out of here and in my realm by mid-morning tomorrow, though, so the remainder of the enchantment should hold by then. We can sleep easy."

Sleep was the last thing on Gwen's mind. From Aidan's trembling hand on her shoulder, she guessed he felt the same. But there was nothing to be done—they couldn't go any farther tonight, in the dark and with Bran's health worsening, and there was no shelter nearby.

"I'll take first watch, shall I?" Aidan said, squeezing her shoulder before releasing it to unroll a sleeping bag. Her shoulder felt very cold and empty when his hand left.

"Okay, thanks," she said, and moved to help Bran into a sleeping bag. She had the feeling it would be a very long night.

***

As Gwen had suspected, it was a very long night.

Every crack in the woods and every rustle of dry leaves woke her from her fitful dozing at Bran's side. Aidan's profile in the darkness showed no signs of sleepiness, and his eyes glinted watchfully. The darkness pressed in on all sides, a cloying mass of suffocating weight. Finally, Gwen sat up and touched Aidan's arm.

"I'll take watch now. You rest."

Aidan didn't answer right away, but shimmied over to put an arm around her. Suddenly the darkness didn't feel quite so malignant against the warmth of Aidan. Gwen relaxed into him.

"Let's watch together for a minute," Aidan said. He glanced at Bran, who lay with his mouth open, utterly unperturbed. Aidan snorted. "Glad to see someone's resting well. Do you think a freight train would wake him?"

"Probably. If only because he'd want to check it out. Something human, you know."

They lapsed into silence. Aidan stroked Gwen's hair lightly, and it was as if every stroke brushed away Gwen's fear and worry. She nestled closer to Aidan.

"Do you think we'll ever be together somewhere normal?" she asked.

"You mean, not in a dangerous parallel universe? Too much excitement for you?"

"Just—yeah, the two of us have always been here, fighting for our lives. What do you think it will be like when everything is regular?"

"Peaceful. Restful. Glorious," Aidan replied easily. He kissed the top of her head. She smiled in the dark, but her anxiety reared its ugly head.

"Do you think we'll be okay?" She fidgeted, annoyed with herself for not clearly stating what she felt. The words weren't coming out right, and Aidan wasn't reading between the lines.

A twig snapped to their left. Aidan's hand paused mid-stroke and Gwen froze. A second later, leaves rustled closer, as if something were walking toward them.

"Oh no oh no oh no," Gwen whispered frantically. "What are we going to do?"

Aidan leaned over and clamped a hand over Bran's mouth. Bran opened his eyes immediately and Aidan brought his finger to his lips. When Bran nodded, Aidan released his hand.

"There's something coming," Gwen breathed into Bran's ear.

Aidan stood carefully, hauling Bran up with him. Gwen threw her backpack over her shoulder and grabbed Aidan's. She left the sleeping bags—it would be impossible to outrun anything with them in her arms, and a lion would have no interest in blankets. Aidan and Bran stumbled toward the path. Gwen turned to follow, but took only two steps before a voice shouted in the silence.

"Get them!"

Gwen's mind worked frantically as she whirled in the direction of the voice. No ghostly lion chased them, but what did they have to contend with now?

She hardly had time to register the sight of two men bursting through nearby bushes before the nearest man grabbed her. He pinned her arms to her sides. Gwen thrashed her body and kicked her legs in every direction, but the man held firm.

Aidan and Bran fared little better. Aidan, hampered by Bran, was captured easily. The second man threw both of them to the ground and knelt on Aidan's back, twisting his arms until Aidan hissed in pain. The men didn't bother to contain Bran, who lay limply where he had fallen during the attack.

When it was clear that her struggling was in vain, Gwen stopped to study their attackers. Who were they? Why did they want to capture their party of three?

Gwen could see little of the man whose arms enclosed her body in a suffocating grip. His sleeves were sewn from rough leather, dirty and with ragged edges in place of a cuff. The other man, perched on Aidan, wore a vest of ratty fur over a coarsely woven shirt. His long hair was unkempt and his eyes were cold. He saw Gwen looking at him and he narrowed his eyes.

"This is what will happen," he said. His voice was low, but Gwen had no trouble hearing the ominous words. "We take your food and supplies. You don't struggle. We don't kill you."

Gwen shivered. The man's tone was featureless, matter-of-fact. This was not his first capture. It was a business transaction, nothing more. She had no doubt that if they didn't submit, things would go badly for them.

"We'll starve without our things," Aidan forced out. The man leaned until his weight lay directly over Aidan's chest. Aidan coughed weakly and lay still, wheezing shallowly.

"Better you than me," the man said without emotion. He looked back at Gwen. "Do we have a deal?"

The man holding her squeezed more tightly.

"Maybe we should change the terms," he said, his breath hot in Gwen's ear. She grimaced and turned her face away from the rank smell. "The girl could come with us."

A cold rush of fear traveled throughout Gwen's body, from her spine right to her toes. Aidan twitched but no sound escaped his compressed lungs. The kneeling man sighed with exasperation.

"Fine. The girl comes too." He pulled Aidan's head up by his hair. "No fighting back."

"I wouldn't do that," Bran said calmly. Gwen jerked her head to look at him. He had pulled himself into a seated position, although the effort had clearly cost him—

his face was as pale as the moon.

"You're not going to start making a nuisance of yourself, are you, cripple?" the kneeling man said with a firm hold on Aidan's hair.

"Not me," Bran said. His eyes flickered briefly to Gwen and then rested on the man's face. Gwen had never seen him so calm and collected. Bran wasn't himself—he was up to something. He said, "It's the others that you might want to worry about."

"What others?" the kneeling man said with a hint of scorn.

"The rest of our party. Most of the able-bodied men and women went ahead to scout for better shelter, but they're due back soon." Bran paused and then said, "Actually, I think I hear them now."

They all went silent. Gwen strained her ears, almost taken in by Bran's story. She wondered what he was up to and desperately hoped he had a plan. To her surprise, a rustling in the distance greeted her ears, followed by the sound of clanking as if many people in armor walked toward them. Murmurs and occasional laughter floated in their direction.

"Help!" Gwen screamed. She didn't know if Bran was doing something, or whether there was actually a small army headed toward them. Either way, playing along had to be better than the situation they were currently in. "Over here!"

A hand clamped over her mouth. She could taste dirt on her tongue. The kneeling man's cold eyes darted warily between Gwen and Bran.

"Come on," he growled at the man holding Gwen. "Grab her pack and let's go. There will be easier pickings farther on."

Gwen found herself thrown to the ground and her backpack wrested from her shoulders. The army noises grew louder as the men made their escape, running through the undergrowth with light feet that disappeared quickly into the night.

With the men out of earshot, the sound of the approaching army stopped abruptly. Gwen and the others were alone in the stillness. Gwen pushed herself up, intending to make sure Aidan wasn't hurt. Before she could crawl over to him, Bran collapsed. His body convulsed with spasms and sparks, and steam of all colors streamed into the air. To Gwen's horror, fire began to flicker along Bran's fingers and down the bridge of his nose between his half-closed eyes.

Gwen scuttled over and held down Bran's shaking torso. Aidan appeared a second later. He floated his hand above Bran's face, his eyes narrowed in concentration. Bran's body shuddered uncontrollably. After a moment, frosty air flowed from Aidan's hand to the flames dancing above Bran's nose.

The dancing of the flames slowed from a tarantella to a waltz before flickering out entirely, leaving black scorch marks in their wake. Bran's body continued to shudder, but at a slower pace. The sparks came at less frequent intervals, and smoke stopped curling from underneath Bran's hair.

Aidan flopped backward onto his bottom and heaved a huge sigh.

"What just happened?"

Gwen placed a shaking hand on Bran's forehead, stroking his clammy skin.

"I think Bran protected us with the sounds of his own made-up army. But it cost him."

The puzzlement on Aidan's face cleared to understanding, swiftly followed by concern.

"He made the sounds by magic, and now he's paying for it." He sighed again and his hands balled into fists. "Dammit, that was a good idea. I might have been able to do it if I'd been thinking straight. And now Bran's out of commission." He stood up and paced away from Gwen and the unconscious Bran, turning back after three steps. "I can't stand being so powerless. I have to step it up. This could have been so much worse."

"But it wasn't," Gwen said. She hated to see the distress on Aidan's face. "You can't blame yourself. Bran's been using magic a lot longer than we have. It's his default skill."

"But now he's even more ill than before. And we can't afford to rely on him. We can't afford to make mistakes like that anymore. This place is too dangerous to be complacent." He turned away again. The only part of his face visible was his clenched jaw.

Gwen didn't have anything to say. Aidan was right. They had jumped in the deep end, and they didn't know how to swim. The thought of the two men with their dirty furs and cold eyes made her shiver.

Bran's head moved under her hand and she glanced at him. He opened his eyes and looked at her with recognition.

"Bran," she said quietly, trying to appear calm. "How are you feeling?"

"Peachy," he replied, wincing as he drew in a large breath. "Did it work?"

"You bet. They ran. Took my backpack, but left Aidan's. And left me."

Bran tried for a grin, but only managed a grimace. Aidan knelt down beside them again.

"Those men were Breenan. Why didn't they see through your trick?"

"They were forest men," Bran said with a ghost of a shrug. "The common people don't have a lot of magical power. What they do have is deeper forest magic. It's useful for hunting and growing things. Not so helpful for tricks." He coughed twice, and red and purple sparks flew out. He continued, "They have a harder time recognizing flashy magic because they don't see much of it. Besides which, we don't exactly look royal at the moment."

"What kind of things can they do?" Gwen asked. "Should we be on the lookout for magic from them? They didn't use any here."

"Perhaps they could encourage animals to come near you, or trees to fall. Might take a while, though. I wouldn't worry about it. Worry about their tackling skills more." Bran closed his eyes, pale eyelashes in contrast to the dark shadows below.

"Okay, have a rest." Gwen stroked his forehead once more and looked at Aidan, whose face was set in grim lines. "Now what?"

"Now we wait until morning, then we get the hell out of here."

Chapter 6

Well before the sun made an appearance in the sky, while the forest was still gray and cold, Gwen and Aidan stuffed the sleeping bags into their single backpack and prepared to depart. Gwen swung the pack over her shoulders and looked at Bran, who shivered despondently on the ground.

"How are we going to do this?" she whispered to Aidan. "Bran looks like he won't last five minutes."

"I don't know what else we can do. We have to keep moving. I'll do my best to drag him along."

"What if we went back to England for a bit, traveled there by taxi or bus? At least we won't have lions and Breenan robbers."

"Now, there's an idea." Aidan patted his pocket enthusiastically, then grimaced. "If I hadn't left my wallet at home, of course. I didn't think we would need money in the Otherworld."

"Damn, and I don't have mine, either." Gwen's shoulders slumped. "So I guess a ride is out."

"And what would we say about the mobile weather

system?" Aidan pointed at Bran's head, encircled by a purple fog that puffed out of his ears. "No, I'm afraid we're stuck here. Bran, is there a spell I can use to move you along? We really need to move today, and well—" he shrugged apologetically. "I'd rather not carry you the whole way. And since we're stuck in the Otherworld, we might as well use magic while we can."

Bran's eyes lit up with a hint of his old enthusiasm.

"Yes! You can falsely lighten me, for a while, at least. Here, I'll show you." He held out his hands.

"No, no. I'll figure it out. Don't use any magic."

Bran's arms drooped and he nodded his head glumly.

Aidan rolled his shoulders and dropped his hands to his side. His face grew still in concentration.

"Do you know what you're doing?" Gwen hissed at him, alarmed. What if he got it wrong, and hurt Bran somehow?

"Relax. I've played with something similar before. It should work."

"Should?"

Before Gwen could protest further, Aidan closed his eyes and released his breath in a forceful sigh.

Bran yelped as he rose off the forest floor. Dry leaves drifted down from where they had stuck to his pants. He hovered there, a foot from the ground, oscillating slightly until he twisted himself back into a seated position.

Gwen laughed. The sensation felt unfamiliar after the stress of the previous night. She whirled around and threw her arms around Aidan, whose face beamed. He staggered slightly from the surprise of Gwen's hug.

"You did it! That's so much better. Now we can actually make some headway."

"Hey," Bran said weakly, but he too was smiling.

"Yeah, it worked," Aidan said. "But it's still a fair bit of effort. Much easier than hauling this deadweight around," he waved at Bran, who feebly flicked his hand at him in a dismissive gesture. "But still, not free."

"We can take turns. We'll trade Bran and the backpack every so often."

"So I'm baggage now?"

"Yes. Be quiet and rest like a good piece of luggage. We'll get you home soon."

Despite her lack of sleep after the perils of the night, Gwen had a spring in her step. Aidan set a brisk pace and the forest passed by smoothly and quickly. The cool crispness of approaching winter still bit at Gwen's bare legs and dead leaves rustled underfoot, but now Gwen felt that they were getting somewhere at last.

After an hour's walk, during which Bran dozed on his bed of air, the canopy of naked branches and coniferous foliage above Gwen's head started to thin. Sunlight slanted in and highlighted craggy bark.

"Is it just me, or are we coming to the end of this bloody forest?" Aidan said, peering forward.

"Oh, I hope so. The sooner, the better. Not that we know what's up ahead. Could be even worse."

"Now there's positive thinking at its finest." Aidan turned and looked at Gwen quizzically. "It's not like you to be so pessimistic. What's the matter?" He walked back to Gwen and took her hands in his. She sighed and gazed into his familiar green eyes.

"I don't know. It's everything, all at once. Bran is sick and Isolde is sick and the realm is sick—now I have to fix everything and I don't know what's coming next, not at all."

"Look on the bright side. You don't have to fix everything by yourself. You have me."

Aidan was right. They were in this together. Gwen's heart, under its heavy load of guilt and fear, lightened considerably. A warm glow that had nothing to do with her core started burning in her chest. She and Aidan had had so little time together by themselves. She had a sudden urge to kiss him—she wanted to feel his arms around her, to press up against his warmth and feel loved and held. His eyes told her he felt the same way. She leaned forward, and her lips met his waiting ones. Her inner heat increased from a gentle glow to a fiery sun. She kissed Aidan intensely and slid her hands up and around his chest to clutch him tightly. His lips responded to hers with equal fervor.

"Ow!"

Bran's voice jolted Gwen out of the haze of the moment. She tore herself away from Aidan, who twisted to look at Bran. Bran sat in a pile of leaves, where he rubbed his bottom gingerly and peered owlishly at them.

"You dropped me," he said to Aidan. His eyes lit on Gwen's burning face and he grinned. "Oh, I see. You thought you'd take a little—break, and lose your concentration. Don't mind me, I'll sit here and wait." He wiggled his eyebrows suggestively at them, but immediately dissolved into a fit of coughing, green and orange sparks forcing out of his mouth in fitful bursts.

Gwen touched Aidan's elbow.

"You take the backpack for a bit. I'll hover Bran."

Aidan didn't argue. He slung the pack over his shoulder.

"Here, let me show you the spell."

Aidan brought his hands up to touch her temples. Gwen bit her lip nervously. She'd seen Bran "teach" a spell to Aidan in the past, through some kind of magical transfer, but had never had it done to herself. Come to think of it, she'd never seen Aidan transfer either. He narrowed his eyes in concentration, staring directly into hers. She gulped.

Her vision fogged over, even though her eyes were wide open. She stiffened, but immediately felt a presence at her temples, a strange and yet familiar warmth that was not hers. It ran through her body and wrapped itself around her core. It squeezed once, twice—then knowledge exploded in her head, a dazzling burst of light that left a vague imprint of a memory, of performing a lightening spell on a heavy bag of flour in a kitchen with shifting patterns of sunlight that danced over brown linoleum.

The sensation of being overtaken by another presence was too much for Gwen. She felt naked, exposed, letting someone deep into the center of her core. She sprang away from Aidan's fingers on her temples. The fog in her eyes cleared and Aidan stood before her, looking puzzled.

"Did you get it? What's wrong?"

"Yeah. Yeah, I got it." Gwen tried to calm herself. Aidan seemed fine—what was wrong with her? Why was she so jumpy? It was just Aidan. She took a deep breath and turned to Bran. "Okay, let's get going."

***

Bran slept while Gwen hovered him down the path. He occasionally sighed, his breath a blue cloud. He was so pale. Every time Gwen looked at him, she found herself walking a little faster, willing Bran to hold on, to not get any worse. Her limbs ached and her head pounded with the effort of the spell, but Bran was in no shape to walk by himself. Aidan trudged silently behind her. They hadn't spoken much since the spell transfer, and Gwen wondered what Aidan thought of her behavior. Perhaps he hadn't noticed. She grimaced. It was unlikely he had missed her abrupt leap away from him.

The trees continued to thin, and a breeze brushed against Gwen's bare legs and across her cheeks. Was it warmer here? The maples they now walked under had denser foliage than the trees of yesterday. Only an occasional leaf drifted down from the canopy, which was filled with brilliant crimsons and golds that fluttered in the gentle winds around an odd pine standing straight and tall.

The path widened imperceptibly, until Gwen stopped watching for errant roots along the flattened, well-maintained trail. When the path was wide enough for Gwen and Aidan to comfortably walk side by side, Bran stirred and stretched.

"Oh, it's nice to be home."

"What? Are we at your house already?" Gwen looked around, but there were no dwellings in sight.

"No, no. We've entered the old Silverwood realm, that's all. Father took it over when Mother died, so it's under Wintertree protection now. It'll be a while yet," Bran said sleepily. He turned on his bed of air and fell back to sleep.

Gwen's shoulders slumped. The leap of hope at Bran's initial words drained out of her and left only the tired weight of the spell on her body.

"We're well on our way," Aidan said. He slid a hand into hers. She grasped it tightly, thankful for his presence, for his ability to forget her twitchiness earlier.

Within an hour, larger and larger meadows divided the forest, which eventually petered out. They were left staring at a vast expanse of rolling hills covered in dry waving grasses. The sun shone brightly overhead, gilding the grass in a welcoming golden light. It smelled heavenly to Gwen, like summer and harvest and fresh open spaces.

"Well, this is different," Aidan said finally. "I can actually see farther than twenty feet. No offense to your mother, but I think I like what Faolan has done with the place."

Gwen squeezed his hand.

"I agree. If I never seen another mist-covered tree, it will be too soon." She squinted across the grassland to a thin trickle of smoke that rose beyond the nearest hill, almost invisible against the brilliant blue sky. "Is that smoke? Do you think someone lives over there?"

She and Aidan looked at each other with identical expressions of concern. Aidan said, "That's where the road goes, so I suppose we'll find out soon enough." He looked around with an appraising eye. "I wonder where we are, in England, I mean. We must be halfway to the seaside by now, but it looks so different."

"I guess the land is mostly the same, but humans and Breenan have done different things to it."

"Yeah, it's a lot more peaceful here. Strange we haven't seen anyone."

They struck out along the path, which had turned into a road of fine round pebbles. It wound up and down tiny hillocks and alongside a burbling stream for a time before it leaped across by way of an arched stone bridge, small and tidy. Gwen was tired from the effort of hovering Bran—her core pulsed with a continuous heat and she felt very hungry from the energy loss—but the road was so much easier than the forest that her burden was bearable.

It would have seemed idyllic but for evidence that a large number of people had recently walked this way. Broken arrows, discarded shoes, even a small straw figurine which looked like somebody's forgotten doll, lay abandoned on the borders of the road.

"What happened here?" Gwen said to Aidan quietly. There was no need to whisper since they were alone, but the discarded evidence of people's lives prompted a hushed response.

"It looks like a migration of some sort. A lot of people trying to get somewhere fast."

"Or get away from somewhere," Gwen said. Her heart sank when she realized what she saw. "This is from Breenan leaving Isolde's realm. Refugees who couldn't find food, or were invaded." She only realized that she was clutching Aidan's hand tightly when he covered her white knuckles with his other hand and stroked the fingers in an attempt to relax her. She released his hand and hugged herself. "I wonder how many passed this way."

Aidan was silent for a moment. Gwen wondered what he was thinking. Finally he said, "Come on. We need to keep moving."

Twenty minutes later found them cresting a small mound in front of the stream of smoke. Below, in a valley nestled between three hills, lay a village. Stone huts surrounded a central open area dotted by small figures, moving about their business. C hildren played a game with a long rope, next to a field beyond the huts. Even from this distance, Gwen recognized ripening orange squash scattered haphazardly among drying vines. They didn't appear to be planted in any kind of order or row. Gwen wondered how they farmed, especially since there were no domesticated animals that she could see. Even so, it was much more recognizably a village than the warren in the forest had been.

A crinkling of plastic drew Gwen's attention to Aidan. He had dropped the pack to the ground and found a package of chips. He offered the bag to her.

"Crisps? I can't possibly face another village without something in my stomach."

"Thanks." She rustled around in the bag and extracted a small handful. "We didn't really do breakfast, did we? I was so focused on leaving the craziness of the forest that it slipped my mind." She carefully lowered Bran to the ground. The release of the spell made her dizzy with relief for a moment. Bran woke up with a moan.

"Time for food," she said.

"I'm not hungry," Bran said without opening his eyes. His fingertips glowed with an eerie red light that flickered faintly. Gwen exchanged a worried look with Aidan.

"Come on, mate," Aidan said cheerily. "Spot of breakfast, then we've a walk through a village. You'll need your strength for that."

Bran blearily opened his eyes, pushed himself upright with a groan, and looked down the road toward the huts.

"Right. I don't know how far I can walk, but I'll try."

"At least if we can hover you in an upright position, it might not be that noticeable," said Gwen. "And you can keep your hands in your pockets."

Bran looked down at his glowing fingers and shut his mouth tight.

"Right," he said again, looking queasy.

"Unless we ask for the villagers' help," Aidan said, looking brighter. "This is your father's realm, which makes you some sort of prince, right? Let's tell them who you are. Surely they'd help their prince."

Bran was shaking his head before Aidan had finished speaking.

"Not like this. My symptoms—they're too similar to spellpox. It's highly contagious. One sparky cough, and we'll be run out of town before we can explain. Or worse, locked up and quarantined."

"All right, fine. We walk through town, quickly, and hope no one bothers us. Cover your mouth with your sleeve."

"Do you want to hover Bran for a while, and make it look like you're supporting him while walking?" Gwen said. "You're better at it than I am. I'd still make it look like he's floating on a cloud." After last night's attack and Bran's warning, Gwen was keen to appear confident and strong in front of the Breenan.

Aidan passed her the backpack and floated Bran with the spell so his feet barely cleared the ground. Gwen nodded in approval. It looked like Bran was walking with Aidan's help, as long as she didn't look too closely at his motionless feet. It would have to do.

It took another ten minutes to reach the village, by which time Bran was visibly limper than at the top of the hill. He rallied when a few of the villagers turned in their direction. Wariness was etched across the villagers' faces and suspicion in the stiff way they held themselves, waiting to see who the newcomers were.

"Nice and confident, now," Aidan said before they were in earshot. "We walk through as quickly as possible. Don't engage."

Gwen nodded and straightened her shoulders in an attempt to portray assured self-reliance. More and more villagers stopped what they were doing to glance their way. When the trio was close enough, Gwen tried to smile and nod. This seemed to appease the watchers, who nodded back and relaxed their vigilant stances.

"Look friendly," she hissed to Aidan. He adjusted Bran on his shoulder for a more realistic look, then eyed her slantwise.

"What, I don't look friendly normally? I thought that's what you liked about me," he said with a grin.

"Very funny. Come on, let's get out of here in one piece. You're doing great, Bran," she added to the barely functioning Bran, who looked on the verge of unconsciousness.

The villagers watched them, but made no move to approach nor speak to them. Gwen preferred this. The warren people had been creepy enough. She didn't need a repeat.

They passed through the circle of stone huts, eleven in total, each one containing a solid wooden door carved with insignias of foliage and curling vines.

"Do you think the doors say something in their leaf writing?" Gwen whispered to Aidan. "I wonder what they mean."

"Perhaps they're names, or family crests."

"Like a totem pole." Gwen considered the carvings with renewed interest, then looked away hastily when she

93

caught the eye of a Breenan man who glared at her suspiciously. She gave a vacant smile and kept her eyes forward.

A small pond lined with trees lay within sight of the huts, past the last field. Aidan managed to stumble behind a graceful poplar before Bran fell off his shoulder onto the pillow of air. Gwen hurried to Bran's side.

"He's glowing even more now," she said to Aidan. Bran's whole hands pulsed red with fiery orange highlights, visible after slipping out of his pockets. "I hope we're almost there."

Aidan opened his mouth to speak, but before he could make a sound a great commotion burst out in the direction of the village. Mouth dry, Gwen scrambled around the tree to get a better look.

Four people ran from the village, holding their arms over their heads for protection. One, who looked like the father of the group, slowed and chivvied two smaller figures along, putting himself between them and the village. Gwen soon found out why. A knot of villagers had banded together and were throwing objects at the retreating family. Gwen couldn't tell what the objects were—perhaps some rotten food, from the way they squashed on the road when the villagers missed their targets. The villagers watched the family run down the road until the four reached the pond where Gwen and the others crouched. Then the villagers dispersed, and the family slowed to collapse at the water's edge.

Gwen sat frozen, petrified. Why had the villagers attacked this family? What could they have possibly done? Were Gwen and the others now in danger?

Gwen had a closer look at the four Breenan and

breathed a little easier. These people did not look threatening in the slightest. The simple skins they wore were ragged and dirty, and the children had no shoes. Only the mother carried anything, and it was simply a small sheet flung over her shoulder with a few lumpy items inside, the bundle no larger than her head.

Aidan cleared his throat to announce their presence. All four jumped with fright. The mother grabbed the children in her arms and the father stood in front, poised for a fight.

Aidan threw his hands up to show they were weaponless.

"It's all right. We're travelers. We don't mean any harm."

A moment of stillness passed while the father's eyes flashed back and forth between Gwen, Aidan, and the sleeping Bran, looking for threats. When he didn't find any, his shoulders slumped and he relaxed his stance.

"Are you also from Queen Isolde's realm?" He looked at them quizzically. "You are dressed very strangely."

Gwen looked down at her shorts.

"No, we're travelers from another land. Did you—did you leave because of the troubles?" She didn't want the answer, not really, but she had to ask.

"Yes. We live in the borderlands where the forest is thin. Our village was invaded a week ago. We left the realm—there was nothing to hunt, nothing to forage. We've tried begging in this realm," his mouth twisted around the words as if they tasted bitter. "But the people here do not take kindly to strangers. They fear being overrun, perhaps. Many of us have come before."

The guilt that had been eating at Gwen's insides ever since they had spoken to Isolde flared up into an acute pain. She vowed not to mention her connection to the queen—she was sure Aidan would follow her lead.

She bent down and opened their remaining backpack, pulling out a bag of chips and a package of pepperoni sticks. Aidan made an almost inaudible grunt of dissent, but she ignored it. She held out the food to the man.

"Here. It's not much, but it's something."

The man took the food gingerly, and examined its plastic packaging with curiosity. Gwen smiled briefly.

"You need to take off the clear stuff. Don't eat that. And rip open the bag—there's food inside."

"Thank you." The man looked up with clear eyes, his gratitude at the small gesture making Gwen feel worse that she couldn't do more. "We thank you."

Gwen nodded, finding nothing more to say. The man turned to share the chips and meat with his family. The children held out their hands eagerly and the woman nodded in thanks to Gwen. Gwen turned back to Bran and Aidan. Aidan's mouth was set in a thin line, but he said nothing. Gwen picked up the backpack.

"Ready to go?" she asked Aidan, who nodded. He hovered the sleeping Bran with a groan of effort and they left the pond's edge. One of the children pointed at them and his parents turned to watch them go. The man frowned.

"You are very skillful." He waved at the floating Bran. "Where did you come from, did you say?"

"A long way away," Gwen said hastily.

"And your friend—is he ill?"

"Yes," Gwen replied, thankful to leave the topic of their magical abilities. "He did too much magic at once. We're taking him to his father to be healed."

"Oh," the man said. The single word carried such a sense of finality and compassion that Gwen winced. "I am sorry for your loss. May the road treat you gently."

"He's not gone yet," Gwen snapped, then composed herself. The man was only being kind. "Thank you. I hope you and your family find some peace, somewhere."

The man nodded, and Gwen and Aidan left the pond to find the road once again—the road that would hopefully lead to Bran's cure and the realm's healing.

Chapter 7

Aidan was silent as they walked. Gwen peeked at him. His face was set in grim lines and he stared ahead without looking at her.

"What's wrong?" she asked, puzzled.

"If you keep giving away our food, we'll be the ones begging soon."

"What?" Gwen was taken aback. How could she have not given some of their food to the family by the pond? "They were starving. They had nothing. I had to do something."

Aidan sighed and ran his fingers through his hair. Then he stopped and turned to Gwen.

"Gwen. You have to stop taking responsibility for everything bad that's happened in Isolde's realm. You didn't know what would happen, and taking the locket was the right thing to do. It's Isolde's fault that the realm fell apart. She was the one who built a house of cards that came tumbling down when the locket was gone." He looked to the sky, as if asking for patience. "But if we're to save Bran, and help the realm, we have to be able to fend for ourselves. We didn't have a lot of food to begin with. Can we agree on not giving any more away, please?"

Gwen felt mutinous, but she didn't have any words to respond to Aidan. There was a hole in his logic, she knew it, but at the moment she couldn't find it. Aidan looked at her face, sighed again, and turned to start walking.

"Come on. Let's keep moving."

***

The road crept by, hour after long hour. Gwen was thankful for her shorts in the bright sun—the late summer heat mirrored the human world's weather more so than Isolde's realm did. Rolling hills were interspersed with small groves of trees and bisected by muddy rivers that meandered slowly through dry grasses. Occasionally, the road branched off and a minor tributary wound between hills and out of sight. Always, the fork in the road was marked by a single tree with a creeping vine wound around its trunk. Sometimes it was an oak festooned with clumps of mistletoe, other times it was a gnarled cherry smothered by clematis, but the combination of tree and creeping plant did not vary. During one of Bran's brief periods of wakefulness, Gwen asked him about it.

"It's a signpost," he said sleepily. "There's a village down the road, the village of Stillwater. There are lots of people living in father's realm."

"Could have fooled me." Aidan gazed around at the empty valley in which they stood. "I thought we were the last ones standing."

"The village folk often don't like being in the thick of things, but there are plenty of them. We'll pass through

99

Leafly soon—it's on the main road. Home is only a day away after that." Bran coughed his customary rainbow sparks. When he had recovered, he closed his eyes and said no more.

Gwen exchanged glances with Aidan.

"A whole day?" she said. "This is silly. Don't Breenan have any other way to get around other than by walking?"

"Yeah, I wish we could make a portal back to the real world and catch the bus," Aidan said.

"Wouldn't that be nice? If we actually knew where we were going, that is. And had money. And if our patient didn't shoot sparks."

"Three tickets to the Wintertree realm, please, driver. And don't mind the combustible lunatic here—he's harmless, really."

Gwen giggled, then looked at Bran and sighed. Aidan coughed and she glanced at him sharply. His face was pale.

"Are you okay?"

"I'm all right."

"No, it's hovering Bran, isn't it? Here, let me take a turn."

Aidan didn't protest. She passed him the backpack and he gently lowered Bran to the ground while Gwen reached into her core and drew on the fuzzy borrowed memory to lift Bran's body in the air. Bran didn't stir. The weight of the hovering magic fell on Gwen's shoulders like a heavy coat.

An hour later, the hills opened up to a wide valley with a large river that flowed steadily through the center. The road ran alongside its banks and met a cluster of low buildings in the middle of the valley. It was a much bigger settlement than the previous village they had encountered—it was still tiny by modern human standards, but Gwen estimated that at least a hundred low dwellings surrounded a large central area. The open square bustled with figures.

"At last, civilization in the Otherworld," Aidan said. He peered more closely. "Is it market day?"

"The square seems really busy." Gwen squinted into the distance. "Yes, that's exactly what's going on."

"Perhaps we can gather some supplies." Aidan looked thoughtful. Gwen frowned.

"But we don't have any money. I don't even know what they use for money here."

"Bran said they don't have money—they trade things. I wonder—if I went down there and played my flute…"

"You mean you want to busk? Put out your proverbial hat and see what people give you?" It sounded crazy, but the more Gwen thought about it, the more it made sense. "Isolde and company certainly put a high value on music. It could be worth a shot. We should ask Bran, though—make sure you aren't breaking the law or something." She moved to Bran and shook his shoulder gently. "Bran, wake up." He murmured groggily without opening his eyes. "Bran, we need to ask you a question. If Aidan played his flute in the Leafly market, would people give him things for playing?"

Bran nodded slowly.

"Yeah, I expect so. Go for it." He rolled over and covered his eyes with his sleeve.

The village grew larger and more imposing the closer they got. Gwen started to sweat. There were a lot of Breenan in this town. The stone dwellings housed many of them, but it was clear that market day had swelled the town's population considerably.

"What's the plan?" Gwen asked Aidan. "Are we just going to march in there and start playing? What about Bran?"

Aidan looked at Bran, whose hair waved in the slight breeze as he lay on his invisible bed, limp and lifeless.

"You'd better stay out of town with Bran," Aidan said. "We'll find somewhere safe for you to hide. I'll play, trade for some supplies, and we'll skirt the town on the way out."

"That sounds too easy. I don't like you going in on your own." Gwen worried her bottom lip as she stared at Bran, then sighed. "But I don't want to be quarantined if anyone spots Bran."

Aidan scanned the riverbank on their approach to the town. Gwen's hands clenched into fists at the sound of shouts and the murmur of a crowd.

"There." Aidan pointed. "A nice cluster of willows. You can hide inside one of them. Try not to have a traumatic flashback."

Gwen laughed in surprise. Aidan referred to the painful marking ceremony where they had received their tattoos and knowledge of their heritage. A large part of it had taken place under the sweeping branches of willow trees such as these.

"I'll do my best."

Aidan rummaged in the backpack to pull out his worn black case. He opened it and assembled his flute, then clutched it in tight hands and stood. Gwen's breath caught when it hit her that Aidan was leaving. She threw her arms around him.

"Be careful, okay? If anything—anything—seems strange or goes wrong, come right back. We can survive another day on chips if we have to."

"One bag between three? I hardly think so." He squeezed her to show he was joking. "I'll be careful, I promise."

Gwen released his body, but clutched his face between her hands to give him a final kiss.

"You'd better be."

He gave her a lopsided grin and paced with long strides toward the town. Gwen sighed at his retreating form and glanced around. There was nobody to see where she went—everyone must be at the market. Determined not to press her luck, she jogged toward the willows with Bran hovering beside her.

The space within the willow's branches was empty, and the yellowing leaves trapped heat to create a humid room that glowed with a golden light. Gwen lowered Bran carefully and sat beside him, relieved that they were safe for the moment.

Less than a minute had passed before Gwen's anxieties returned. She and Bran were safe, yes, but what about Aidan? What was happening out there? Was he successfully playing for an adoring audience, or had a different scenario played out? Gwen's mind flashed her a grim series of images—Aidan captured, Aidan shot with an arrow, Aidan's tattoo and half-human status exposed…

Gwen looked at Bran. He was peacefully sleeping, with no sign of waking up any time soon. The willow was as safe a hiding place as she could find. Bran would be fine here. She just wanted to check on Aidan, make sure he was okay. She would come right back.

Her mind made up, Gwen tucked the pack against Bran's back. She hoped that if Bran woke up, he would take the presence of the pack as an indication that they would return. Unencumbered by either the pack or Bran for the first time in a long while, Gwen peeked out of the willow to check that the coast was clear. She stole through the swaying fronds and sauntered casually toward the town.

It wasn't difficult to locate the market—the road led directly to the market's noises. Hardly anyone stood at their front doors to see her pass. One or two older Breenan sat on chairs beside dark doorways or empty alleys and stared at her as she strolled by, but none spoke to her and she passed them in silence, sweating. She felt distinctly out of place in her shorts, and vowed to stay in the shadows and leave as soon as she saw that Aidan was safe.

The din from the market square grew louder and louder on the deserted street until she emerged through a stone archway between two closely spaced houses. A melange of bodies and colors and smells dazzled her momentarily and she stopped to absorb the scene. There were no carts or stalls. Instead, woven blankets of greens and deep blues and vivid reds lay strewn over half of the marketplace ground. Spread on the blankets were goods for trade, large gourds and strange leaves and roots that Gwen didn't recognize. Some blankets held stoppered clay bottles, others were scattered with carved wooden utensils, and one even had a few daggers and other metal instruments. The Breenan crowd in the marketplace stepped lightly around the blankets to inspect goods and chat among themselves. The warm autumn air swirled throughout, scented with the earthy soil of root vegetables and the fragrance of unfamiliar herbs. Occasionally, one of the Breenan presiding over a blanket would exchange goods with their neighbor. It seemed simple enough to Gwen. Confusing to implement, but simple in theory. She wondered uneasily how Aidan would "trade" his music for food.

Thinking of Aidan brought her back to the dangers of the marketplace. It was so busy that no one had yet spared her a glance, but it wouldn't be long before she was noticed. She backed into the shadows of the nearest house and her eyes darted around frantically. Where was Aidan?

She heard him before she saw him. A melody soared high above her, achingly sweet and utterly different from the noises of the chattering crowd. The Breenan looked around with interest, and those who spotted Aidan pointed him out to their neighbors. Gwen followed the fingers with her eyes to find Aidan, his copper hair flaming in the sun and the silver flute glinting brightly. He stood, highlighted by the sun, on the outer edge of the marketplace where the blankets were less frequent.

Gwen's heart nearly beat out of her chest in fear and admiration. What it must have taken Aidan to bring flute to lips, to draw attention in such a dramatic way, all eyes fixed on him? Gwen couldn't think of anything worse, but Aidan looked calm and relaxed. He swayed slightly to his own melody with his eyes half-closed.

The haunting music drifted through the listening crowd for only a short while. Aidan didn't let the last note linger before he launched into a lively tune that made Gwen want to move her feet to the music. She kept still, but the Breenan crowd nearest Aidan had no such qualms. They quickly cleared a small area by folding blankets and rolling gourds out of the way. Immediately, eight Breenan lifted their feet and swung each other around in a Breenan-style jig. Gwen didn't hide her smile when she imagined Aidan's inner reaction to the Breenan, whom he insisted danced all the time. They certainly weren't proving him wrong today.

When the jig ended, the crowd cheered. Aidan gave a theatrical bow with no attempt to keep the grin off his face. Gwen shook her head, laughing. Aidan was enjoying every minute of this. He didn't let the cheering finish before he brought the flute to his lips and began another infectious tune. While the Breenan danced, filling the impromptu dance floor with their wild leaps, a small pile grew beside the swaying Aidan. Gwen watched, fascinated, as a Breenan woman placed a short stack of flatbreads next to a woven basket of berries and a striped yellow squash.

"It's working," Gwen whispered out loud. She shook her head in disbelief at their stroke of good luck. Good luck, and Aidan's skill and courage.

After the tune ended, the crowd clapped and Aidan gave another bow, then he waved to indicate that the music was done. The Breenan looked disappointed, but moved blankets back and continued with their market day as if nothing unusual had happened.

Aidan's pile of traded goods was too large for him to carry on his own. Gwen edged her way around the circumference of the marketplace to join him without being noticed. By the time she was within shouting distance, Aidan had already tucked his flute under his arm and bent to gather his spoils.

Gwen froze when a Breenan man walked toward Aidan

106

and stopped behind him. Who was this? Had their luck come to an end? She strained her ears to listen as the man spoke to the unaware Aidan with a booming voice.

"Musician. You have great talent."

Aidan whirled around to face the speaker. The man was tall, with wide shoulders and the beginnings of a gut, although he looked strong and fit. His hair was as copper as Aidan's own, which wasn't unusual—half the Breenan here had matching locks. He was dressed well in a finely woven shirt and a short cape, better than the majority of the market-goers. Gwen wondered if he were a local leader or noble. Aside from Isolde's social hierarchy of queen-courtier-forest people, she realized that she knew nothing about the strata of Breenan society in the Otherworld.

But if this man had any power, he probably wasn't a good person to be noticed by.

"Thank you." Aidan looked the man up and down with wariness.

"Where did you learn your music? I confess, I have not heard the tunes before."

Gwen tightened her fists, awaiting Aidan's answer.

"I found a human in another realm, and learned everything I could from him." Aidan delivered his lie without hesitation. "It seemed a shame not to take the opportunity."

The man nodded, respect written on his face.

"Indeed. That is a worthy point of view. I wonder—musician, would you be willing to play for my family tonight? You will be well-fed with a warm bed. My dwelling is not far to the northeast. You would be most welcome."

Aidan pretended to consider the offer, but eventually

shook his head with a show of regret.

"I'm sorry, I have to be moving on. Thank you for your offer."

"Well, if you change your mind in the next while, let me know," the man said, disappointment clear on his face. "I would dearly like to hear more. I am particularly fond of music."

Another well-dressed Breenan strode up to the man as he turned to go.

"Our negotiations are complete, my Lord Declan. Shall we depart?"

Aidan froze at the mention of his father's name. Gwen's heart skipped a beat. Had the other man said "Declan?" How common was that name here? The Declan before her was the right age to be Aidan's father, and their coloration was similar. Gwen studied Declan's face. Now that she looked, there were striking similarities between Aidan and this Declan. She leaned back against the wall of the nearest house, stunned. Could they really have found Aidan's father? A thought hit her—if Declan was anything like Gwen's mother, then Gwen needed to start worrying.

Declan sighed and glanced at Aidan, who stared at him in confusion.

"Yes, I'm ready to depart." He addressed Aidan. "Unless you have changed your mind?"

Aidan's eyes darted around the marketplace, obviously at a loss of what to do. Gwen sympathized completely. This was his chance to meet the man who had been an enigma his whole life. Despite the troubles after meeting Isolde, and the realization that Isolde was not who Gwen had hoped her to be, she still wouldn't give up their meeting for the world.

During Aidan's frantic searching, his eyes met Gwen's. They opened wide with relief. Gwen nodded, trying to convey her approval of Aidan going with Declan, but she also put her finger to her lips. Until they knew more about Declan, there was no reason to tell him about Gwen and Bran. He had to prove that he was on their side first. Aidan paused with indecision before he turned to Declan, who waited for his answer.

"On further thought, I'd be honored to join your family tonight," Aidan said slowly and formally.

Declan's face broke open in a wide smile, and Gwen shook her head in amazement at the resemblance to Aidan.

"Excellent! We'll leave at once." He gestured to the man with him. "Here, Tiernan, help the musician with his goods." Declan removed his cape with a flourish and laid it on the ground next to Aidan, and Tiernan bent to move the food and other offerings into the cape. When he and Aidan had finished packing the cape and Aidan had slung the package over his back, Declan said, "My home is in the Wintertree realm proper. I presume you are on foot?"

Aidan nodded mutely. He'd been tongue-tied ever since finding out Declan's name, but his eyes hardly left his father's face. When they flicked to Gwen, she backed away. That was her cue. She needed to collect Bran and make her way to the northern edge of this town. Following Aidan was her only option—she cursed herself for not having a tracker ring for him. How could she be so stupid? She had just assumed they would never be parted.

Once she had carefully sidled her way back to the archway, she fairly flew down the road toward the willow. Except for the few elderly Breenan who didn't look in any condition to follow her, no one saw her run by. She raced across the meadow and ducked into the willow, panting.

"Bran! Bran, we've got to move. Aidan found his father, but we need to follow him so we don't lose him." She picked up the backpack and clipped Bran's head in her haste. "Oh Bran! I'm so sorry." She swung the pack over her shoulders and bent down to Bran, then frowned. She'd hit him with enough force to wake him up, even if he had slept through her voice. He lay still, his sleep undisturbed, but an unhealthy sheen of sweat and a glow of greenish light emanated from his skin. He looked much worse than before. Gwen's lips tightened. Was this foolishness, to have let Aidan go with Declan? Did they really have time to spare? At least they were still traveling in the right direction. Gwen's only hope now was that Declan would prove more sympathetic than her own mother had been, and would help them with Bran.

Gwen dug into her core and brought out the magic she needed to hover Bran. It was a struggle, this time—the magical warmth oozed sluggishly out of her core. She attempted to drape Bran's arm around her neck to appear more natural, but he flopped back to his bed of air, a deadweight. Gwen dithered for a moment, arranging his limbs into a fetal position to reduce his apparent size. Unable to do more, she parted the willow branches and they passed through. She desperately hoped that no one would see them circumnavigate the town.

Luckily, the town borders remained as deserted as before, with all inhabitants at the market. The town was larger than it looked. Gwen began to sweat, nervous about losing Aidan and the weight of hovering Bran heavy on her body. She was completely alone now, without even Bran's company. Her legs stumbled into a jog, and Bran floated eerily before her.

Finally, too late for Gwen's taste, she spotted a party of three men leading two horses. Aidan's loping stride was recognizable among them. Gwen's heart hammered from exertion and from a release of pent-up panic that had threatened to escape ever since she had left Aidan. She slowed and let the group move farther along the road to avoid detection.

Once the party rounded the top of a small hillock and disappeared from view, Gwen pounced on her chance. She jogged with Bran's unconscious body toward the road and along its packed-dirt surface. Her panic emerged again when Aidan was out of sight. She puffed and gasped her way up the hill, determined not to lose the trail. When she reached the crest, she slowed and crept forward.

Aidan and the others were halfway across the next grassy valley already, the dull thud of their horses' hooves barely discernable. Gwen huffed out through her teeth, exasperated. How was she supposed to follow Aidan covertly when there was no cover for her to hide behind? Was the entire trip going to be a mix of waiting and panicked running?

When the group was halfway up the next mound, Gwen decided to risk her descent. She tried to be quiet as she crept down the road, although they were far enough away that she doubted they could hear her. As soon as Aidan and the others were out of sight over the hill, she raced across the valley.

After an hour of this pace, Gwen's endurance had almost reached its limit. The backpack pulled on her shoulders unbearably and made each step a fight against gravity. Her core flickered, unused to sustained magic. She gritted her teeth during her climb up yet another hillock. The landscape contained more trees now, small stands of spreading maples, their green leaves touched by yellow and red with the beginnings of a beautiful fall display. Gwen was too tired and annoyed to enjoy the picturesque vista. She looked at Bran. His skin glowed brighter than before, a green light exacerbating his already unhealthy pallor. She swallowed and pushed up the hill with greater determination.

The hill was crowned with three massive maples, whose trunks formed a tight wooden triangle. Gwen stole toward the trunks and lowered Bran into place behind one. She peered out from another, and breathed a sigh of relief. Declan had passed the reins of his horse to a small boy who had materialized nearby, and waved Aidan toward the door of a large cottage. The dwelling sat snugly in the arms of a woodland that blanketed the surrounding hills. Its wooden face with white trim glowed in the warmth of the afternoon sun that slanted across a meadow of swaying golden grass. Behind it was an impressively large outbuilding with a row of half-doors inhabited by horses munching hay. Even through her sweaty weariness, Gwen felt a twinge of pleasure at the scene. It looked so cozy and welcoming.

To the left of the door a group of children played at a game Gwen didn't recognize, that involved sticks and two balls the size of fists. At Declan's call, which Gwen could faintly hear on the breeze, the children stopped their play and clustered around him. Declan dispensed kisses and hair ruffles, and his booming laugh echoed in the meadow. Aidan stood to one side, awkward and out of place. Even from Gwen's perch on the hill, Aidan's discomfort was evident on his face. The man accompanying them, Tiernan, waved to Declan and trotted his horse in the direction of a line of smoke within the woodland.

Declan gestured to Aidan and said something inaudible. The children looked at Aidan with interest, and a couple of the braver ones moved to Aidan and gestured to his flute. Aidan held it out for inspection and the children touched it gingerly.

Gwen wanted to know what was going on. She looked at Bran with a moment's indecision, then laid the pack at his back. Unburdened, Gwen stretched briefly in pleasure before peeking out of the trees once again. The group at the cottage was busy inspecting Aidan, so she took her chance. She ran in a crouch to a lone maple halfway between Bran and the cottage. The tall grasses helped to conceal her, but if anyone looked directly at her she knew she'd be seen.

Once at the tree, she pressed her back against its trunk and gasped for breath. Her heart pounded and her head swam. No shouts of alarm followed her dash, and she tightened her jaw to conquer her fear before she poked her head out from the tree trunk.

"Where's your mother?" Declan's voice was clear and resonant. Gwen hunched lower in the grass and watched the little group.

"She's picking berries by the river with the older girls," a young boy with blond hair replied. "We're having them after supper."

"Excellent. And the others?"

"Tristan and the others will be back from their hunt soon."

Declan pushed the boy toward the cottage door.

"Fetch our honored guest a drink, my boy." He waved at two of the other children. "Come, bring us benches. And put his bundle inside—he's carried it far enough."

The children scampered to do their father's bidding. They relieved a bewildered Aidan of his bundle of market goods and dragged solid wooden benches from inside the cottage to form a semicircle. Declan gestured at Aidan to sit and poured golden liquid into a metal goblet from the pitcher carried by the blond boy.

"Drink, my new friend Aidan. To your health, and to the dexterity of your fingers. May they be ever nimble."

Aidan raised his glass to mirror Declan and sipped at the liquid. He watched Declan warily. Declan gulped from his goblet.

"Oh, I've been waiting for this moment. We've been too long on the road."

"What were you doing?" Aidan asked.

Declan leaned back on his hands. One of his children shuffled toward him on the ground to lay a head on his knee, and he brushed her hair absentmindedly.

"Border patrols. The troubles in the west are making the borderlands unstable. I'm a marshal for the king, so I must do my rounds. But there's nothing like coming home." He ruffled the little girl's hair and she giggled. "Is there, my little acorn?"

Aidan's lips tightened and he looked lost. He collected himself before anyone but Gwen noticed and picked up his flute.

"I promised I'd play for you. Shall I play something now?"

"If you're rested, by all means," Declan said. He looked surprised at Aidan's alacrity. "I would never object."

Aidan stood and moved to the opening of the semicircle. The children sitting on benches or against Declan stopped their chatter and watched Aidan intently. Aidan took a deep breath and half-closed his eyes. His flute at his lips, he began to play.

He didn't play the jigs from the market this time. A low, sad melody emerged from the silver instrument. It reached into Gwen's heart and brought out feelings of loss and longing—for what, she didn't know.

Gwen glanced at Declan, who appeared wholly absorbed by the music with his eyes closed and his chin raised. A couple of the younger children fidgeted, but the older ones watched Aidan raptly.

After a minute, quiet footfalls announced the arrival of the hunters, three young men and a young woman about Gwen's age who carried the swinging carcass of a deer between them. They laid it down gently at the threshold of the cottage and moved quietly to the group. A minute later, an older woman accompanied by a gaggle of girls emerged from around the left side of the cottage, all of them carrying woven baskets of purple-black berries. The girls looked curiously at Aidan, but they moved quietly to the benches and arranged themselves to listen. Aidan didn't appear to notice, absorbed in the music.

When the breeze carried the last note away, Aidan finally looked up. He seemed surprised by his growing audience. Declan began to clap and his family soon joined him.

"Well done! I haven't heard its like in many years. You have a tremendous gift, my friend."

Aidan bowed his head slightly for an answer. The older woman, who Gwen presumed was Declan's wife, looked sharply from Aidan to Declan.

"Another one of your by-blows, is he?" she said to Declan. Her head jerked toward Aidan.

Aidan froze. Declan shook his head.

"No, of course not." He glanced at Aidan and frowned. "I don't think so."

Aidan said nothing, but he stood tense with the wide eyes of a hunted deer. Declan rose slowly. He walked over to Aidan. Aidan looked ready to bolt.

"Let me see your mark," Declan said quietly to Aidan.

Aidan stepped backward.

"Why?"

Declan held out his hand in a gesture of peace.

"Please."

Aidan paused a moment before he released his breath in a sigh and tilted his neck to the right. He reached up and yanked at the neck of his shirt. A tattoo appeared, green leaves stark against the white of his pale skin.

Declan leaned in closely to examine the mark. When he straightened, he looked puzzled and his eyes raked Aidan's face.

"You are. You are my son."

Aidan wouldn't meet Declan's eyes now. He focused instead on hills in the far distance.

"But your mother—it says nothing about her." Declan peered at Aidan, trying to make Aidan look his way. "Who is your mother?"

Aidan's jaw tightened.

"Her name is Deirdre," he spat out. "If you remember."

Chapter 8

"Deirdre?" Declan said slowly. "Deirdre. But that would mean…" He looked incredulous, and studied Aidan's tight face in fascination. "You're partly human."

Aidan turned his gaze to Declan, but only glared at him by way of an answer. Declan's family behind him gasped and broke out into excited chatter. The older ones on the benches peered furtively from their perches, and the younger ones actually crawled to the side to get a closer look at their strange new brother, born of another world.

Declan's eyes glistened brightly. He grasped Aidan's forearms with two large hands and gazed at him.

"My son! The son I never knew. I don't know how you came to be here, but I'm so glad you've arrived at last." Declan beamed at Aidan with wet eyes and spontaneously wrapped him in a crushing bear hug. Aidan stayed stiff and unresponsive in his father's arms, although he made no attempt to escape. Gwen wondered if it were even possible to wriggle free of Declan's muscly arms.

When Declan finally released him, Aidan stepped back to create some distance between them.

"How did you get through?" Aidan asked, his voice strained. "Why did you come to my world?" Gwen noted the attempt at separation, Aidan's rejection of the Otherworld. She wondered if Declan noticed.

Declan shook his head, clearly trying to understand Aidan's perspective. He looked bewildered, but answered Aidan readily enough.

"A good friend of mine knew how to get through the portals. He never told me how. His name was Finn—I haven't seen him for ten years or more. It was just a lark, going to the human world. It was so different from anything I knew. I stopped going after—after Deirdre, in fact. I never knew…" He looked misty again and Aidan stiffened as if in fear of another embrace. Declan refrained, perhaps sensing that the first one had not been well-received. He asked instead, "How did you come here?"

"I know how to get through the portals too," Aidan said. He didn't elaborate, but said only, "My Breenan friend is sick. We're taking him to his father to be healed."

"What? Where is your sick friend?" Declan looked around before he asked, "And who is 'we?'"

Gwen guessed that this was her cue to emerge. Declan looked safe enough. She hoped they had judged his character well. She rose from the tall grasses and picked her way toward the benches. Aidan saw her first and his whole face blossomed with relief and happiness at the sight of her. She could hardly stop herself smiling in return, despite the circumstances. Declan looked puzzled at his reaction until he whirled around in the direction of Aidan's gaze. His family followed and their mouths dropped open. Gwen was suddenly too aware of her grubby arms and unusual shorts. She tossed her hair back and feigned a confidence she didn't feel.

"Hello," she said to the waiting group. "My name is Gwen."

Aidan moved swiftly to her side, grabbing her hand and giving it a firm squeeze.

"Where is he?" he asked quietly.

"Oh, right." Gwen turned and pulled the necessary magic out of her core. She had just enough strength left to reach Bran's immobile body and the backpack behind the maples and float them toward her. She leaned against Aidan. "Ugh, I've been doing that all afternoon. I'm exhausted." The overwhelming urge to cough shook her body. Aidan looked at her in concern.

"You're too pale. Here, I've got him." The pull on her core lightened considerably when Aidan took over the hovering. She let go with a sigh of relief. Bran's inert body floated their way until he lay in front of them. Gwen noted unhappily that his skin still glowed and his breaths were short.

Declan and his wife hurried to Bran's side with the rest of their clan following close behind. They ranged around Gwen and Aidan, forming a circle around them. Gwen didn't like feeling trapped, and she continued to lean against Aidan, comforted by his solid heat and the fact that they were together again.

"Wait," one of the hunters said, her bright eyes narrowed in a confused frown. "That's Bran. Prince Bran. Our Prince Bran."

Declan leaned forward and his wife gently brushed Bran's fringe off his forehead. Although Bran was now pulsating with green light and a sheet of sweat glistened on his cheeks, he was unmistakeably himself. Declan shook his head in confusion and looked at Aidan.

"Why do you have Prince Bran? And what's wrong with him? Is it spellpox?"

Aidan hesitated. Gwen rescued him.

"Bran's our friend. We met him when we first stumbled into the Otherworld. He made it to the human world by himself, but used too much magic while he was…" Gwen paused. It seemed like too much work to explain North America. "He overspent himself, and now he's sick. We're taking him to his father to be healed."

Declan looked grave.

"I've never heard of a cure for overuse of magic." He sighed. "Well, if anyone knows, it will be the king. Bran looks in bad shape, though. How long has he been like this?"

"He got sick yesterday, and he's been getting worse ever since. I haven't been able to wake him up since this morning," Gwen said. She bit her lip. Why did everyone keep saying that there was no hope? Could Bran really be dying? She repeated more forcefully, "We need to get him to his father. Soon."

"Of course," Declan said distractedly. "The castle is a half-day's ride from here. You can leave at first light. Bran will be all right until then—we can make him comfortable. My wife Morna has some remedies that will subdue the sickness, although not cure it." He gestured at his older sons. "Carry him inside and we'll clean him up."

Declan's children and wife funneled into the house, Bran in the arms of the eldest sons. Gwen and Aidan were left outside with Declan. Declan sighed and rubbed his face.

"I'm sorry, I didn't have a chance to properly greet

you," he said to Gwen, bowing formally. "You're a friend of Aidan's?"

"Yes."

"I see you also have a mark." Gwen reached up to her left shoulder self-consciously. Declan asked delicately, "Are you also partly human?"

"Yes." Gwen saw no reason to lie. She glanced at Aidan, whose brooding face was preoccupied. She said to Declan, "Would you like to read it? You might find it interesting."

Declan looked puzzled, but moved closer to inspect Gwen's tattoo through the thin strap of her tank top. He frowned, and his eyes opened wide in astonishment.

"Queen Isolde's daughter? From the realm of the Velvet Woods?"

Gwen blinked in surprise. She hadn't realized her mother's realm had a name. She snorted. Of course it would be mysteriously fanciful. How typical of Isolde.

"That's me. Not a publicly acknowledged daughter, but still. We're also on another mission." She decided to throw caution to the wind. Aidan glanced at her, but she carried on. "Isolde's realm is in trouble, because—well, there are reasons." She swallowed, not wanting to go into those reasons. "There might be a chance for me to make things right. We're going to Isle Caengal to find a solution."

Declan studied her for a moment. What was he looking for? He seemed to find whatever it was, because he said, "If you can restore the Velvet Woods to its former self, the Nine Realms would be indebted to you, Gwen. The troubles are causing turmoil throughout the south." He nodded as if coming to a decision. "Tomorrow I will give you horses and transport for Prince Bran. I will have two of my children accompany you for protection. Tristan and Rhiannon will do, I think. They will help you take Bran to his father. I wish I could accompany you myself, but I resume border patrol tomorrow."

Aidan only nodded tightly, so Gwen said, "Thank you. We need all the help we can get around here. Now that Bran's unconscious, our Breenan knowledge is very limited."

Declan laughed sadly.

"I'm sorry you never had a chance to know your Breenan side. Both of you." He glanced at Aidan, who looked away. Declan sighed, and said, "Come in. The sun will set soon. Let us eat and prepare for your journey tomorrow."

"Eating sounds like a good plan," Gwen said, her stomach reasserting itself with a growl. Declan laughed again. Cheerful seemed like his natural state.

"There's always more than enough at our table. Come."

Declan waved Aidan and Gwen toward the door to the cottage. Aidan walked stiffly and clutched his flute with a tight grip. Gwen slipped a surreptitious hand into his free one and gave it a gentle squeeze. It was clear that Aidan wasn't taking this reunion very well, and she wished they had a few moments alone to talk.

That was an impossibility—Declan's children streamed through the door and surrounded them. They chattered excitedly and stared with curiosity in their direction. She and Aidan were on display, and Gwen would have happily crawled into the shadows if Aidan hadn't been there, needing her. She squared her shoulders and looked around the room they had entered.

The cottage was entirely one room on the first floor,

with great wooden pillars holding up the ceiling at intervals. Wood prevailed. Gwen was reminded of a rustic hunting lodge. Windows on every wall allowed light in from the setting sun and warmed the browns to a deep, gleaming golden. The huge room housed a kitchen of sorts at one end, with counters and a large pottery basin in lieu of a sink. Ensconced in another wall was a fireplace tall enough for Gwen to stand in, mercifully unlit in the warm summer evening. It was surrounded by heaps of cushions of various shapes and fabrics. The majority of the room was filled by a massive wooden slab of a table, glowing in sunbeams from the western windows. Gwen's eyebrows rose in amazement. It was large enough to seat all of Declan's family, with room for guests. Gwen hadn't counted, but there couldn't be any less than twenty-four in the house now. The table stood, unconcerned. Everyone would have a place. Gwen compared it to the kitchen table next to the window at her father's apartment, and considered the little house Aidan grew up in with his mother. She and Aidan were both entirely out of place here.

Declan evidently disagreed.

"Sit, please! You've traveled far." Declan pulled out two chairs for Aidan and Gwen at the head of the table and sat himself in a third next to Aidan. His wife and children began a well-choreographed routine to prepare dinner. The eldest arranged themselves at the table comfortably, sliding gloves off and leaning back in their chairs. Morna and the older children, girls and boys both, moved in and out of the kitchen area through a small door at the back. Even the smaller children moved with industry to place knives and plates on the wooden table. Gwen's attention was half on the ordered bustle of preparations and half on Declan while he spoke.

"I can't tell you how happy I am to learn that I have another son." He gazed at Aidan in delight. Aidan shifted uncomfortably. "I'm only sorry it wasn't sooner. Tell me, how is your mother? How is Deirdre?"

"She's fine," Aidan said shortly. "It's not easy being a single mother, though. She's worked hard to provide for us."

Declan's face grew sorrowful.

"I wish I'd—well, there's no use regretting what we can't change, is there? I remember when I met her. It was twilight. Deirdre was with friends, walking down the road to a party. I remember she called it a fancy-dress ball, but it looked no different from a regular ball to me. Finn and I joined her group, and what laughs we had that night! Deirdre's smile in the moonlight, the way she danced with such abandon, as if she could dance all night—I was smitten. Finn and I visited that place many times during those weeks we were posted at the southern borders. Finn grew bored but I pleaded with him, just one more time, just once more..." Declan sighed. "I had to eventually leave, and I never saw Deirdre again. The human world didn't call so sweetly without visiting Deirdre, and I ventured into it no more, despite Finn's invitations."

Aidan stared at Declan's face the entire time he spoke, soaking up every word. Gwen recognized his hungry expression—she had felt the same when Isolde had spoken about meeting her father. When it was clear Declan had finished his tale, Aidan spoke.

"She never told me about you, you know. I never even knew your name until I got my mark." He looked down to his lap. Gwen ached to see Aidan's hurt and confusion, but didn't know how to comfort him. Declan looked saddened, but he nodded.

"She was angry, I expect. I understand."

A red-headed girl of about thirteen approached Declan with a tray containing a pottery pitcher and numerous blown-glass cups.

"Thank you, Aina. A drink, after a long day and new surprises." He poured glass after glass of a dark red liquid and passed them to those seated, starting with Gwen and Aidan. He lifted his own in a toast. "To family, and to new beginnings."

They raised their cups and drank, Aidan more slowly than the rest. Gwen slid her hand to his leg and rubbed it in small circles, trying to comfort. Aidan reached down and clutched her hand fiercely, as if it were the only thing that kept him grounded.

Morna came to the table from the kitchen to speak to Declan about dinner. She casually sipped from his wine as she did so. Gwen thought that she and Aidan might have a few seconds out of the spotlight, but one of the eldest sons leaned forward to speak to them. He was a tall man with chestnut-brown hair, a few years older than Aidan. Gwen admitted to herself that he was very good-looking, but from his confident bearing and self-assured expression, it was clear that he knew it.

"Well-met, brother. I'm Tristan, eldest son of Declan and Morna. This," he pointed to a young woman across the table, her ash blond hair bright above sharp eyes. "Is Rhiannon, daughter of Declan and Bedelia. We'll be coming with you tomorrow to take Bran to the castle." He shook his head. "It would be Bran, wouldn't it?" He aimed this remark at his sister. She raised one eyebrow in a high arch.

"This is no time to be cavalier, Tristan. Bran doesn't have long for this world. Show some respect." She sipped from her glass and turned to Aidan. "Ignore him. Thankfully, bad manners aren't infectious. I'm afraid he's always like that. I should know—we're hunting partners. Someone has to keep him in check."

"We're a good team," Tristan said easily, taking no offense at his sister's words. "I shoot the deer, Rhiannon guts them."

In a strange, jerky movement, Rhiannon flicked her finger toward Tristan. Half a second later, Tristan winced and slapped at a tiny spark on his cheek. The extinguished spark left a trail of soot on his skin.

"That's not quite how it goes," Rhiannon said calmly, as if nothing had happened. "I'm the best shot in the family. Tristan's not bad."

"Well, who would dare to argue?" Tristan said smartly, although his eyes were smiling. "You know you'll pay for that later."

"Perhaps. If you can catch me off guard."

Gwen and Aidan glanced at each other. Gwen wasn't sure what to make of the two siblings. They seemed so at ease with each other and themselves, and she felt out of her element. They were their new guides through the Breenan world, but they weren't Bran.

The older children brought out huge platters of roasted venison and root vegetables, slightly charred from a fire that Gwen guessed was outside. The rest of Declan's brood arranged themselves noisily around the table on various stools and chairs, and speared food with long

126

prongs from the platters. Conversation faded with the arrival of the food.

Gwen cautiously filled her plate. Everything was simple, with a mild smoky flavor from the fire, but her ravenous stomach screamed for more. After two days of increasingly stale buns, sweaty cheese, and greasy chips, Gwen reveled in the full meal. Once their initial hunger had been satisfied, Declan turned to Aidan once again.

"So, Aidan, tell me more about yourself. What is your life like in the human world? I remember it to be a very strange and different place from this one."

Tristan, Rhiannon, and others sitting nearby paused and leaned forward to hear Aidan's answer. Aidan didn't appear to notice. His focus was entirely on his plate, until he raised his eyes to a candle in the center of the table and shrugged.

"I grew up in a small village, went to school. I visit the city occasionally, play music, work in a pub." Gwen poked Aidan and he looked around in surprise. Confused faces greeted him. "A pub? You know, where you drink beer and have a good time?" Heads nodded and Aidan continued. "I met Gwen in the spring and we fell into this world for a few days. Now I'm moving to Canada to study music." More confusion reigned, and Aidan clarified. "Canada is a land very far away. It's where Gwen lives. I have to fly there."

"You can fly?" A red-headed girl said incredulously, while the others looked both shocked and impressed. Gwen laughed and even Aidan's mouth briefly twitched out of its solemn expression.

"Yeah, the human world has a few tricks, too."

Declan looked at Aidan wistfully as Aidan ate the last

few bites of his roasted squash.

"A school just for music? What a wondrous place that must be."

Aidan smiled for the first time all afternoon. Gwen's heart squeezed to see it.

"Yeah, I'm looking forward to it." He glanced around at Declan's family, most of whom had finished eating. They idly licked forks and leaned back in their chairs. "Would you like me to play for you again?"

"Oh, there's no obligation. You're my long-lost son come home, not simply a wandering bard."

Aidan shrugged stiffly, retreating back into himself at the mention of his being Declan's son.

"That was our agreement. Music for food and a place to sleep. But if you don't want to listen…"

"Please, play if you wish. I would never turn down a chance for music in this house."

Aidan stood to pick up his flute that lay on top of the battered backpack by the door. Declan smiled at Gwen.

"Do you play as well?" he asked. His kind eyes brightened. Gwen laughed.

"No, not anymore. Aidan's the musical genius, not me."

"Ah, well. We all have our talents. I attempt to play the harp, but my feeble pickings are hardly worth the name of music. And I know only a few ballads, not nearly enough to satisfy."

Aidan walked purposefully to the empty fireplace, centering himself for maximum effect. Already he looked more relaxed, away from the curious questions of his new siblings and father, with an instrument in his hands. The room fell quiet, the older children hushing the younger ones. Gwen settled back in her chair to listen.

From the first notes that fell upon the waiting ears of Declan's family, Aidan had them enchanted. The music enveloped the room, its plaintive melody haunting and sad. Aidan closed his eyes, lost in his own spell and entirely at ease, as if the crowd of onlookers had disappeared. Gwen glanced at Declan, whose face had fallen into confusion and longing as he watched his strange new son. Gwen sympathized. Meeting her mother for the first time had been bewildering, although Isolde's callous treatment of Gwen and her friends was vastly different to Declan's cheery welcome. She understood Aidan's reluctance to let Declan play a fatherly role, when he had never been there for Aidan. She wondered if Declan understood how Aidan felt. He seemed like a man of simple feelings, used to a cheerful home filled with loving children.

Aidan played four songs, each punctuated only briefly by sighs from his captive audience. A couple of the youngest fell asleep in the laps of their sisters. At the closing of the fourth, Aidan brought his flute to his side, gave a small bow, and walked back to join Gwen.

"Thank you for dinner," he said formally to Declan.

"No, you have given us a gift beyond compare. Dinner was the least I could offer." Declan looked carefully at Aidan when he said this. Aidan looked down at Gwen.

"We should go check on Bran." He looked back to Declan. "Where is he?"

Declan pointed at a staircase to the second floor.

"He's in the first door on the right." He looked as if he wanted to say more, but refrained when Aidan nodded stiffly and led the way to the staircase. The eyes of Declan's family burned a hole in Gwen's back as she

129

followed Aidan.

Aidan had softened up to Declan just enough to be cordial, but Gwen could see his discomfort in the tenseness of his shoulders and his careful words. The Aidan she knew was easy and joking, not tight-lipped and quiet. She sighed, and wondered how best to reach him.

She took his hand when they entered the room where Bran lay. Morna had applied a poultice of strange-smelling herbs to Bran's wrists. It seemed to be working, if Bran's color was anything to go by—it had faded from a vibrant green light to a barely visible glow on his skin. He breathed more easily now, although his forehead still gleamed with sweat.

"He looks better." Gwen reached down to tuck Bran's blanket more securely around his chest with her free hand.

"Yeah," Aidan said in a distracted tone. Gwen turned and touched Aidan's cheek. He brought his eyes to her own and focused slowly from his inner thoughts to her face.

"How are you doing?" Gwen asked. Aidan looked about to burst with unexpressed emotions. "Talk to me."

Aidan sighed explosively, his breath coming in short bursts.

"I don't know. I don't know what to think. I'm just— I'm just…"

He broke away from Gwen and paced across the room only to encounter the far wall. He turned around, distracted, like a caged animal. He stopped in front of Gwen again, his eyes distressed. Without further words, he leaned down and pressed his lips to hers. Gwen was startled, but responded in kind. Aidan's kiss was intense, heated, as if he were trying to express himself physically since words failed him. He wrapped his arms around her and clutched her to him, as if desperate for her to understand what he was trying to say. Gwen thought she did, a little, and then she wasn't really thinking at all.

Aidan pushed against her and they shuffled until Gwen's back hit the wall. Aidan's hands were everywhere, all over her, and she pressed herself up and into him, letting everything else go, allowing him to show his emotions in the only way he felt he could, until a voice interrupted them.

"Like father, like son, is it?"

Gwen and Aidan broke off from their embrace, breathing heavily. Gwen looked past Aidan's shoulder— Morna had entered the room with an extra blanket for Bran. Aidan blinked out of the fog of desire that had clouded his eyes a moment before. His face darkened as the import of Morna's words struck him.

"I am nothing like him," Aidan spat out, his voice husky.

Morna shrugged.

"Perhaps." She looked at Aidan curiously. "It's not always a bad thing. He's a good man, despite his faults. I know you feel some injustice was done to you, but if Declan had known you existed, you can be sure he would have been a part of your life, somehow." She unfolded the blanket and spread it over Bran's legs. "Will you be staying on? Most of Declan's other children do, at some time or other."

"No," Aidan said vehemently. Morna pursed her lips.

"Don't be too severe on Declan. He has a good heart, and he'll be a good father if you let him." She moved out of the room and left Aidan staring after her. Gwen slid her arms around him for a hug.

"Whatever you want, just know I'm here for you. Okay?"

Aidan looked down at her, his mouth almost hovering on the edge of a smile, the first she'd seen all day. He was calmer now, his outburst of the previous moment subsided. Gwen didn't know whether she or Morna's words had had more of an effect.

"Thanks, Gwen." He kissed the top of her head, and sighed.

"I suppose we should go to bed," Gwen said. "Long day tomorrow."

"That'll be a change. I was enjoying being lazy."

Gwen laughed, relieved more than she could say to hear Aidan's usual lighthearted tone. She squeezed Aidan's middle and let go.

"Come on, slacker. Time for bed."

***

Too soon, Gwen was shaken awake by a firm hand on her shoulder.

"Gwen? Gwen, it's time to wake up. It's almost dawn."

Gwen struggled to open her eyes. She was so warm, so intensely comfortable, that it was a huge effort to turn her head and see the perpetrator of her awakening. Rhiannon stood in the dim of the early pre-dawn light that filtered through the shutters.

"Here are some clothes for you. They're mine—they should fit. We're close in size." Rhiannon tossed a bundle on the bed. "You'll be less conspicuous. And the king won't be as suspicious. Come downstairs when you're ready—we'll leave at once."

Feeling disjointed and out of place, Gwen rolled off her mattress onto the wooden floor and pushed herself up with a quiet grumble. She didn't want to wake the other girls, slumbering silently in their various beds, but she was so achy all over. She groped for the bundle Rhiannon had left her and shook it out. A pair of fitted pants, a linen shirt, and a soft suede coat fell out, along with a pair of leather shoes that landed on the mattress with a thump. Her bra and underwear, clean and dry, were easy to spot in the pile. Less than a minute had passed before she crept downstairs, combing her hair with her fingers and braiding it as she went.

The main room was empty in the gray light of early morning, but a clinking and huffing sound from outside alerted Gwen to Rhiannon's whereabouts. Gwen ducked through the open door to where four horses stood, snorting and swishing their tails. Tristan sat on one, natural and at ease, a large bundle balanced on his horse's rump. Rhiannon swung smoothly into the saddle of a second horse when Gwen emerged from the cottage. Aidan stood next to a third horse, eyeing it with distrust. He was dressed similarly to Tristan, in a blousy white shirt and leather vest, with slim brown pants under calf-height boots. Gwen approved the look—he cut a rather dashing figure.

Declan strode over to Aidan from his place beside Morna, who tucked a few cloth-covered bundles into saddlebags on Tristan's horse.

"You should have everything you need," Declan said with a worried crease between his eyes. It was an unnatural expression on him. "There is plenty of food, as well as all of your earnings from the market yesterday. Rhiannon and Tristan know the way to the palace and will take good care of both of you."

Aidan nodded, a mix of emotions warring on his face, but he said nothing.

"I'm glad we had this chance to finally meet," Declan said haltingly. "Know that you are always welcome here, whenever you wish. Please, don't be a stranger." He hesitated before raising his arms to place his hands on either side of Aidan's head. Aidan looked startled for a moment. Gwen realized that Declan was attempting the formal farewell that Bran had taught Aidan. Aidan returned the gesture and the two touched foreheads lightly. Declan stepped away with moist eyes.

"Thank you for letting us stay," Aidan said. Then he smiled, a genuine smile that Gwen was happy to see. "Hopefully we'll meet again one day."

Declan's face broke into a broad smile at Aidan's words.

"That would please me more than I can say."

Aidan turned to his horse, tucked his foot into the stirrup, and awkwardly heaved himself into the saddle. Gwen looked sourly at her horse. Aidan made it look relatively easy, but he had the advantage of height. The closest she'd ever been to a horse was a pony ride when she was five. Before she attempted to mount, Declan moved to her side.

"Let me help." He held his hands in a foothold and Gwen gratefully placed her foot in them. As she pushed off the ground, he lifted his hand until she landed with a thump on her stomach across the saddle. She swung her leg around with her cheeks burning, and Declan laughed good-naturedly.

"I remember, horses are out of fashion in the human world, aren't they? You have those splendid machines to ride around in now." Tristan and Rhiannon looked curiously at Gwen as Declan bowed. "Safe travels, Gwen. May you find what you seek."

"Thank you," Gwen said, before Tristan kicked his horse to a trot. He moved past Gwen and revealed that the bundle jostling behind him was Bran, curled in a fetal position under a blanket on a thick leather platform.

"Is Bran okay on the horse?"

"He won't fall off," Declan said. "He's tightly secured, and Tristan has a mild cushioning spell on him, so the bouncing won't bother him. And Morna's poultice will keep him from worsening until the king sees him."

Gwen gripped the leather reins with white knuckles and glanced at Aidan. His face was set in grim lines as he stared at his horse's mane. He looked at her.

"Do you know how to start this thing?"

Gwen shook her head, terrified yet on the verge of laughter. How did she find herself in these situations? She kicked the horse gingerly with her heels. The animal leaned down to munch grass and pulled the reins almost out of her hands. She bent forward to avoid losing them.

"I have no idea."

Laughter behind her from Declan and his wife burst forth a moment before Gwen heard a sharp smack. Her horse's head whipped up and it jolted forward, almost jerking Gwen from her seat. A wave of cold sweat left her with a precise appreciation of exactly how far away the ground really was. Her horse now in motion, she briefly looked back to see Rhiannon give the rump of Aidan's horse a flick with the end of her reins. Aidan clutched the saddle when his horse joined Gwen's in a reluctant trot.

"Farewell!" Declan shouted. "Come back soon!"

Rhiannon trotted beside Gwen and Aidan.

"So you two can't ride, it looks like." She glanced curiously at Gwen's white knuckles and Aidan's tight jaw. "Little Cuinn looks more comfortable on a horse, and he's only three."

"Yeah? Well, I'd like to see little Cuinn drive down the M11 on a bank holiday," Aidan said. "Give me a car any day."

Gwen had to agree. The horse's bouncing gait had her flopping in the saddle with an uncomfortable jolting motion. Her bottom had already grown sore and they hadn't been riding for more than a few minutes. An idea came to her, and she dug into her core for the necessary power. Her core felt less full than normal, somehow. She concentrated on the hovering spell, and nearly passed out.

"Gwen! What are you doing?" Rhiannon said from behind her.

Gwen clutched the saddle and frantically kept herself from sliding off the horse. A wave of nausea washed over her and she swallowed.

"I don't know. I tried to hover myself because my butt hurt, and I almost fainted."

Rhiannon frowned.

"Did you float Bran all the way from the Velvet Woods?"

"Yeah," Gwen said. Her vision stopped tunneling, but her core pulsed uncomfortably.

"You can't work that kind of magic on yourself, not without a huge power drain. And you can't use a power-hungry spell for so long without consequences. Notice how Tristan's making the horse carry Bran? You have to know your limits or you'll get yourself into trouble."

Gwen nodded contritely. She shivered at the thought of ending up in Bran's predicament. Rhiannon shook her head.

"No more magic for you for a day or so, or you'll end up like Bran. You two are a menace to yourselves, without proper training."

Rhiannon's chastisement made Gwen feel like a foolish child. She changed the topic.

"Rhiannon? How far is it to the castle?"

Rhiannon laughed. It briefly softened her sharp features and reminded her slightly of Aidan.

"Are you tired of riding already? It's another few hours yet, sorry to say. Better get comfortable." She must have noticed Gwen's woebegone face, because she relented. "Try squeezing your knees into the horse. It will give you more stability. Don't worry about directing her—she'll follow ours. She's lazy, but not stupid."

Aidan spoke then, his voice distant as if in deep thought.

"Bran said he was my cousin. What's the relation?"

"His mother is our father's half-sister through their father. He and Aunt Evelyn are both from the old realm of Silverwood, before Faolan annexed it a few years ago. Faolan married Aunt Evelyn, long ago now—she shared a mother with King Landon. Landon died years ago, from a tusk to the thigh, I think it was. During a hunt." Rhiannon glanced forward to Bran, hovering insensible in front of Tristan. "Bran and his brothers used to visit sometimes. Aunt Evelyn was lovely, I remember. She died a few years back, and the visits dried up. We've met up with Bran at the castle sometimes, though. He can be maddening, but good fun."

"That sounds about right," Aidan said to Gwen. "I suppose that explains why my mark says I'm from Landon's tribe. I wondered."

"Breenan politics sound as confusing as human ones," Gwen said. "My realm is simpler than your realm. You're going to have to get a history book for yours."

"If they had books, that is."

"What's a book?" Rhiannon asked.

"Exactly," Aidan said.

"It's a—" Gwen had a hard time putting a definition of a book into words. "It's a bundle of papers that have words on them, writing, so you can record things for the future."

"Ah," Rhiannon nodded in understanding. "Like a memory garden."

It was Gwen's turn to look puzzled. Rhiannon tossed her braid over her shoulder as she thought how to explain.

"It's a garden where the plants tell a story. The story may change from day to day or year to year, but don't all stories change a little in the telling? The essence is the same. Morna's herb garden tells the story of the family—how she and Father met, who the children are, when they were born or arrived or left, what their temperaments are like. I have my own ivy plant in the garden, trained to record that I arrived in the Wintertree realm when I was eight."

Tristan fell back to join the conversation.

"Remember when you forced that vine behind the cottage into the shape of your name and that boy from the village? You were so in love." Tristan drew out the vowels

138

of this last sentence for a sing-song effect.

Rhiannon didn't blush or look embarrassed, the way Gwen was sure she would have. Instead, she said calmly, "Watch it, dear brother. I know too much about you—I'm sure our new brother and his friend would be interested to know."

Tristan threw back his head and laughed, lighter yet eerily similar to Declan's booming chuckle.

"Do your worst, Rhiannon. I have nothing to hide."

"You're not from this realm?" Aidan asked Rhiannon.

"No. I was born in the Longshore realm, where my mother and I lived in a small fishing village. Father visited us when he was nearby. She died when I was eight—there was a storm at sea and many drowned that day—and Father brought me to the cottage, where I've lived ever since." She said all this in a matter-of-fact way. Gwen didn't think she had ever met someone quite so collected and self-assured. She was a little intimidated by Rhiannon, if she were completely honest with herself. Rhiannon nodded at her brother. "Tristan's the first-born son of Father and Morna, and his mother's favorite."

Tristan shrugged.

"Who can blame her? I'd be my favorite, too." He dodged, laughing, when Rhiannon threw a ball of green flames in his direction. It narrowly missed his shoulder. "Don't be sore, Rhiannon. You know you're one of Father's favorites."

"I'm not sore. You were due for one of your daily fireballs, that's all. Someone has to keep your ego in line."

Gwen let out a surprised laugh before she clamped her mouth shut. She didn't want to offend Tristan at the very start of their journey. Luckily, Tristan laughed as well.

"Thanks, Rhiannon. Now our beautiful new companion thinks I'm arrogant." He gave Gwen a winning smile. Rhiannon rolled her eyes.

"You did that on your own, dear brother."

Tristan and Rhiannon bantered back and forth while Gwen's focus centered inescapably on her increasingly sore bottom. After several minutes, she tentatively spoke.

"Can I walk for a minute? My butt feels like it's on fire."

Rhiannon looked at her pityingly, but slowed her horse.

"For a bit. We should keep up the pace as much as possible, for Bran's sake."

"Of course. Just for a minute, I promise." Gwen looked guiltily at Bran, but her bottom screamed at her. She swung her leg over the horse's backside and slid awkwardly to the ground. The stirrup dug into her stomach on the way down.

Aidan joined her on the ground a moment later, and they led their horses as quickly as Gwen could hobble. Tristan and Rhiannon's horses walked leisurely at their side, the two siblings at ease in the saddle.

Rhiannon pulled up to the backside of Aidan's horse, which carried his backpack. She reached out and traced the brand lettering on the backpack's cover.

"What's this?" She leaned in for a closer view. Aidan looked back to see what she referred to.

"It's the writing Gwen mentioned. That's what goes into books, to tell stories. That's how we record information."

"How strange. Tristan, come look at this." Tristan glanced over briefly, but his interest was minimal. Rhiannon asked, "What does it say?"

"It's a name, of the people who made the backpack. We don't use flowers to write at home."

Rhiannon stared at them with interest. Gwen felt uncomfortable under the scrutiny.

"Will you teach me something in 'writing?' How do I write my name?"

Aidan grinned at Gwen.

"Sure. We'll need to stop for a minute first, if Bran is all right. Find some dirt to draw in."

Rhiannon wrinkled her nose daintily. Aidan looked amused.

"I assume you don't have paper on you, so dirt will have to do. It's not something we commonly do, so you can stop feeding your internal stereotypes of inferior humans."

Rhiannon looked affronted.

"I was doing no such thing."

"Looks like our new brother has a chip on his shoulder," Tristan said from his perch on his horse. "Although, I bet you wouldn't swear on the sacred mountain that you weren't thinking it, Rhiannon."

Rhiannon glowered at Tristan but didn't answer. To keep the peace, Gwen bent down and traced Rhiannon's name in the dust of the road with her finger. Rhiannon swung down from her horse for a better view.

"See? Rhi—an—non." She pointed at each letter when she sounded it aloud. "Each letter has a different sound. When you put them together, they spell out your name."

Rhiannon studied the channels in the dirt. She squatted to trace them in the air above each letter.

"How strange," she said, half to herself. She shook her head and straightened. "Fascinating. Clumsy and inefficient, but fascinating."

"Inefficient?" Gwen and Aidan exchanged raised eyebrows. "It works pretty well for us."

"I suppose. But with plants, so much can be said by how a leaf curls, or the precise angle of a branch. There is no 'sound' of 'letters.' One can simply look at the pattern, and everything is known." Rhiannon pointed at Gwen's tattoo. "Take your mark, for example. This area of the pattern, here," she touched a region with three overlapping leaves. "It signifies that you belong to the realm of the Velvet Woods. The way the third leaf folds indicates the location of the realm, and the top leaf with a vine curling over, just so, is Isolde's signature. See, here it is repeated in the region that explains your parentage."

Gwen craned her neck to see the areas that Rhiannon's finger traced. Sure enough, a pattern of three leaves lay just below her collarbone, and the leaf and vine of Isolde repeated itself on her shoulder. Aidan shook his head.

"Perhaps you can say more, but it's ridiculously complicated. It must take forever to learn."

Rhiannon shrugged.

"Everyone manages it." She looked forward to Bran. "Come on, we'd better move. We've stopped long enough."

Aidan helped Gwen back into her saddle before he climbed into his own. Tristan nudged his horse into a brisk trot. Gwen felt her bottom complain instantly.

"How steady do you two feel?" Tristan asked with a grin. Gwen grew wary at the mischief in his eyes.

"Not bad," Aidan replied, heedless of the warning signs.

"Then hold on," Tristan said, and he kicked his mount.

The horse leaped forward, and Rhiannon kicked her own horse to follow. It was enough to awaken Gwen's and Aidan's own animals. Gwen clutched at the mane of her horse as it surged underneath her, its powerful legs pushing forward in a rolling canter. She let out an involuntary shriek of surprise and tightened her knees so forcefully that she was amazed the horse didn't complain.

Hooves thundered on the hard-packed earth. Rhiannon's hair in its long blond braid tossed and thumped on her back. Bran's platform swayed smoothly, cushioned by the spell. Tristan turned around in his saddle and laughed when he saw Gwen's wide eyes.

"Isn't this living?" he shouted.

***

At mid-day, they crested a small hill. Below them lay a valley, one half forested and the other carpeted by golden meadows. In the center of the valley, where trees met grass, a castle stood sentinel.

Unlike Isolde's solitary palace nestled deep within brooding trees, this castle was surrounded by a town, the largest Gwen had seen in the Otherworld. The castle was constructed of wood instead of stone, and rose a few storeys above the surrounding dwellings. The town had no discernable roads—instead it presented a jumble of rooftops liberally interspersed with crowns of trees and climbing vines.

When they drew closer to the city gates, Tristan and Rhiannon swung down gracefully from their horses and continued to walk on foot. Gwen and Aidan dismounted, if not smoothly, than with more ease than previously. Tristan turned to Gwen.

"Once we've passed Bran off to the king, you're headed east to the Longshore realm?"

"Yes. That's where Isle Caengal is, right?" Gwen's heart gave an uncomfortable jolt when she recalled the people of Isolde's realm, the starving children and the refugees on the road. At least they had almost delivered Bran to his father. Then he would be in safe hands, and they could continue on to find a cure for the realm. It sounded simple, in theory. Plans always did.

"So they say. Never been, myself."

"I've seen it," Rhiannon said, her voice hushed. "It's only an hour's walk from the village where I was born. No one ever makes land there, though. They say the island is guarded by an enormous sea serpent."

Gwen and Aidan exchanged skeptical looks and Tristan laughed.

"A sea serpent? Really, Rhiannon. They're all extinct by now. I'd love to see one—could you imagine?"

Aidan raise his eyebrows in disbelief.

"You mean sea serpents actually existed here? At some point?"

"Yes, of course. They turned on each other once they'd hunted all the selkies. The last one died three hundred years ago, I heard."

"You can laugh," Rhiannon said darkly. "There are plenty who swear they've seen it. And there must be a reason why no one ever visits the island." She turned to Gwen. "You really have to go there to find some 'cure' for the Velvet Woods?" Rhiannon snorted. "You like impossible quests, I see. First Bran, now this."

Gwen had nothing to say in response. Her shoulders

sagged. Rhiannon had a point—everyone said that Bran was incurable, and that no one ever visited this island where a magic spell might or might not be, that might or might not fix the realm.

Aidan put an arm around her shoulder as they approached the gate.

"We'll figure it out," he whispered in her ear. "We've made it this far, haven't we? We've only almost died twice on this trip. That's good odds for us."

Gwen chuckled weakly despite herself. She leaned her head briefly against Aidan, acknowledging his touch. She straightened when two guards approached their party, and Aidan's arm slipped off her shoulders.

Tristan greeted the guards.

"Good day, gentlemen. We have an urgent need to see the king. He will want to receive us—we have his son, Prince Bran." Tristan waved at Bran, wrapped tightly in his blanket cocoon. The guards leaned forward to inspect the unconscious prince. They both leaped back when they recognized Bran's face, and pointed sharp spears at the four.

"Guards!" one of them shouted, and three more guards ran out of the gates with spears at the ready. The horses shuffled and snorted, uneasy by the commotion. Gwen couldn't blame them. Why were they being received like this? Didn't the king want his son back?

"He's very ill," she said, speaking loudly and calmly. "We need to take him to his father."

One of the guards, an older Breenan with a close-cropped graying beard, leveled his spear at her face. Aidan made a motion to pull Gwen out of danger and two more spears swung close enough to graze his clothes. Aidan froze.

"Move along," the older guard said in clipped tones. "The king will want to deal with the kidnappers himself."

Chapter 9

Gwen's stomach dropped. Kidnappers?

"No, you don't understand…" she blurted out.

"Quiet," the older guard said. "And start walking."

Guards seized the reins from Gwen and waved her forward. Aidan gulped beside her. Even Rhiannon's normally calm face was marred by a slight frown. Tristan appeared relaxed, but his shoulders were tense.

"Don't worry, Gwen," he said lightly. "We'll sort it all out at the castle. The king knows us. These guards," he let the word shimmer with the faintest hint of contempt. "They're only following orders."

Gwen nodded tightly but said nothing further. The spears looked wickedly sharp and the points were dipped in a dark liquid. Was it poison?

The guards did not speak, but marched them along at a hurried pace. Even through her growing fog of fear— would the king believe Tristan that they had nothing to do with Bran's condition?—Gwen's surroundings grabbed her attention. Here was a small city, reminiscent of a medieval village but with drastic differences. Plants and gardens grew in abundance in front of every building, and vines climbed their way over every windowsill. The one or two storey buildings themselves were constructed entirely of unpainted wood, which Gwen could hardly see behind the foliage. A profusion of vibrant flowers, orange and purple and bright crimson, flourished in the late summer warmth and carpeted the houses with color. The road remained hard-packed dirt, refusing to make their boots dusty despite the dryness. Gwen wondered if it had a spell on it.

The people they passed looked more affluent than those in the villages, with clothes of leather and fur taking precedence. Many of the men and women they passed had brilliant fall foliage tucked in their hair. Leaves fluttered in the breeze, past onlookers who stared at Gwen and the others in open curiosity. The guards did not pause, but hustled them forward at an ever-quickening pace before too many passersby could gawk.

Despite the number of houses surrounding them, the road was wide and led in a winding fashion to the castle, which towered above the wooden shakes of the roofs encircling it. Gwen was surprised at its construction—she had expected a stone castle similar to Isolde's, with crenelated towers and flying pennants. Instead, a five-storey wooden mansion greeted her eyes. Oiled panels gleamed and large airy windows glinted in the sunlight. It had an understated appearance, but was so much larger than the houses in the surrounding town that there was no question of its status.

The road ended at a massive doorway. Heavy wooden doors studded with metal rivets were propped open invitingly, although sentries on either side discouraged casual entry. The relaxed sentries snapped to attention when they spotted Gwen and the others escorted by their fellow guards. The older guard halted at the doorway.

"Prisoners to see the king. We have Prince Bran in our custody."

Their guards lifted Bran's platform off of Tristan's horse. The sentries at the doorway took their horses and fell back to let them pass, one shouting ahead for more guards to accompany their group. Gwen was sweating now, and she sought out Aidan's hand for comfort. The guard behind her swatted at her groping hand.

"Do not interact. You will not escape."

Gwen glanced at Aidan, whose face was white over a tight jaw. He grimaced at her but didn't speak.

The guards swept them through a wide corridor, two-storey ceilings oppressive with dark wooden paneling. Both walls were liberally covered with mounted animal heads of all descriptions. Some were antlered deer, some the massive rack of moose, some a type of enormous ox. Gwen remembered Bran's interest in hunting, and then the tapestry in Isolde's castle of a human hunt. She kept her eyes down from then on, in case there was a human head mounted among the glassy-eyed animals.

The corridor ended with another open door. Light streaming from the room beyond hardly penetrated the dark corridor. A babble of raised voices floated on motes of dust in the air and grew louder as they approached.

Gwen blinked when they stepped through the doorway. The room they entered was bright from a plethora of floor-to-ceiling windows, which minimized the wood paneling of the walls. The windows were translucent to prevent visibility from the outside, but did nothing to reduce the brilliant sunlight refracting through bubbles in the glass.

The cavernous room was sparsely furnished with a few ornate chairs at the end and a long table along the side. Seven men clustered around the table. Some shouted and gesticulated wildly, while others hunched over maps.

At the entry of Gwen and the others, the eldest man turned to examine the arrivals. He was dressed similarly to the others, in slim trousers and shirt with a leather vest. His vest, however, was trimmed with a narrow strip of white fur around the neckline, and the buttons were of soft gold. More than this, Gwen could see he was important by his bearing, upright and casually confident, and his expression, firm and uncompromising. This must be King Faolan, ruler of the Wintertree realm—and Bran's father.

"My lord uncle," Tristan said, sweeping low in a deep bow.

"Ah, Tristan," Faolan said. "Well met. And, remind me again of your name, girl."

"Rhiannon." Rhiannon looked resigned.

"Yes. Rhiannon. You will forgive me—there are so many of you, it is difficult to remember." Faolan's eyes glanced at Gwen and Aidan, then came to rest on the curled form of his son. After a frozen moment, Faolan threw off all dignity and ran to his son's side. "Bran! Bran!" He turned to Tristan, his impassive expression vanished in the panic of an anxious parent. "What happened?"

Before Tristan could formulate an answer, Faolan's eyes swept their little group. He took in the guards with spears that pointed toward Gwen and Aidan, and his face hardened.

"You've captured the degenerates who took my son,"

150

he spat out, his tone brooking no argument. He pointed at Gwen and Aidan. "Those two, take them to a holding cell. Get them out of my sight!"

Guards grabbed Gwen's forearms roughly and dragged her backward. She stared at Faolan, his face twisted with rage while he watched them get dragged away. Aidan's shouts and Tristan and Rhiannon's attempts at explanation faded as a thick buzzing filled her ears. How could this be happening? They had traveled so far and risked so much— why couldn't Faolan see that?

Too quickly, they were pulled out of the lit chamber and back along the dark corridor with only the eyes of mournful dead animals to follow their progress. Another passageway, this one even darker and only large enough for three abreast, led along a winding path to a wide room with a ceiling so low that Aidan had to duck. Numerous round trapdoors dotted the floor in a pattern of grim polka-dots. A guard yanked up the furthest on the left to reveal a dark opening.

"In you go." She jerked her head toward the hole. "You can stay there until the king decides what to do with you."

Gwen looked at Aidan, panicked. Things were moving far too swiftly. Was there any way they could escape? Aidan was shoved to the hole and spears leveled at his face. He backed away slowly until his heels met the edge of the hole. He knelt down and felt with his feet. There must have been a ladder, because he descended with only one more anguished glance at Gwen.

A guard shoved Gwen and she stumbled toward the hole.

"Off you go, down the hatch. No complaints, and no tricks."

When Gwen looked down, the faint glint of Aidan's fiery hair lent her a tiny measure of relief. She sat at the edge of the hole and dangled her legs until she felt the rungs of a rope ladder. When she put her weight on the topmost rung, the ladder swung alarmingly. Hands reached up to steady the ladder and arms brushed her calves reassuringly.

"Come on, we don't have all day. Down you go." The guard pounded his spear butt against the floor impatiently. Gwen felt for the next rung and stepped down into the hole, her hands sweaty on the wooden floor. The darkness smelled dank and musty, as if they were underground.

Once her head sunk below the level of the floor, one of the guards slammed the trapdoor shut with a thud. The noise was muffled, with an earthy finality as if they were buried alive. The surprise of the trapdoor closing startled Gwen and she lost her footing on the ladder. She screamed, and fell backward into Aidan's arms. He held her close and she wriggled around to clutch him. Her terrified gasps filled the airless cell.

***

"Clear the table," Faolan ordered. Three of his sons scrambled to sweep away maps and cups. The guards lifted Bran to the table and gently laid his platform down on its surface. Faolan bent over his son and examined him, touching his forehead, feeling his pulse, laying a hand on his chest and closing his own eyes to sense Bran's core.

Tristan started to speak, but Rhiannon put a hand on his forearm.

"Don't," she whispered. "We'll sort it out in a minute.

152

Let the king calm down first."

Faolan continued to study Bran. To Rhiannon's right, two young men talked quietly.

"You know it'll be your fault, Crevan," a man with a blond ponytail said conversationally. "It always is."

"Shut up, Owen. Don't give Father any ideas." Crevan shook his head, somehow expressing both sadness and exasperation in the motion. "Of course Bran would get himself into trouble like this."

Faolan must have heard this last pronouncement, because his eyes flicked open. He turned his head sharply to look at his eldest son.

"Do not blame Bran for this tragedy. Why, it was only in the spring that you let him wander loose in the Velvet Woods. Or have you forgotten?"

"Of course not, father," Crevan muttered. "But you must admit, it is very like Bran to get into mischief. It's his nature."

Faolan's eyes softened, and he looked past Crevan with unseeing eyes.

"Your mother was just the same. He reminds me so much of her." He snapped back to attention and glared at his sons. "Unlike the rest of you. Come, examine him while I speak to your cousins." He walked toward Tristan and Rhiannon as the rest clustered around the unconscious Bran. "Thank you for bringing Bran to me, and escorting the criminals to my door. Tell me, what happened? I must know everything, so I can know how best to treat him."

Tristan glanced at his sister before he answered.

"From what we can gather, he exerted himself too far magically."

Faolan's face grew still. A few of his sons behind him

drew in their breath, but otherwise the hall was silent.

"How could this happen? Bran knows his limits as well as anyone. He should never have extended himself beyond his capabilities."

"This is Bran we're talking about," Owen said from the table.

"Silence," Faolan said sharply without turning to his son. To Tristan he said, "There is more. Tell me." His voice was firm and commanding, a voice that was used to being obeyed. Tristan bowed his head.

"Bran was in the human world when he overexerted himself."

The hall erupted in exclamations and gasps. Faolan remained still, although his face grew stony.

"Tell me how my son entered that world. Did the prisoners take him there?"

Tristan shook his head vehemently.

"No. No, Bran became friends with them in the spring, when they traveled here from the human world by accident and joined the Wintertree marking ceremony." Crevan closed his eyes as if the news pained him. Faolan slowly turned his gaze to his eldest son, and then back to Tristan without a word. Tristan continued. "A few days ago, Bran followed them into the human world without their knowledge. He attempted a translocation spell. That's when he fell ill." Tristan looked at Rhiannon helplessly. "That's all we know."

"And who are these two prisoners? If they are human, how is it they can travel to our world? If they are Breenan, what are they doing in the human world?" Faolan looked skeptical. "There must be more."

"Aidan and Gwendolyn are both half-human, half-

154

Breenan," Tristan said finally after a glance at his sister, who nodded briefly. "Aidan is our father's son by a human woman. Gwen is of the Velvet Woods. Queen Isolde's daughter."

At this Faolan's icy demeanor dissolved. His breathing grew heavy and his eyes flashed with anger.

"So. Isolde is not content to merely ravage the countryside and foist her people upon our unsuspecting villages. Now she harms my son? She is playing a very dangerous game, one she will not win. I promise her plot will not succeed. The Velvet Woods will cease to exist by the time I am finished with it." By the end of this speech, Faolan was almost shouting. His voice rang clearly through the hall. Tristan's mouth gaped and Rhiannon grew pale.

"No, sire, you don't understand," Tristan cut in when Faolan took a breath. Faolan turned his furious gaze upon him. Tristan quailed, but said, "Gwen is Isolde's unacknowledged daughter. There is no plot—Gwen is simply friends with Bran. That's all."

"I don't believe that for a moment. Humans are a weak and contemptuous people. Isolde must be behind this."

"It's not their fault. Bran followed them into their world. And besides, I sincerely doubt they could have overpowered Bran in any way. Their magic is present but pitifully undeveloped. They have no skills in fighting and can barely ride a horse. They risked their lives to bring Bran here, without any protection or conveyance from Isolde. They are no threat, I assure you."

Faolan breathed heavily as he stared at Tristan, whose face showed nothing but earnestness. Faolan turned back to Bran, who lay motionless on the cleared table. A few moments passed, during which no one dared to speak.

"The human world is fundamentally different from ours in a number of ways," Faolan said finally. "Bran would not have known his limits there. It would have been a simple matter of using magic at the edge of his ability, but with a new, unexpected boundary in place." He paced slowly to Bran and stroked the hair from his forehead. "There is so little I can do. I am still not convinced that Isolde had nothing to do with luring Bran into the human world."

"Gwen's intentions are pure," Tristan said, a pleading tone in his voice. He paused for a moment, as if unsure what to say. "She is on a quest, after bringing Bran to you, to save her mother's realm. She has some plan to find the ultimate cure on Isle Caengal. If she can, then the Velvet Woods will cease to be a problem on our borders. Gwen is trying to help, in whatever way she can." Rhiannon nodded in agreement at her brother's words.

Faolan stared at Tristan for a long minute. Tristan held his gaze. Eventually, Faolan spoke to the guards at the door.

"Bring me the prisoners."

***

While Gwen caught her breath, Aidan conjured a blue flame in his hand to drive away the darkness and rolled it onto the dirt floor. The cell looked as unwelcoming as it smelled, moist and earthy, dank and tiny. Aidan shouted up at the impassive trapdoor.

"Come back! There's been a mistake! Let us out!" He climbed up and pounded on the trapdoor, but the solid wooden slab did not shift.

Gwen slid down against the wall until she sat on the earthen floor, and hugged her knees tightly to her chest. She felt sick—her heart beat too fast and her stomach roiled. She and Aidan had tried to do the right thing—why were they being punished? Why was Faolan deaf to reason? Why hadn't Bran warned them that his father might react this way?

Aidan paused his shouting and leaned his head against the wall, panting. The silence was absolute, and his forceful breaths the only break in the stillness. Gwen didn't say anything. What was there to say?

"Wait," Aidan said, his voice excited. Gwen wondered tiredly what he could possibly be excited about. "Gwen—make a portal!"

Gwen gazed at Aidan in the flickering light of Aidan's blue fire. Confusion gradually gave way to understanding. She leaped up.

"Yes, of course." A smile of triumph crept over her face, mirroring Aidan's own grin. "Why didn't I think of that before? We can escape easily."

"Give it a go," Aidan said with determination.

"I can't, remember? Rhiannon said not to use magic today. I don't want to end up like Bran."

"Right. I suppose I can try, now that we're in the Otherworld. My mum is my anchor from this side."

"Give it a try. We have nothing to lose."

Aidan nodded and raised his arm. A flash of worry crossed his face, replaced by concentration. With a soft ripping noise, a rent in the fabric of the world emerged. Gwen smiled, then frowned as she processed what she saw.

"What is that?" Aidan examined the portal more closely. "Did I do it wrong?"

Gwen joined him at the fluttering portal. She reached forward tentatively to brush the human world. Instead of an open space leading to a forest, a room, a road, or anything else recognizable, solid rock met her questing fingers. Gwen racked her brain, trying to understand what they looked at. The truth slowly dawned on her.

"We're in a mountain," she said quietly. The portal mended itself with a swish. Aidan frowned and held out his arm in the opposite direction. The resulting portal opened to a similar view, but this time a vein of sparkling white crystals ran from the top to the bottom of the sheer rock wall. Gwen waited until the portal mended before she turned to Aidan's crestfallen face. "We can't escape." The full weight of her own words hit her and she sank back to the floor under their burden.

Aidan joined her on the floor after a minute. There was little else to do, after all.

"I suppose we wait and hope that Tristan and Rhiannon can get us out of this mess," he said finally into the silence.

Gwen nodded.

"At least we brought Bran back. Maybe Faolan can save him. And if Bran wakes up, he won't let us stay down here."

"No. If he doesn't wake up, though..." Aidan left the thought unfinished. Gwen shivered.

***

The half hour that elapsed felt like years before the

silence in their prison was interrupted by the scraping of the opening trapdoor. Gwen and Aidan leaped to their feet. Light streamed in from the round hole. Silhouetted against it were the heads of two guards.

"The king wants to see you," one of the guards said without preamble. "Come."

Gwen climbed up the rope ladder, swaying precariously until she grasped the top. The guards hauled her up unceremoniously by her arms and deposited her on her feet. Another guard encircled her forearm with a tight grip.

"Nothing tricky," the guard said. "You won't get far."

When Aidan had been hauled up and his arm firmly ensconced in another guard's hand, they proceeded back down the hall. The great double doors loomed menacingly ahead, and Gwen's hands trembled. What would happen? Aidan tripped behind her and the guard cursed. Gwen winced when Aidan grunted in pain. She turned to look, but her guard wrenched her forward.

Gwen was pulled through the double doors again, to a similar scene as before. Faolan paced in the center of the room. His sons still clustered around the table, but this time they were focused on Bran, who lay supine on the wooden slab as if for a viewing. Tristan and Rhiannon were among them, but looked up with concern once Gwen and Aidan were in sight. Faolan ceased his movement at their entry.

"Bring them here," he said. The guards roughly brought Gwen forward and left her, ten paces in front of Faolan. Aidan landed beside her and brushed off his sleeve where the guard had gripped him. Faolan moved toward them slowly, with deliberation. Gwen stiffened, unsure what to do. Would he hurt them somehow? Gwen couldn't see any sign of a weapon, but Bran had said that his father was particularly adept at magic. He could be capable of anything.

Faolan approached Aidan first and reached out to his left shoulder. Aidan flinched.

"Hold still," Faolan said, iron behind his words. Aidan froze and allowed Faolan to draw down the neck of his shirt. Faolan considered Aidan's mark for a moment, his eyes raking over the green tattoo, before he stepped back and nodded.

"A son of Declan, that is certain." He turned to Gwen and reached for her shoulder. She tensed, but tried not to show her discomfort as Faolan's cool fingers traced her skin to expose her shoulder. He spent longer on her mark than Aidan's, and she took the opportunity to study him. It was puzzling to recognize the shape of Bran's grinning features in the unforgiving lines of Faolan's face.

"And a daughter of Isolde, of the Velvet Woods," Faolan said. He stepped back and regarded her. Gwen shrugged her shirt back into place. "Tristan informed me of your journey thus far, and your self-appointed quest to restore your mother's realm by seeking out Isle Caengal." He looked at her thoughtfully. "The spells on that island are reputed to be many, and diverse. But rumors tell of a spell beyond all others, a powerful spell of restoration for those of pure intention. This spell, if it exists, would indeed heal both the Velvet Woods and my youngest son. I will permit you to leave my realm, on the condition that you continue to seek out this restoration spell and first use it to restore good health upon Bran. Then you may restore the Velvet Woods if you wish."

"Do you know anything else about Isle Caengal?"

Gwen asked. She had a hard time believing Faolan would let them go. He sounded as if he knew more about the island than anyone they had met so far, though, so she wasn't going to let an opportunity pass to find out more.

Faolan shrugged.

"The Isle is veiled in dark rumors and stories meant to frighten. I have had little reason to investigate until this point—the Isle does not lie within my realm, and I have power enough to rule without resorting to outside aid. Besides, I have no desire to face the trials."

"Trials?" Aidan said.

"The legends state that the Isle does not give up its secrets easily. Some form of testing is in place to ensure only those of purest intent may pass. A cousin of mine attempted to access the Isle many years ago. He was a simple-minded fool, and no doubt wanted the power to overthrow me. He never returned. Of course, you two will not face the same issue." Faolan smiled thinly. "However, I have one condition. Declan's son I will take on faith, despite his dubious half-breed status. But you," he said to Gwen. "You must prove your sincerity. Find the cure and I will release you." He waved to a servant on the edge of the hall, who came forward bearing a golden bracelet of fine filigree. She grasped Gwen's arm and slid the bracelet onto her wrist. With a smooth gesture, the woman wound her fingers around the bracelet. Horrified, Gwen watched the bracelet shrink and mold itself to fit her wrist perfectly. When the reworking was complete, the woman stepped back without a word.

"What is this? What did you do?"

"A device of my own invention," Faolan said. He watched her without expression. "The magic within is connected to Bran's life. If he ceases to be, so do you. It's simply a precaution on my part, to ensure you do your best to obtain the cure and do not return to the human world before you heal my son. Time is not a luxury he has at present. Oh, yes, one final touch." He strode forward and grasped Gwen's wrist before she had time to react. A yellow light shimmered over his fingers and onto the bracelet, where it sunk into the metal and disappeared. Faolan released Gwen's arm with a contemptuous flick. "Do not attempt to re-enter the human world while you wear this bracelet. You will not live long enough to regret the decision."

Gwen's mouth gaped open incredulously. Did Faolan think she was a heartless monster? Hadn't her actions up until now shown her dedication to helping Bran?

"I want Bran healed and Isolde's realm saved as much as anyone. That's all I've been doing since I arrived in the Otherworld. What else do I need to do to prove myself?"

"Succeed in your quest," Faolan said simply. "Find the cure. Do it quickly."

Chapter 10

Faolan's dispassionate eyes gazed at Gwen. Gwen felt numb, but horror flickered at the edges. She looked around wildly at Aidan and Tristan, both of whom appeared shell-shocked, and at Rhiannon, whose calm face had creased in a small frown of concern. Gwen's eyes darted back to Faolan, her mind still at a loss for words.

"I suggest you hurry," Faolan said. "Bran's health is rapidly deteriorating, and your mother will not survive for long."

Gwen frowned, her mind whirling.

"What do you mean, my mother won't survive for long? What's wrong with her?"

Faolan looked at her with mild curiosity.

"Are you not aware of how the defenses of the Velvet Woods are arranged?" Gwen shook her head. Isolde hadn't looked well, but Gwen had thought that it was due to another sickness, or perhaps sadness at the state of the realm. "So much of the realm is supported through magical means. When all is well, this method ensures strong defenses and lasting prosperity without the need to maintain armies and farms. However, when the magic is disrupted, there is little to be done. The magic to support the realm arises from the current ruler—in this case, your mother. The realm and Isolde are irrevocably linked while she still rules. If the realm suffers, so does she. And from the reports of my border patrol, failure of the realm is imminent. Already, the realms of Whitecliff and Riverside prepare to invade the Velvet Woods, along with my own army, of course. The day the realm fails and outside armies march within, Isolde's reign and life will end."

Gwen blinked in disbelief at Faolan's words.

"She didn't say anything. I mean, she looked sick, but..." Why had Isolde not told her? Did she not want to worry Gwen? Or did she think Gwen wouldn't have cared? Gwen wasn't sure what she felt. Isolde was her mother in the biological sense, but she had never been a part of Gwen's life. When they had met, Isolde was not the loving mother-figure Gwen had longed for. Still, she felt a strange bond with the arrogant, beautiful woman her father had once loved.

Another consideration sprang to Gwen's mind. Without Isolde, Gwen was cut off from entering the Otherworld. Isolde was Gwen's anchor to the Otherworld, her only tie to the Breenan lands and the reason she could make portals. Her father flitted across her mind's eye. What if she were barred from entering the human world? Her anchors, Isolde and her father, now seemed so fragile. What if she were trapped in the Otherworld forever?

All of these unwelcome thoughts spun through Gwen's mind in a second, leaving her disoriented and shaken.

Faolan looked impatient.

"You may travel freely through my lands and in the

Longshore realm, with whom I have a peace treaty. Go, now. Your hours are numbered." He nodded to Tristan and Rhiannon, gave Aidan a passing glance, and walked over to Bran on his table.

A hand tugged Gwen's elbow. She turned, and Tristan pulled her toward the door.

"Come on, Gwen. It's time to go."

Gwen looked back once after the guards had surrounded their party and walked them through the double doors. Faolan stood at Bran's head. He stroked his son's hair back from his forehead with an expression of naked fear. Gwen shivered.

***

Crevan shifted his weight back and forth a few times before he spoke.

"Father, why didn't you send us to accompany the half-bloods? If there is a way to cure Bran on the isle, should we rely on inexperienced half-humans?"

"It's a fool's errand," Faolan said shortly without looking up from Bran's face. "The powerful spells on Isle Caengal are almost certainly no more than legend. Allowing the half-bloods to continue their quest removes them from here in an honorable way. Declan and Isolde will have no cause for blame."

"But what about the bracelet?" Crevan asked, his attempt to match Faolan's impassive tone not entirely succeeding. "If the quest is impossible, the girl will die."

Faolan shrugged.

"It was a reasonable precaution. I did not say the quest was impossible, only highly unlikely to succeed given the lack of verifiable information about the isle. Perhaps they may yet succeed, and Bran will be saved due to their efforts. If not, well, Isolde is hardly in a state to bother about the welfare of an unacknowledged half-breed child." He looked at Crevan. "I need you—all of you—to alert Lord Maddoc, Lady Oriana, all of the most powerful magical Breenan in the realm. I need them here, to consult about possible healing measures for Bran."

"But no one has ever recovered from overuse of magic," Crevan said quietly.

"Silence!" Faolan thundered, his eyes wide and his calm extinguished. "Leave now and bring me who I require!"

Crevan nodded silently, pity in his eyes. With a last look at his youngest brother, stretched on the wooden table with a peaceful expression on his face, he nodded at his other brothers. They filed out and left Faolan to kneel at Bran's head in the empty hall.

***

Gwen's heart pounded and her stomach was hollow during their march to the gates of Faolan's house. The treacherous bracelet was cool on her skin—how long would Bran last? Gwen began to shake. Aidan looked at her in concern, but didn't approach her until the guards pointed them out of the double doors into the brilliant sunlight of Faolan's bustling town and handed Rhiannon the reins of their horses.

Rhiannon passed Gwen her reins, but remained silent. Tristan swung himself into his saddle before he spoke.

"We'd better get moving. The border of the Longshore

realm is still a few hours away, and we don't have much time."

Gwen gazed at him, her mind turning this declaration over. She tried to extract meaning through her fog of dread.

"You mean—you're coming with us?"

Tristan and Rhiannon glanced at each other before Tristan turned to Gwen.

"Of course. We're not about to abandon you now. Besides," he cracked a strained version of his usual jovial grin. "Impossible adventures are just my style."

"You'll need our help," Rhiannon added. "You're both very underprepared for life here. Besides, Aidan is family—and we don't let family down."

Aidan, quiet until now, said, "Thank you. Thank you both." He touched Gwen's arm gently and offered his hands as a foothold. She squeezed his shoulder and mounted her horse, grateful he was here. Tristan and Rhiannon would be invaluable, but she needed Aidan's presence.

"Tristan," she said. "Can't we do something about the bracelet? Magic it off, somehow?"

Tristan shook his head.

"Faolan is uncommonly powerful. There's no way I'd have the ability to thwart a spell of his making. And I wouldn't want to try, in case my meddling set the spell in motion."

"Gwen." Aidan pointed to her hand. "What's happened to your ring?"

Gwen glanced at Bran's tracker ring on her thumb. The once bright copper was now pale and somehow insubstantial. Tristan grabbed her hand and examined the ring.

"Is this Bran's?"

"Yes."

Tristan sighed and let go.

"As Bran's health worsens, the ring will fade—it's made of magic, and is connected to him. When he passes, the ring will disappear."

Gwen stared at him in horror.

"But it's so faded already."

"Then we'd better move quickly."

Their ride out of town was silent amid the noise of the bustling townsfolk. No one gave them a second glance now that they were no longer being dragged through the streets by guards.

Past the main gates of the town, the noise of the multitudes faded behind them until the soft clopping of their horses' hooves on the earthen track was the only sound. Gwen wanted to break the silence, but she didn't know what to say. The bracelet was heavy and unyielding on her wrist.

At a fork in the road, Rhiannon trotted to the forefront of their group.

"This way to the Longshore realm. If we speed up a little, we can be on the shores near Isle Caengal by dusk."

"Good," Gwen said through her dry throat. Her voice was tight and strange in her ears, as if long-unused. She cleared it roughly. "What else do you two know about this island? What's its story? Why the trials?"

Tristan pointed to his sister.

"Rhiannon will know more than me. She used to live near it, after all."

Rhiannon frowned, but it was an expression of

thoughtfulness, not annoyance.

"There are legends, nothing more. I'm trying to remember, but it's been so long since…" Her lips tightened almost imperceptibly, and Gwen remembered with a pang that Rhiannon only went to live with Declan in the Wintertree realm when her mother died. Rhiannon continued, ignoring the pause. "If I remember rightly, the stories say that there were two queens, hundreds of years ago. One was a Breenan, Lady Maeve, highly skilled in magic. The other was a human woman, a powerful queen in her own land. This was many years before the closing of the portals, back when it was simple to travel between the worlds, if you knew the way.

"The queens were great friends, one often staying with the other for long stretches. The human queen was an inventor, constantly dreaming up new ways to better the worlds, often using the magic of the Breenan queen. Together they created many new, powerful spells." Rhiannon shrugged. "That's all the stories say. Oh, and that Lady Maeve raised Isle Caengal from the sea, built her castle on it, and put a strong protection magic over it all. That's why no one can set foot on the island."

"Protection for what, I wonder?" Aidan leaned forward with interest. "Protection for this restoration spell?"

"I don't understand," Gwen said. "Why does it need to be protected? It sounds like a decent spell. What's the harm in letting it loose on the world?"

"It's probably not the only spell there. Who knows what the queens dreamed up? Assuming the legends are true, that is." Rhiannon clamped her lips shut after a glare from Tristan, and she looked contrite.

Gwen's interest in the island's history subsided once

169

the bracelet again rose to the foreground of her mind. The spell had to be real. Any other possibility didn't bear thinking about. A fierce hate rose in her for Faolan, not tempered in the slightest by the knowledge that he had done what he did for love of his son.

Aidan glanced at the changing passions on Gwen's face with a worried expression.

"How far to the island?" he asked Rhiannon.

"A few hours yet," she said quietly. Tristan turned to grin at Aidan.

"Better get comfortable on that horse."

***

By the time the sun approached the horizon in the cloud-streaked sky, shooting rays of magenta and fiery orange across the zenith, Gwen was too tired and sore to worry about the bracelet. They had crossed the border only an hour before, but to Gwen it might as well have been a week. Her legs and bottom screamed at her, and her inner thighs were rubbed raw from the hours of straddling her horse.

The landscape after the border was not substantially different from the Wintertree realm, with rolling hills alternately covered by sweeping, deciduous forests of vibrant autumn hues and dry, waving grasses. There were no signs of habitation until the scent of the sea wafted into Gwen's nostrils with the stiffening breeze.

"Look, Gwen," Aidan said. He pointed to the left. "Do you reckon it's a house?"

Gwen squinted into the setting sun in the direction of Aidan's finger. At first she didn't know what she looked

170

at. In the crevasse of two barren, exposed mounds of bedrock, a clutter of driftwood had collected. Aidan's comment made her look more closely. There was, perhaps, a wild structure to the pile, the faintest hint that the grayed logs had not gathered there by happenstance. That large, flattish log might be a door, and maybe the layers of wood on the top could act as shingles on a roof. A cluster of seashells adorned the space beside the door, too artfully displayed to be random. Gwen was certain that the gaps in the structure at chest-height were covered in sheets of translucent seaweed, perhaps acting as a windowpane.

"I think you're right," she said at last to Aidan. "They're good at camouflage here, aren't they?"

Rhiannon raised an eyebrow, but said only, "We'll camp on the shoreline, over the next hill."

Gwen's heart dropped, but before she could say anything, Aidan cut in.

"We're stopping for the night?" he said, his voice tense. "What about Bran's health? We don't have long." He looked at Gwen's hand and his jaw worked.

"We can't do anything in the dark," Gwen said tersely. As a matter of fact, she agreed wholeheartedly with Aidan's sentiment—how many hours did she have left?— but his concern made her even more worried, which left her angry and grumpy. She grew annoyed at herself for snapping at Aidan when she caught a glimpse of his hurt expression, which only soured her mood more. She kicked her horse into a trot to put some distance between herself and Aidan, and winced when the increased pace aggravated her sore legs.

When Gwen crested the low hill, her senses were assaulted by the overpowering presence of the sea. A

171

barrage of sound hit her from a cascading torrent of waves that crashed on the pebbly shore. The sulfurous scent of exposed seaweed drifted past her nose, and moist air collected on her skin in a salty dew. Even the sunset was more vibrant here—the foaming waves glowed red and pink under an incandescent sky, which was only separated from the sea by a dark mass of land that jutted out of the water.

Rhiannon stopped her horse beside Gwen's.

"Isle Caengal," she said reflectively.

"Bit gloomy, isn't it?" Tristan said as he and Aidan rode up to the girls.

Rhiannon flicked her braid back from her shoulder.

"Well, it isn't shrouded with mystery and intrigue for nothing." She swung down from her horse and unclipped her pack from the saddle. The rest of the horse's tack came off next, and Tristan proceeded to follow his sister's lead.

"What are you doing? Are we stopping here?" Gwen asked.

"We won't need the horses anymore," Rhiannon said. "We'll send them off to roam while we're on the island."

"They won't run away? How will we get back home?" Aidan remained seated on his horse.

"No problem, brother," Tristan said, an easy smile on his face. He hauled his saddle to a nearby scrubby bush, out of sight. "Unhitch your gear, will you? We'll clip a bit of mane off the horses, and call them back with magic when we need them. They're wily creatures—they won't get caught by thieves for a few days."

Aidan looked at Gwen, who shrugged and slid off her horse. She stumbled until her numb legs supported her unsteady weight.

"I think I'm okay with abandoning the horses for a while—I miss walking."

"And being able to feel my arse," Aidan said. He winced when his feet hit the grass.

They stowed their gear under the bush with the growing pile of tack, and Tristan stroked the nearest leaves briefly. The topmost foliage knit together to create an impenetrable barrier of green.

"Keeps water off the leather," Tristan said when he spotted Gwen's curious stare. Rhiannon faced the other three.

"How are we getting to the island? Any thoughts?"

Gwen started. Of course they needed a way across the water. Aidan frowned.

"Can't you magic us across somehow? Make us walk on water or something?"

Tristan laughed.

"Don't know that one, sorry. Magic is not a free pass, you know. Far too much power needed, especially over that distance and over water."

"A portal would have been perfect," Aidan said, his face glum. "Faolan didn't do us any favors with that bracelet."

"What if we made a raft?" Tristan said. "I can probably enchant one together. It'll take some time, and I don't know if it will hold…"

"Yes, and then what?" Rhiannon arched an eyebrow. "I can probably swim the distance, but the rest of you don't stand a chance. It's much farther than you think. Distances are deceiving over water."

"So swimming is out?" Aidan said. "That was my next suggestion."

During the discussion Gwen had been scanning the shoreline. She cut in now.

"Is that a village down there, or just a pile of driftwood? If there are people, maybe we could borrow a boat."

Rhiannon's head whipped around in the direction of Gwen's outstretched arm.

"Yes, that's a village. Best idea so far. Actually, I can see plenty of boats from here. May need some persuasion for the fishers to part with a boat, but I'm sure we can strike a deal."

They stumbled down the sandy embankment, which was filled with windswept scrubby bushes and driftwood. The crashing waves were loud enough to discourage unnecessary chatter. Their destination was a massive cluster of driftwood piles, tucked beside a grass-topped cliff. It was well protected from the wind and placed above the high tide line. They drew nearer and Gwen could make out doors and windows. They were easier to spot after seeing the lone dwelling from before, but instead of one house, these windows and doors were a part of a greater abode. Gwen was reminded of the warren in the Velvet Woods.

They saw nobody until they had come within twenty paces of the nearest door. Gwen jumped violently when she heard a voice.

"Evening, strangers."

Aidan leaped almost as far as Gwen, and even Tristan's head jerked around. Rhiannon maintained her usual calm.

"Good evening. Do the fish swim well today?"

"Straight to the net, and never out."

Gwen was puzzled by the question and answer—

174

perhaps it was a form of greeting in this realm. The speaker had seemed to expect the question. Every part of him was long and thin, from his elongated legs to his lank blond hair, and he had folded himself onto a jutting piece of broken sandstone above the high tide line. He was dressed in a faded blue shirt and gray trousers that shimmered in the dying light. When Gwen looked more closely, she realized that he was liberally sprinkled with fish scales that glittered and shone. A fine-meshed net draped across his lap, and his fingers continued to make knots around a rip in the mesh while he spoke. His eyes never strayed from the foursome.

Rhiannon cast her eyes out to the water and scanned the waves and clouds critically.

"Stormy tomorrow, I reckon."

"No fishing at dawn. You have an eye for these things." He glanced at her with appreciation.

"I was born beyond the Mereless headland." She paused. "We're in need of a boat tomorrow."

"Dangerous waters, if you want to travel to the fishing grounds. And the fish will be too deep from the storm. I have a boat, indeed, but I am leery of lending it out in the coming weather. Even if you are a 'Shorian."

"We don't want to fish. We wish to make land on Isle Caengal."

The previously stoic man burst out in laughter. A few heads popped out of doorways, curious, but retreated swiftly when Gwen looked their way.

"No one lands on Isle Caengal," he said once he had caught his breath. "The monster sees to that."

Gwen glanced at Aidan, whose face paled.

"What monster?" Tristan said. His attempt to sound

175

casual was a thin veil that did not disguise his unease.

"Have you not heard that no one lands on Caengal?" Tristan nodded, and the man said, "Did you never wonder why? It's guarded by a sea beast, so hideous, so powerful, that no boat has ever passed through its territory in living memory. I've seen two attempts in my life, one when I was a boy and one other, ten years ago. The entire village stopped to watch the carnage."

Gwen broke out in a cold sweat. Was this it? How could they get past a sea monster, when no one else had ever done it?

"How do you fish, with a monster in your bay?" Rhiannon said.

"The monster is no true beast of the sea. It is bound to the island, to guard it for eternity. It never ventures past the two rocks, there." He pointed at two tiny islands in the bay, between the shore and Isle Caengal's looming darkness. The islands were only large enough to host twenty birds each. "We don't bother it, and it doesn't bother us."

Rhiannon nodded slowly.

"We are still in need of a boat for tomorrow. We can give you gifts in exchange for the loan."

Tristan shifted from foot to foot, but remained silent. Gwen wanted to say something, but what? What Rhiannon serious about taking the boat to the island? But what other choice did they have?

"It won't be a loan," the man said. He continued to mend his net without looking at it. "As it happens, I have a second boat that I don't use anymore. She's in rough shape, but she holds water. You can take her off my hands, for the right exchange."

"I'd like to see the boat first."

The man nodded, and his fingers finally ceased their endless knotting. He slid the net over his shoulder and unfolded himself from the rock. His head jerked for them to follow, and they set off along the beach toward the headland.

Dried seaweed crackled under Gwen's feet. She drew close to Aidan.

"Do we have anything to trade for the boat?"

"I don't know. I presume Rhiannon has something. Declan would have sent them with provisions, I suppose."

"So Declan is paying our way?"

"Yeah, well, it's not as if he's ever done anything for me before. It's about time."

Gwen didn't like to hear the bitterness in Aidan's voice, but she understood where it came from. She brushed his hand with her own lightly, and he twined his fingers through hers, as if grateful for the gesture. Rhiannon glanced at them, and her eyes landed on their connected hands. She turned back without expression.

Beyond the driftwood warren was a tiny bay, tucked between the warren and the headland. A dozen tiny coracles bobbed in the water, protected from the crashing waves by a breakwater of crushed rock at the mouth of the bay. The man waded into the shallow water and pushed the little round boats until he grabbed the one he searched for. It was far bigger than the others, elongated rather than circular, with multiple tarred hides stretched around its hull.

"Here she is. Isn't she a beauty?" His smile was mocking. "I won her off a fisherman down the coast, in a bet. She's far too large for my purposes, but she'll take all of you, and hold water too. At least until you're capsized."

Gwen clenched Aidan's hand tighter. Rhiannon didn't react to the man's comment, but waded into the water to join him. She looked at the coracle with a critical eye and turned it around in the water to examine every inch.

"It's certainly seen better days, but it will manage the journey." She opened the satchel that swung at her side and drew out a clay whistle on a leather strap. It was round, no larger than her palm, and had four holes to play different notes with. Rhiannon presented it to the man.

"It has been spelled to bring seven days of good fishing. All you need to do is play a few notes when you reach the fishing grounds, and your catches that day will be the best of your year."

The man looked at the whistle on Rhiannon's outstretched hand.

"Who did you say you were?"

"We didn't."

He gave a slow nod.

"A fair trade." He picked the whistle up and hung it around his neck. "The boat is yours."

The man helped Rhiannon float the coracle to the water's edge and lift it to her shoulders, and Tristan hoisted the other end in his arms. Aidan took the offered paddle, and they trundled along the shore like a large beetle crawling on the sand.

Silence reigned until they arrived at the beach near their hidden saddles. Rhiannon and Tristan dropped the coracle above the high tide line. Rhiannon sat down and Tristan stretched his shoulders.

"So, battling a monster tomorrow, are we?" He bent down to rummage in his saddle bag. "Should be fun."

"You don't have to do this," Gwen said. The siblings had no reason to risk their lives for her. If she died, what was it to them? Some regret, a few days of sadness, perhaps, but no lasting damage.

Tristan looked at her, puzzled. He held a long dagger in one hand and a whetstone in the other.

"We're not going to leave you to battle a sea monster on your own."

"But we'll probably die," Gwen said. Her throat closed as she choked on the import of her own words. What about her father, back in the human world? He would never know what had happened to her, would always be waiting for her to return.

"It's clear that Aidan is going, no matter what. And Aidan is family. We don't leave family behind. We'll face this monster, and we'll win or we won't. Did you think it would be easy to get the restoration spell? We were expecting obstacles. Rhiannon and I knew what we were signing up for." He started to sharpen his dagger on the whetstone. "What do you think, Rhiannon? Any old sea monster tips for us landlubbers?"

"Depends on the type of monster. It's a pity the fisherman wasn't more forthcoming. With some sea serpents, you had to be careful of the teeth—too sharp by far. Others had poisonous spines that could rip boats apart. Death by drowning and poison—not the most pleasant way to go." Gwen was growing more horrified by the minute, but Rhiannon lay back calmly on her elbows and continued to speak as if all this information were theoretical. "Sea squids, of course, you need to keep track of all the tentacles."

"Any success stories battling sea monsters? Anything

179

we can learn from?" Tristan said.

"Mmm, there was one man who took down a squid. How did he do it again? Oh yes, he jumped in the water and swam below the squid while it was occupied with his boat, and pierced its eye. Brave, but lucky as well. A last-resort move."

"You don't say," Aidan said. "What do you aim for if it has poison spines everywhere?"

"The snout, perhaps? I don't know, I'm no expert. I left these shores when I was eight. Battling squids was not in my repertoire at that age, and sea serpents are extinct."

"How far do you reckon we could float ourselves magically, if the boat sunk?" Aidan asked Gwen.

"I haven't practiced that one much," Gwen said, a heavy lump in her stomach. "Probably not far enough."

"Only the most powerful can hover their own bodies over water," Tristan said. "None of us qualify. Solid ground is much easier. And Gwen's still recovering, although she's probably back to full strength by now. Here, I have extra daggers for you. You'll have something to defend yourself with, at least. Just remember to slice, not stab. That's the best way to do some damage." He gave Rhiannon a worried glance. She shrugged.

Gwen thought she might be sick. To distract herself, she turned to the saddlebags.

"Anyone hungry for dinner?" Gwen doubted she could force anything down her tight throat, but it gave her something to do. Aidan moved to help. She said, "I've got it." She was surprised by the coldness in her voice.

"How are you feeling? About all this, and the bracelet?"

"I'm fine," she said, louder and harsher than she meant

180

to.

Aidan backed off, looking bewildered.

Now she had hurt his feelings. Gwen clenched her fists, annoyed and disgusted with herself. She wasn't treating him the way he should be treated. She wasn't good for him—not only was she not sure about their relationship, but now she was dragging him and his new-found family into very real danger. It was her fault. She was the one who wanted to help Isolde. He didn't have to be here, but he was, anyway. He deserved better, and she was leading him to his probable death. She turned away and busied herself in the bag.

"We could use some seafood to liven up our meal," Rhiannon said from behind her. "Tristan, take Aidan to search for oysters or mussels."

"You're the expert collector."

"I've taught you well enough. Go on, we'll start a fire."

Gwen didn't watch Aidan trudge down the beach, accompanied by Tristan. Her gut squirmed with guilt. She had made a bad situation worse, and hurt Aidan even more in the process.

Rhiannon stood and collected small pieces of driftwood that surrounded Gwen. When Gwen felt more in control of herself, she joined her. Rhiannon let a few minutes pass in silence while they gathered. Then she spoke.

"What's going on between you and Aidan?"

Gwen looked sharply at Rhiannon, but the other girl made no eye contact. She squatted down beside their driftwood pile and calmly assembled the wood over bunches of dried grass.

"What do you mean?"

Rhiannon sighed.

"You obviously care about each other. I assumed you were a couple, but every so often you lash out and push him away. So, what's going on? Aidan seems like a decent person, but is there something I don't know about him?"

Gwen's eyes pricked with tears. She blinked hard to dash them away. Now even Rhiannon thought she was callous and uncaring. She stayed quiet, not sure what to say.

"Look, you don't have to talk to me." Rhiannon spread her fingers over the neat pile she had made. A flame burst up from the grasses. "But you clearly have something bothering you, and Aidan is suffering for it. It would be best for everyone if you got it off your chest. We have a battle tomorrow, and we need to be a team. No hidden drama."

At the mention of a battle, Gwen's mind filled with images of terrible monsters gleaned from movies.

"But that's the problem! It's my fault Aidan is here. If it weren't for me, he wouldn't be risking his life, and yours too. He's so wonderful to me, and I treat him like his life is worth nothing. And if we make it out of here alive, somehow, he's going to move away from everything he knows to follow me to another country. He's so certain about us. What if he's wrong? What if it doesn't work out? What if I stop caring about him, and I've dragged him away from his life to follow me?"

Gwen stopped, her breath coming in ragged bursts. She hadn't meant to say anything to Rhiannon, but the words had flowed out of her in a torrent. Perhaps it was Rhiannon's calmness, her lack of reaction, which induced Gwen to say so much.

Rhiannon didn't answer right away. She blew on the

little flame to encourage the driftwood to catch fire. Gwen turned to the sea, the red sky now a grayish pink and fading fast.

"I thought Aidan was traveling to your land to attend this school of music," Rhiannon said at last.

"Well, yeah. But he could go anywhere for that. He doesn't have to come so far."

"But he would still have to leave his home, wouldn't he?"

Gwen nodded.

"I just feel that so much hinges on whether we work out."

The driftwood now on fire, Rhiannon fed the flames from her pile. Gwen watched the dancing flames in silence.

"Aidan has a gift," Rhiannon said. "At least, he is unusual in this world. Does the gift of music come so commonly in your world?"

"Oh, no, Aidan has a remarkable talent. He's really amazing."

"Is the school in your land so terrible, that he wouldn't learn anything there?"

"No, I don't think so. I think it's pretty good."

Rhiannon finally looked up at Gwen. She gave her a puzzled smile.

"Then let Aidan follow his passion for music, and combine it with love for you. He's of age. He can make his own decisions. It sounds to me that there is more to take him to your land than just you, so your conscience can be clear."

"But he could go anywhere."

Rhiannon studied Gwen.

"Do you care for Aidan?"

"Of course I do. But we've known each other for such a short time. What if it doesn't work out?"

"Let him come. Perhaps he's not right for you. But how will you know if you don't try? Sometimes you have to jump in with both feet, especially in love. If it doesn't work out, then you'll find someone else. But what if it does work out? Don't you want to know what that would be like?"

Gwen's lip trembled. Was it that easy?

"So you think I'm being silly?"

Rhiannon gave a rare, genuine smile.

"I think you care enough about him to worry like this. That's a good sign." She poked at the fire, now burning merrily. "But I do think you need to talk to Aidan about your fears. I expect he'll do a better job at convincing you than I will."

A crunching sound alerted Gwen to the approach of Aidan and Tristan. It was dark now, too dark to see far. The fire glowed bright, a beacon on the dusky beach. Tristan held up a handful of oyster shells.

"Success! Let's eat."

Aidan deposited his handful of oysters next to the fire with Tristan's and sat down on the sand near Gwen, but avoided her gaze. She fretted at her lower lip. How could she mend this?

"Gwen, could you find some bread while these cook?" Rhiannon said. "Mmm, it's been too long since I've had good oysters." She prodded the fire to expose some coals, and nestled the oysters in glowing embers. Gwen rummaged in a saddle bag until she found loaves of flatbread, wrapped in waxed cloth.

When the shells sprang apart, Tristan rolled the oysters out of the fire and pried them open with his dagger and his sleeve as a glove. Despite her fears and worries, Gwen's stomach finally rumbled with hunger. It had been a long time since they'd eaten. The oysters smelled heavenly, and the flatbread was divine to Gwen's hungry taste buds.

The four didn't speak much over dinner, and after they had eaten Rhiannon pulled out her blanket.

"I'm done," she said, a yawn overtaking her words. "Better get an early start tomorrow. No point in wasting daylight hours." She glanced pointedly at Gwen's wrist.

Gwen, relaxed from dinner, clenched her jaw at the reminder of the deadly bracelet. Without a further word, Rhiannon rolled over. Tristan dug out his own blanket.

"Night, you two. Sleep well—you'll need it."

"So encouraging," Aidan muttered. Tristan grinned and closed his eyes. Before long, both siblings were breathing quietly and rhythmically in sleep.

Aidan said nothing, but stared into the fire with a brooding expression on his face. Night had fallen in earnest and stars began to glow, one by one, in the dark sky. Gwen fidgeted. What did she want to say?

"Look, Aidan," she said. He continued to gaze at the dying fire. "I wanted to say—I'm sorry for how I've been acting. I haven't been very nice to you lately. You're doing this for me, and I've treated you badly. I'm sorry." She scuffed her toes together, back and forth, the boots making a muffled scraping sound.

Aidan shrugged.

"It's been a tough few days. We've all been on edge. You, especially, with that thing on your wrist."

"I know, but it's no excuse."

185

He looked at her then, and gave her a wry smile.

"You're forgiven."

Was it that easy? Gwen didn't know how to talk to Aidan about the reason for her temper. It was too late to discuss it, though, so she shuffled over to him and he held out an arm for her to snuggle into. They lay back together and contemplated the stars.

"We'll figure this out tomorrow," Aidan said. "I know we will."

"Oh, let's not talk about it." Gwen shivered and clutched him closer. "I was enjoying just lying here."

"Do you reckon Tristan and Rhiannon are asleep?" Aidan raised his head to look at his siblings.

"I think so."

"Good." Aidan turned swiftly and pressed his lips to hers. Gwen smiled through her returning kiss.

Chapter 11

The lightening sky awoke Gwen. She was still wrapped in Aidan's arms, and when she sat up, he stirred.

"Morning," he said, his voice thick with sleep.

Gwen smiled down at him before she looked at Isle Caengal with a frown. Even in the morning light, it looked forbidding and unwelcoming.

Aidan followed her gaze.

"Let's wake the others and get this show started." He sat up with a groan. "Oh, why is the ground so hard?"

Gwen crawled over to Rhiannon.

"Rhiannon? It's light out. Should we get moving?"

Rhiannon blinked awake and sat up quickly. She was alert in seconds.

"Yes, of course. Have a bite of food, and we'll leave at once." She picked up a piece of driftwood and lobbed it at her brother. He grunted awake. "Wake up, Tristan. Time to go."

"Such a delicate flower, you are." He rubbed his back where she had hit him.

After bread and dried fruit, Tristan and Aidan carried

the coracle to the water's edge. Rhiannon and Gwen followed with a satchel of food. The rest they stowed in the bush with the hidden saddles.

"We'll need provisions for the ride home," Rhiannon said briskly. "We shouldn't be on the island for long. We won't need much."

Gwen appreciated Rhiannon's optimism, but stared bleakly at the ocean before them. There was no sun today. Dark clouds had coalesced into a thick blanket of gray above their heads, and the sea roiled unsteadily under a fitful wind.

"Does anyone know how to steer this thing?" Aidan said. He prodded the coracle doubtfully with his foot.

"Make a figure-eight in the water," Tristan said. He swiped the paddle through the air to demonstrate. "Sit in the front, and use the motion to pull us forward." He handed the paddle to Aidan.

"I'm driving, am I?"

"Rhiannon and I need our hands free, in case the monster decides to make an appearance. And I assume you're not going to make Gwen paddle while you sit idle in the back of our leisure cruise?" He winked at Gwen. Aidan huffed and mimicked Tristan's motions with the paddle in midair.

Rhiannon waded into the cold water and held the coracle steady.

"Come on, Gwen. Hop in."

Gwen shrugged at Aidan, and waded in. The bitingly cold water sloshed into her boots, and she gasped involuntarily. She grabbed the edge of the coracle and was astonished by its instability. It rocked with every wave that hit its side, and reacted to her slightest touch.

"How am I supposed to get into this thing? It's going to tip for sure."

"I'm holding it," Rhiannon said. Her voice was as calm as always. "You'll be fine."

Gwen hoisted a leg over the side and pushed off with her other foot. She tried to throw her weight toward the center of the little boat, but overcompensated. The boat rocked violently. Tristan whistled.

"This'll be a wild ride."

Aidan followed Gwen into the boat. Gwen clutched the edges of the coracle with whitened hands, sure they were about to tip into the icy water. Aidan managed to shuffle to the bow without mishap, past their satchel and another shapeless sack made of oiled canvas. Tristan followed more gracefully, and Rhiannon joined them with a leap as if she were born in a coracle.

"All right, Aidan," Tristan said. "Show us your skills."

Aidan dipped his paddle into the water hesitantly and pulled a figure-eight. The coracle shot forward, unencumbered by a deep keel. A wave splashed into his face and he sputtered.

"Keep paddling!" Rhiannon called out. "We need to get past the wave break."

Indistinct muttering emerged from the bow, but Aidan dug his paddle in resolutely and the coracle rode the incoming waves as it bobbed away from shore.

The boat grew steadier when they had passed the foamy waves and Aidan's paddling grew surer. Halfway to the barrier rocks, Tristan winked at Gwen and said to Aidan, "Is that all you have? Put some muscle in it."

The only reply Aidan gave was a sheet of water directed at Tristan from his well-aimed paddle. Tristan grinned and threw up his hand. The water froze in place, then poured diagonally to fall back into the water.

Gwen surprised herself by grinning, but her smiles quickly subsided. The entry rocks grew nearer. Three seagulls perched on the leftmost island, their cold, beady eyes following the progress of the coracle. When their little boat approached, all three birds took to the sky with large, ponderous wings, shrieking their displeasure to the skies. The melancholic cries struck Gwen with a sense of foreboding, and she shivered.

Aidan slowed before they reached the entry islands, and they rocked in the sloppy waves. He turned to face the others.

"What's the plan?"

"You'll paddle quickly but calmly in a direct path to the beach." Rhiannon pointed to a small opening in the cliffs of Isle Caengal, where a stony beach received the lapping ocean. "Gwen will keep a lookout for any disturbances, and Tristan and I will have our weapons ready. At the slightest sign of attack, we fight. No matter what, Aidan, keep paddling. The sooner we get there, the less time anything will have to attack us."

Aidan swallowed and nodded. He gave Gwen a wan smile which she tried to return, and faced forward once more. Tristan unsheathed his dagger and handed the satchel to Gwen.

"Better put this on your back. I'd rather not lose it in a commotion."

Gwen's hands shook as she slung the satchel over her shoulder. She gripped the small dagger Tristan had given her yesterday with white knuckles. Was this it? Was this how people felt going into battle, like they might faint and vomit and scream all at the same time? Would they come out of this alive? She should have kissed Aidan one last time.

Rhiannon looked at her and smiled faintly.

"We can do this, Gwen. Tristan and I have been in tighter spots. Have some faith."

Gwen nodded, but couldn't speak through her tight jaw. Aidan began to paddle. The coracle glided through the water with every swift pull. The bay's gray waters and choppy waves made it difficult to scan for disturbances, and Gwen's imagination pictured a fin or tentacle in every trough.

They approached the islands, drew level to them, and crossed the invisible line spanning the two. Nothing happened.

"Do you see anything?" Gwen whispered, her voice high and thin.

"Perhaps it's asleep," Tristan said quietly. "Keep paddling, Aidan. Nice and smooth."

The rolling waves pitched them from side to side as they swept between the rocks in front of Isle Caengal. Gwen scanned the water, her heart hammering. She allowed herself the faintest ray of hope. Maybe the monster was a legend after all. Maybe they would complete their journey unmolested.

The water to her left bubbled and frothed.

"Oh no, oh no, oh no," Gwen said. She pointed with a frantic finger. "What's that?"

Tristan and Rhiannon's heads whipped around and they held their daggers at the ready. Aidan spared a glance at the writhing sea before he dug his paddle in with greater intensity and force. The coracle shot past the disturbance, which slowly faded.

"Where did it go?" Gwen whispered.

Something rose out of the water on their right. Gwen screamed before she clapped a hand to her mouth, afraid of alerting trouble. Was it a tentacle? In the split-second that the object hung there, dripping, her brain registered the sight. No suckers, no slimy flesh—instead of a squid arm, hardened greenish scales covered a thick appendage that tapered to a point. Studded along its length were sharp spines the length of Gwen's hand. The appendage—was it a tail?—emerged from the murky water without a known source.

Before she could take in much more than a cursory glance, the tail whipped toward their boat with incredible speed. It lightly touched the side of the coracle, but its long spines tore a sizeable hole above the water line. Rhiannon had no time to react before the tail slithered back into the stormy water, leaving no ripples on the surface.

"Breach on starboard," Rhiannon called out. "That bag, Gwen—it has mending putty in it. Shove some in the hole, quick."

Gwen lunged for the sack at the bottom of the coracle and ripped it open. Inside was a small mound of grayish putty that glowed faintly. Was it infused with magic? She tore off a chunk and smeared it over the rent in the hull. Instantly, the putty adhered to the hide and the water stopped its relentless flow.

"Be ready for the next attack!" Rhiannon shouted. "Keep paddling, Aidan."

Aidan needed no reminder. His shoulders heaved with every stroke, faster and more powerful than before. Gwen shouted.

192

"Look out, Tristan!"

The tail whipped again and left another hole, this one at the water line. Tristan lunged after the tail, but only succeeded in slashing the water with his dagger. Rhiannon yanked at his shirt.

"Don't fall in, idiot! We can't save you in there."

Gwen pressed more putty into the new hole. Water pooling at the bottom of the boat rocked from side to side. Gwen thought that Rhiannon's movement had destabilized the coracle, until the whole vessel lifted in place. The animal hides below Gwen's feet heaved and stretched from the outline of a broad back that pressed against the bottom of the coracle. Aidan shouted when his paddle left the water, and Tristan fell to the side of the boat. A spine rubbed against the hide and poked a hole through the skins. The damage done, the monster sank and left the coracle bobbing once more in the waves. A steady spurt of water fountained into the boat.

"Here!" Gwen tossed a piece of putty to Tristan. "Shove this in the hole. And keep paddling, Aidan!"

Gwen twisted to look behind her at the sound of rushing water. She screamed.

The monstrous head of a sea serpent rose from the waves. It looked prehistoric, with bony plates covering its face and two horny ridges lined with spines that ran down the length of its head and body. Huge, sunken black eyes, like those of a shark, focused on her—merciless, remorseless. The gaping mouth had far too many rows of teeth that curved inward, allowing no escape for its prey.

There was no time for defensive measures, even if Gwen had been capable of raising her dagger. The sharp teeth crunched down on the stern of the coracle, which splintered the wooden frame but miraculously did not break it. Just as quickly, the serpent released the boat and was gone, sunk back into the cold waters below their feet.

Gwen's chest heaved. She couldn't get enough air into her lungs.

"Now what? Where is it coming from next?"

They didn't have long to wait. A tail emerged from the depths and whipped the coracle again, faster than Rhiannon could react. It tore a gash in the hide, this time below the water line. Water poured in and Rhiannon stuffed the hole with putty from Gwen, her face white. Again, the tail lashed toward Tristan who whirled around to meet it, but to no avail. The tail disappeared and left a line of punctures in its wake.

"More putty, Gwen!" Rhiannon yelled, her calm demeanor evaporated.

"I don't have much more!" Gwen reached out with the last of the putty and spread it quickly over the tear.

The water stopped streaming in, and Gwen was momentarily relieved until she realized why. The serpent's back pressed into the coracle's bottom and lifted the little boat high above sea level. Three spines broke through this time, and when the monster sank back into the waves, water poured in relentlessly.

Gwen dug through the satchel, desperate to find anything that would stopper the holes. She ripped apart a cloth that covered some of their bread, and knelt forward to block the fountains. Tristan yelled above her.

"Look out!"

She turned from her kneeling position at the bottom of the boat and saw the serpent's head loom over her from the stern. It bit down on the coracle's frame with a sickening

194

crunch, then released its hold and withdrew. The splintered frame was reduced to a narrow fragment of its former self. The coracle creaked ominously.

"The boat won't hold for long, not without a proper frame," Rhiannon said. "We need to keep moving!"

Aidan's muscles strained and his neck was taut, but he had no breath to answer Rhiannon.

The island was still so far away. Gwen looked at their rapidly decaying boat with horror. Water leaked in from the breeched hull that she had stuffed with rags, and their boots slopped around the growing pool at their feet. The broken frame was sunk low in the water, only a hands width above the roiling sea. They weren't going to make it. The serpent was too fast for them. It was too unpredictable…

"Wait," Gwen said. Her mind whirled and she scanned the water for the next attack. "It's a pattern. The monster is attacking in the same way every time." Tristan looked at her, confused. Gwen warmed to her idea. "Yes! That's it. Rhiannon, it's going to attack with its tail from your side next. Be ready with your dagger."

Rhiannon looked incredulously at her brother, but Tristan only shrugged.

"I don't have a better idea."

Seconds after Rhiannon turned to the water, dagger at the ready, the dripping tail rose and lashed out toward the boat. Ready for it, Rhiannon let out a yell and sliced at the appendage. The tail halted in mid-whip, a long bloody gash clearly visible. It writhed in pain on the surface of the water before it jerked back to the depths.

"Okay, Tristan, be ready for the tail again, but this time on your side!" Gwen shouted. Tristan gripped his dagger in one hand and the edge of the boat in the other, ready to attack.

He didn't wait for long. The tail rose once more, the gash dripping with blood and seawater, and lunged to pierce the boat. Tristan slashed at the tip and the tail writhed back into the water. The tapered end of the tail flew in an arc through the air and landed with a splash.

"Now what?" Rhiannon said. She looked to Gwen for instructions.

"Now it's going to pick us up with its back," she said. She felt calmer and more in control than she had for days. She knew what was coming. Tristan and Rhiannon were attacking the monster, and every stroke that Aidan paddled drew them closer to the island. Maybe this was possible after all.

"What do you think? Try stabbing it?" Tristan asked Rhiannon.

"We don't need more holes in the boat."

"Stab it through a hole that's already there," Gwen said. "Then we don't make any new ones."

The coracle shifted as the serpent rubbed against the bottom. Aidan yelled when his paddle left the water and he clung to the frame of the coracle. The monster's back strained against the hide, but Tristan and Rhiannon were ready. With a concerted blow, they stabbed through the putty in pre-existing holes and forced their daggers deep into the serpent's back before they swiftly drew them out again. The monster spasmed and dropped the coracle with a splash. Water poured in over the sides and through new holes in the hide.

They were fighting well, but they didn't have much time before the valiant coracle gave way and sunk into the cold waters of the bay. Gwen yelled, "Okay, now its head will come from behind!"

"Stab the eyes!" Rhiannon shouted. Gwen scrambled toward the bow and Tristan and Rhiannon positioned themselves at the stern. As Gwen had predicted, the head soon rose from the water, its mouth opened wider than ever before. This time, the serpent would bite straight through the coracle, frame and hull and hide. This was the killing blow.

"Now!" Rhiannon screamed, and together the two lunged forward as far as they could reach. They aimed their daggers for the cold, black eyes of the serpent.

Their aim was true. Deep into the sockets the blades slid, in and out again with sharp accuracy, deep enough to penetrate the brain. The motion halted the serpent. It threw its head back in agony and thrashed back and forth. Its death-throes churned the water and plunged the beleaguered coracle into a chaotic wash. The twitching head jerked erratically, until it slowly sank into the water. It left only a few ripples that were soon swallowed by wind and wave.

The serpent was dead. Gwen could hardly believe it, but she didn't have time to dwell on their victory.

"We need to plug the holes!" Rhiannon threw herself to the bottom of the coracle and pressed the rags firmly to the holes. Gwen ripped apart more of the cloth that covered their bread. Tristan followed behind them with his hand above the leaking plugs. His magic took the edges of the rags and sealed them to the coracle's hide. At the bottom of the boat, putty and rags were under the water that sloshed between their knees.

Once they had plugged most of the holes, Gwen started

to bail with her hands. Rhiannon moved to stabilize the coracle's broken frame at the stern. Tristan took over the paddle from Aidan, who joined Gwen, his face red and arms shaking from his efforts. Gwen touched his shoulder and gave him a brief smile.

"We did it," she said.

Aidan cupped water between trembling hands and threw it overboard.

"Yeah, that was clever, you figuring out the pattern. Nicely done. And some fine dagger work from the wonder team. Look, the water's fairly low now. We'll make it to the island after all."

"Yeah." Gwen finally let herself feel elation from their win. "Yeah, we will. Against the odds. That's—kind of amazing, actually." Her face cracked into a smile, and she hugged Aidan spontaneously. "We did it!"

"First obstacle down, unknown number to go," Rhiannon said from behind her. When Gwen turned around, Rhiannon smiled faintly. "Sorry, I didn't mean to spoil the moment. It was a good victory. How did you know where the serpent would attack?"

"It was following a pattern. I figured out the pattern, and then it was easy to predict."

"Really?" Rhiannon looked mystified. "I wouldn't have guessed that."

Gwen raised an eyebrow at Aidan.

"Perhaps it's a Breenan thing?" he said. "Not so good at creative thinking?"

Within minutes, the coracle scraped against the stony beach. Tristan leaped out first.

"Be careful," Gwen said. "What if there's another obstacle?"

Tristan stood still for a moment. Then his shoulders shrugged and he turned to them with a laugh.

"So far, so good. Come on, we won't get this quest done by quivering in that moth-eaten old coracle."

Gwen gingerly scrambled over the edge of the coracle, relieved to be on solid ground once more. Her knees were weak after the stress of the sea battle, and she stumbled twice before she regained her footing on the loose pebbles of the beach. The beach was short, walled in on both sides by cliffs that plunged deep into the water, and by a grove of trees parallel to the water's edge. A path bisected the trees. It was clearly the only way forward.

Aidan helped Rhiannon drag the damaged coracle up the beach so the tide wouldn't sweep it away, then he joined Gwen to consider their next move.

"I wonder where to next? So many options," he said. She nudged his shoulder with her own and started toward the opening in the trees, in the wake of Tristan's eager footsteps.

Tristan stopped at the treeline. A tree directly to the left of the path, a scraggly oak, stood out from the other trees. The rest were bare, but this tree was covered in a twisted ivy sporting vibrant orange and red leaves. Strands swayed in the stiffening breeze. Tristan narrowed his eyes in thought.

"The signpost has a message."

"Signpost? Do you mean the vine?" Gwen wasn't sure how Tristan knew to look for plant-writing in the vines. Was it obvious to him what was a message and what was just a plant?

"See here?" Tristan pointed at an intricate curl of vines, snaked together. "That's the sign for Breenan, beside the sign for human. They're above this," he pointed at a burst of leaves in a fan-shape. "Which means connecting, working together. And this bare vine, twisted just so, is the sign for unselfishness, next to the leaves of peace."

"Okay. But what does it all mean?"

"The message reads, 'Those who come in peace, with altruistic intent, will find what they need most. Friendship with their otherworld brethren will aid them on their quest.'"

"Well, that sounds good. Doesn't it? We're here for Bran and Isolde, and we're all mates now," Aidan said. "Cryptic as always, of course. I expected nothing less in the Otherworld."

"Not super helpful, is it? I guess we press on. It didn't say not to," Gwen said. She glanced at Rhiannon, stoic as always, and at Tristan, who grinned.

"Let's move. Our spell awaits us."

The path was neatly laid with a covering of crushed seashells that glowed faintly under a dull and stormy sky. Ash trees loomed over the path in a tangled canopy. Light was dim in the ravine between the two steep cliffs. A bird twittered in the distance, unseen through thick branches. Leaves were colorful in the autumn coolness, but few had yet dropped. Wind from the approaching storm rustled dying foliage ominously.

The path curved and twisted, and they could see no farther than ten paces down the trail. Their way inclined gradually. After a few minutes of climbing, they rounded a bend where the monotony of the forest was broken.

"What's that?" Gwen pointed to three flat stones, laid into the soil beside the path. The largest was wide enough to kneel on, and the other two, placed farther back from the trail, were smaller. Carved into their surfaces were the shapes of two handprints. Beyond the stones spread a tiny patch of low groundcover, its miniscule leaves a delicate, velvety green. A dangling clematis vine swirled around a single bloom, and Gwen guessed that there was a message in the swirls.

"The Garden of Love Made Visible," Tristan said. He tilted his head in thought. "I wonder what that means." He stepped forward and prodded the nearest stone with his foot. Gwen held her breath, but nothing happened.

"Perhaps it's one of the queens' inventions," Rhiannon said. "This is Lady Maeve's island, after all."

"This place is probably littered with remarkable magic," Tristan said. "Look, you can see signs all up the path. This one doesn't sound too bad. Let's give it a try."

"Are you serious?" Gwen said, but Tristan already kneeled on the larger stone. He grinned up at her with a wink, and placed his hands on the prints.

Gwen couldn't believe it. What if the spell were dangerous, or a trap? What would they do if he were hurt, or paralyzed, or one of a thousand things that could possibly go wrong? Aidan sucked in his breath beside her, but Rhiannon only sighed.

"Typical. This is why Father sends me with you—so someone competent can pull you out of trouble."

Tristan didn't answer, but instead stared intently at the patch of green. Gwen drew nearer, fascinated despite her misgivings. Where once there had been a monochrome carpet of green foliage, blooms now formed in a staggering array of colors. Miniature flowers opened out of nowhere, blues and reds and violets and golds, dazzling her eyes.

The colors were not random. A clear picture formed of a man and a woman. The man sat in a chair, smiling, and the woman walked behind him with a basket in her arms. When the man turned to speak silently to the woman, the flowers shrunk and bloomed to create a dynamic picture.

"That's Father and Morna," Rhiannon said. As soon as she said the words, the picture changed, and two young boys scuffled in the grass outside Declan's cottage, their panting, happy faces silent in the flowers. Tristan smiled.

"And the twins, little scamps." He leaned back and pulled his hands off the stones. Instantly, the multitude of petals closed and sunk out of sight. Only the woolly green leaves remained. "Well, that was a tidy little spell. Showing us those we care about, what they're doing right now." He got up and dusted off his hands. "Give it a go, Rhiannon. See who else we can see."

Rhiannon didn't need further encouragement and knelt in position. The flowers bloomed once again and showed a closer vision of the same smiling Declan, but cut away swiftly to a burly young man with yellow hair, cutting wood. When this vision emerged, Rhiannon jerked her hands away from the stones as if they burned, her face red. Tristan laughed.

"Still in love with Angus, are we? I don't know why you hide it. He's a bit dim, sure, but you could do worse."

Rhiannon stood up and flicked her fingers at Tristan. He hopped around and swatted at his trousers until a mouse fell out of the leg.

"So sensitive, sister." He winked at Gwen. "Do you think Gwen will be as shy when I appear in her vision?"

Gwen laughed at the absurdity of his comment, but Aidan looked confused and annoyed, although he tried to hide it. Rhiannon huffed.

"You're so vain," she said to Tristan, and then turned to Aidan. "Your turn." She tried to appear unruffled, but her cheeks were still pink. "See if it works for humans, too."

Aidan glanced at Gwen, and she nodded back. There didn't seem to be any harm in it. Both Tristan and Rhiannon had come through unscathed, except for a mouse bite or two. Aidan knelt down on the stone and carefully placed his hands on the prints.

The flowers bloomed, but instead of a face, a multicolored swirl twisted in front of Aidan. After a few seconds, it settled into a picture of a woman, although the image was jumpy and not as clear as the previous ones. Gwen recognized Aidan's mother, Deirdre. She stood against a kitchen sink and looked at a refrigerator. She was safe and whole, but sadness was etched on her face. On the fridge was a picture of Aidan.

Gwen's lips tightened, but before she could say anything comforting the image changed to a sharp representation of herself in the forest looking worried. Aidan sat back on his heels and Tristan laughed.

"We don't need to see Gwen. She's right here. You think the queens could have fixed that."

"Why was it so unclear when we saw that woman?" Rhiannon said.

"She was in the human world," Aidan said. "Perhaps it takes a greater magical effort to see there."

Aidan stood up with a solemn expression. Gwen brushed her hand against his in an attempt to comfort, and took his place on the rock. She drew in a deep breath and gingerly rested her hands on the stones, one finger at a time. The rock was still cool, despite Aidan's hands before hers. She gazed at the groundcover and wondered what she would see.

She didn't wait for long. The flowers swirled as they had for Aidan, in an attempt to penetrate the veil between worlds. They settled into an image of her father in his studio. He dabbed paint onto an easel with a contented smile on his face. Gwen's heart leaped, but she barely had time to register the image before the picture changed to one of Ellie in a dance studio, followed by an image of Aidan standing behind her. She almost pulled her hands away then, but the picture changed once again. This time the flowers showed a dark room. Gwen peered closer with curiosity. Who would the flowers show her now?

The image zoomed in on a figure seated on a carved wooden chair. Gwen gasped. Isolde appeared in the flowers with her head hanging and her hair limp. Her face was painted by the palest white flowers, and the blossoms of her hands trembled as if they swayed in a breeze. Behind the chair, a large hole in the crumbling castle walls revealed fires burning in the distance, and smoke drifted through the gap in the stonework.

Gwen drew her hands back. Isolde looked so ill—was Gwen too late?

"Those fires didn't look good," Tristan said. "Looks like the other realms are attacking already."

Gwen glanced at Bran's ring, her thumb visible through the ghostly circle. Aidan's hand touched Gwen's shoulder gently, and she let herself lean into its solid comfort for a moment before she stood.

"We need to get moving," she said. "We're running out of time."

Chapter 12

They trudged up the path again, Tristan and Rhiannon in single file. The sun overhead filtered through a canopy of autumn leaves. Gwen brought up the rear with Aidan beside her.

"Are you all right?" he asked quietly.

"Did you see her? I don't think she's long for this world." She paused, and Isolde's white face swam before her eyes, backlit by raging fires in the forest. "I don't know why I should bust my gut to help her—she's not exactly a model citizen. But then I think of those orphaned children—"

"And your bracelet."

"And Bran. Oh, I don't know. Maybe Isolde is cruel and uncaring, but I still can't sit back and watch her die."

"Because you're a better person than her."

"I hope so. Although it wouldn't take much." Gwen looked at the path ahead. "How much farther do we have to hike up? I didn't think the island was this high."

A few minutes later, Tristan called back.

"There's a sign over here."

Gwen sped up and joined the others at a small clearing on a plateau. She leaped back as the sight before her eyes registered.

"Whoa!"

They stood, precariously perched, on the edge of a cliff. It plunged sheer and precipitous into icy ocean water, which slurped and crashed at a great distance below. Another cliff rose directly ahead of them. A fringe of trees crowned crumbling sandstone level with their own vantage point. Winds whistled menacingly through the gap and lifted Gwen's hair. Isle Caengal was not one island, but two. A channel of water split the land in half, invisible from the shore. Tristan laughed.

"Careful. It's a long fall to a cold swim." He pointed to a tree on his left, which Gwen hadn't noticed in her preoccupation with the cliff's edge. "There's the sign. But I think it's only half a message. It doesn't make sense otherwise."

The tree was an oak, stunted and gnarled but obviously ancient. It clung to the cliff's edge, and Gwen wondered how it could possibly still be standing. A flowering vine draped from one twisted limb. The vine was not alone, however. Bound by a swollen and knotted rope, a wooden sign swung beside the vine. Burned into the weathered wood were words.

Over the void, to find

Gwen frowned.

"There's a message in human writing, too. On that wooden sign."

"Really? What does it say? I hardly noticed it."

"It says, 'Over the void, to find.' Mean anything to you?"

206

"Perhaps." He pointed to a cluster of flowers above a drooping tendril to the right of the sign. "This says, 'The castle of Lady Maeve.'"

Aidan chuckled behind Gwen.

"Those two queens were really trying to promote inter-species cooperation, weren't they? You can't read the entire message unless you know both Breenan and human writing."

"Over the void, to find the castle of Lady Maeve," Gwen said slowly. "Well, that's clear enough."

"The 'what' is clear, but what do we do about the 'how?'" Rhiannon pointed past the cliff's edge to the other side.

"That's a little less clear," Aidan said.

"Well, there's only one way that I can see," Tristan said. He pushed up his sleeves and walked to the edge of the cliff. "Let's stop talking and start climbing. It's a long way down and up again."

Rhiannon rolled her eyes.

"Don't be ridiculous. There are hardly any handholds, and the cliff is crumbling just to look at it. Even if we had a rope to get down, which we don't, there's no way we could climb up again." She glanced sideways at Gwen and Aidan, as if to say that Rhiannon and Tristan might have a chance at climbing, but she and Aidan had no hope. Gwen privately agreed. Rhiannon said, "What about swimming around? It's far, but we might have a better chance."

"Assuming that monster was the only one," Aidan said. "And that there's another beach on that part of the island. And that we don't freeze to death first."

Rhiannon scowled, then brightened.

"What about flying? You said you could fly, back in

207

the human world."

Aidan and Gwen laughed.

"Not by ourselves," Aidan said. "We need a machine for that."

"Why isn't there a way over?" Gwen said. "I guess this is another obstacle. What do they want from us?"

"They want us to work together, I reckon," Aidan said. "The message was in Breenan and human, so we have to find a way over that uses the strengths of both."

"Like the sea serpent—I figured out the pattern, Rhiannon and Tristan stabbed it."

"So we're the brain, they're the brawn?"

"Hey," Tristan said.

"No offense meant," Aidan said. "So, how do we get across?"

"A bridge would be best," Gwen said.

"Made of what? Metal is out, wood—a possibility, but difficult—rope, but we don't have any."

"Rope, yes! What about vines?"

"Indiana Jones-style?"

"We could twist together some vines, magic it across, and voila!"

"Perfect!" they said in unison, and turned to the other two. Tristan looked bewildered, and Rhiannon's eyebrow was raised.

"Do we have a plan? I didn't quite follow."

"Pull down as many vines as you can find," Gwen said. "We'll twist them together into one big rope. Then you and Tristan can magic it across the canyon and tie it to a tree on the other side."

"I'm not sure how to send it across the water," Aidan said. "And then tying to the tree securely…"

"No problem," Rhiannon said. "Leave that to us."

Ivy was plentiful in the forest, and they soon collected great armfuls of it, glossy and dark green. Gwen grabbed six ends and braided them together, aided by Rhiannon who weaved new ends into the braid as the old ones finished. Aidan laid the rope out in a neat line and wrapped the end around the sign-tree. Tristan inspected the rope as it was made, and strengthened weak connections and Aidan's knot with a wave of his hand. When they were finished, Tristan beckoned Rhiannon to his side.

"We'd better do this together. Make sure we have enough power to secure the knot on the other side."

Rhiannon took both of Tristan's hands in his, and they stared at the end of the ivy rope. It slowly twitched, then slithered like a green, rustling snake toward the edge of the cliff. Instead of tumbling off the edge, it traveled through the air along an invisible path. The canyon was so narrow and the cliffs so steep that the rope reached the opposite side in no time, and wrapped itself sinuously around the trunk of a sturdy-looking beech. Rhiannon and Tristan separated and Tristan looked pleased with himself.

"It's ready. Who wants to take the maiden voyage?"

Gwen hadn't considered this part of the plan in detail until now. The ivy rope was hardly a bridge. To cross to the other side, they would have to cling upside down and shuffle across on hooked knees. Her legs trembled with dread, but the bracelet hummed on her wrist.

"I will," she said.

Tristan nodded in approval, and Aidan squeezed her hand. She secured the satchel more firmly on her back and swung herself up on the rope. She felt like a sloth creeping along a branch, and vowed to herself to move more quickly than one.

Hand over hand, knees shuffling behind, hands again—it wasn't so bad until she passed over the cliff's edge. Immediately, a sense of openness and distance hit her back, and stronger winds from the coming storm brushed past her face and made her hair dance. She froze for a moment, petrified, not daring to move, to look, to do anything. The bracelet hummed. She moved her hand incrementally, and then again.

"You're doing lovely," Aidan called out behind her. She gritted her teeth and brought her other hand forward, then each knee.

"Don't think about it," she said out loud. "Just keep going. Be the sloth. Be the quickest sloth ever."

The rest of the journey was at once excruciatingly long and a blur. Air movements changed when she shuffled over the opposite cliff, but she didn't let go until leafy branches waved above her and her hands hit the trunk of the beech. She unhooked her knees and collapsed to the ground in a heap. Her whole body trembled from exertion and adrenaline, and her head was woozy and light.

"You all right?" Aidan shouted. His voice sounded very distant through the roaring blood in her ears. She waved back, not trusting her voice to speak, and watched Rhiannon swing onto the rope and lightly traverse the chasm as if she climbed rope bridges in her spare time. Aidan followed, much more methodically and with plenty of white knuckles, and dropped beside Gwen. She grasped him in a fierce hug and he clutched her with shaking arms.

Tristan crawled across without incident and they sat on the ledge, with only their panting breaths to break the silence. Finally, Rhiannon spoke.

"Since we've stopped, we should eat. Who knows what obstacles are next? I'd prefer to meet them on a satisfied stomach."

Gwen wasn't sure she could eat, but by the time Rhiannon passed around dried meat and bread, dusty from rolling around in the satchel without a cloth cover, her stomach was growling. Breakfast on the beach had been at daybreak, and it was now a few hours past noon.

They tore into the food in rapturous silence. Gwen finished before the others and stared across the canyon. Her brain glazed over and she blissfully thought of nothing—no dying Isolde, no sick Bran, no monsters or cliffs or other dangers. Especially, no bracelet. Her mindlessness didn't last for long.

"What are you thinking about, Gwen?" Tristan popped the last of the bread in his mouth and chewed. "It's me, isn't it?"

"Of course. How did you guess?" She smiled at Aidan to bring him in on the joke. He grinned back, pleased at the inclusion.

"Because Tristan thinks everyone is in love with him." Rhiannon stood up and slung the satchel over her shoulder. "Come on, and bring the egomaniac. We need to keep moving."

Aidan pulled Gwen to her feet and they followed Rhiannon and Tristan, who disappeared along a path away from the canyon. Gwen glanced at Aidan's profile, wondering how else to bridge the gap between them. She wanted to make amends for the way she had been treating him recently.

"It's too bad you didn't bring your flute to the island. Not that we have time, but still. I'm looking forward to

211

hearing you play more." That was as much mention of the future as she could say without thinking of the bracelet and their as-yet unfinished quest, but Aidan's face lit up.

"Really?"

"Yeah, of course. You're so good, you're going to be great in your courses when you start university. Top of the class, for sure."

Aidan beamed.

"Oh, I doubt that. Classes will be full of child prodigies, and I'll be the dunce in the corner."

"Hardly." Gwen ran her hand down Aidan's arm to interlace her fingers with his. They smiled at each other. Connected, they continued down the path in the direction of their travel companions.

The incline was shallow, and the trees were thin enough that they could see some distance ahead. Rhiannon and Tristan had stopped to stare at another sign. When Gwen and Aidan approached them, still holding hands, the sign became clearer. A single word on a wooden placard was surrounded by a profusion of fiery orange honeysuckle blossoms.

Trust

"What do the flowers say?" Gwen asked.

"Trust," Rhiannon replied. "That's it."

"Same here," Aidan said. "That's not very helpful. Even by cryptic Breenan standards." He peered ahead. "Is there a fog rolling in, or are my eyes playing tricks on me?"

Gwen glanced ahead. Aidan wasn't seeing things. A distinctly purplish haze formed a cloud directly in their path. It grew thicker by the second, eerily unaffected by the stiff breeze.

Tristan shrugged.

"Probably another obstacle. We made it past a sea serpent, let's not worry about this. We can handle a little fog."

He strode forward confidently. Hesitant, Gwen followed Aidan, and Rhiannon brought up the rear. As soon as she stepped into the cloud, Gwen's world grew dim.

"What's happening? Where's the sun?"

"It's too early for sundown," Aidan said. His footsteps stumbled to a halt beside Gwen.

"What are you two talking about?" Tristan's voice came from the front. "Nothing's happened to the sun."

"Am I going blind?" Gwen's surroundings had turned into a world of shadows. Her companions were indistinct shapes next to her, and beyond them the forest faded into blankness. Panic lapped at the edge of her mind. She swallowed. She couldn't afford to lose her nerve now. But if she were going blind... Her heart hammered in her chest.

"The fog must have done something," Rhiannon said behind her, her voice calm and thoughtful. "Affected your vision. Tristan, we'll have to lead them through. Hopefully they recover once we're out of it." Rhiannon's firm hand gripped Gwen's shoulder. "Come on, Gwen, walk forward. I'll lead you. Trust me."

"Trust," Gwen whispered. "This is another test."

"Looks like it. Lift your feet high, there are tree roots."

Although Gwen could see the path directly in front of her feet, little was visible beyond. She was grateful for Rhiannon's steady guidance, and walked with confidence. Tristan and Aidan's passage was marked by stumbling footsteps ahead of them as well as the occasional muffled curse from Aidan and laugh from Tristan. Rhiannon was a patient leader, and Gwen grew more relaxed despite the rough terrain.

"What is that?" Rhiannon said a few minutes later.

"What?" Gwen was instantly on high alert. "What is it?"

"Daggers out, Rhiannon!" Tristan shouted. "Get down, Aidan."

"What's happening?" The terror of not knowing what was happening was ten times worse that seeing whatever it was. Dark shapes rocketed toward them through the air. Rhiannon pushed her down and grunted. A dagger soared above Gwen's head. She screamed and covered her head with her hands.

Flapping sounds whooshed above and a strange bird shrieked, hugely magnified in Gwen's ears. A few passes of the dagger sliced the air by her head. There was shrieking from above, more and more until the air was filled with the discordant music of attacking birds.

"Run!" Rhiannon shouted, and she hoisted Gwen up by her forearm and dragged her forward. Gwen tripped every second step, and it felt like her arm might dislocate from the force of Rhiannon hauling her upright. The shrieking was louder than ever, and black flapping shapes filled the air around them.

Then—silence. The birds vanished as if they had never been, and all Gwen could hear was the beating of her own heart and Rhiannon's panting breath. Rhiannon stopped and twisted around.

"They've gone. Just—disappeared."

Gwen blinked. Vertical lines bisected her vision

through the fog. They gradually coalesced into the shapes of trees.

"Hey, I'm starting to see better!"

Rhiannon let her arm go. Gwen looked around with a squint until her focus sharpened. Aidan and Tristan stood before her, none the worse for wear. Aidan rubbed his eyes and Tristan sheathed his dagger.

"As I told you," Tristan said. "We can handle a little fog."

Gwen looked down the path, and her heart sank.

"That's good," she said to Tristan. "Because there's more where that came from."

A greenish haze filled the trees, only ten paces beyond where they stood. Gwen turned to Rhiannon.

"Can you take my other arm this time? I think my shoulder's about to fall off."

Rhiannon gave her a half-smile, and clamped her hand around Gwen's opposite arm.

"Take out your dagger again, brother. We're not done yet."

Gwen squared her shoulders and they marched forward. She wasn't looking forward to this, but Rhiannon had brought her through without mishap. She trusted the other girl now—Rhiannon's characteristic calm was paired with patience and steely determination. It had kept them safe last time, and it would keep them safe again, Gwen knew.

They entered the green haze and Gwen braced for the inevitable mist. The trees surrounding her grew indistinct. Rhiannon's firm grip on her arm became a tightening vise.

"It's all dark," she said, her voice high with a quaver at the end. "I can't see."

"Oh, great. Now we're both half-blind."

"Not half-blind. My eyes—there's nothing. Only blackness. What will we do? We can't—I have to fight off the birds—" Rhiannon's panic bubbled under her words. Gwen looked at her unseeing eyes through the murk and frowned. Was this the same girl who was always so calm and collected? Had the loss of control unsettled her this badly?

"It's okay, Rhiannon," Gwen said. She reached over and pried the dagger out of Rhiannon's clenched fingers. The other girl opened her hand slowly and unwillingly. "We'll get through this. You can trust me. I'm not entirely useless, you know. I can see well enough to defend us."

Rhiannon didn't look convinced, and Gwen couldn't blame her. The dagger felt foreign and heavy in her hand. The closest she'd ever come to knife work was in the kitchen. Somehow, that didn't feel like enough preparation.

"Lift your feet high," Gwen said. She eyed the path as best as she could through the fog. Only an occasional root protruded from the hard-packed soil, but she knew from experience that occasional was far too often when one couldn't see. Rhiannon cautiously placed each foot in front of the other, guided by Gwen.

Tristan and Aidan were in the same predicament, although Tristan's footsteps were more confident than Rhiannon's.

"Keep your eyes to the skies," he said to Aidan. "And hold that dagger at the ready. Remember—slice, don't stab."

"All right," Aidan said. He turned to peer at Gwen through the gloom despite standing almost at arm's reach. "How are you faring back there?"

"We're coming," she said. "Slowly but surely."

After a few minutes of their stumbling gait, the terrain changed from soil and tree roots to a multitude of jagged rocks strewn haphazardly on the path. Rhiannon stumbled again and again, and Gwen kept up a running commentary about where to place her feet.

"Oh no," Aidan said. Gwen's heart stuttered, and Rhiannon's hand almost cut off the circulation in Gwen's arm.

"What's happening?" she said, her voice an octave higher than usual. "Are the birds coming?"

Beyond Aidan, long brown shapes slithered in the dim. It was hard to tell through the haze, but they moved sinuously around rocks and over roots toward the four.

"It's okay, Rhiannon. No birds. Snakes instead, but they look pretty small. Keep walking."

"No. Don't let down your guard. They'll attack."

"Okay." Gwen patted Rhiannon's hand. Aidan yelled.

"Argh! It leaped at me!"

A splatter of blood stained the rocks nearest Aidan, where one of the snakes writhed with a deep gash along its side. The other snakes lifted their heads. One by one, each wide mouth opened to show a set of wickedly sharp fangs and a flickering tongue.

Gwen gripped her dagger in her shaking hand. The snakes were going to attack. Was she ready for them?

"Keep moving forward," Tristan bellowed. "We need to get out of this fog!"

"Come on, Rhiannon," Gwen said. "Just stay close, and I'll keep the snakes away."

Rhiannon seemed past speech at this point. Her blue eyes darted sightlessly in every direction. Gwen pulled her forward and Rhiannon stumbled behind. The snakes closed in.

One leaped at Aidan, but Gwen didn't see the outcome before another slithered her way. Its open mouth displayed the full extent of its fangs, and its eyes glistened cruelly. Gwen didn't have time to think, only to react. She sliced the dagger in a shallow arc to greet the oncoming serpent. To her surprise, the dagger made contact. The snake hissed and darted away. Blood dribbled from a wound on its side.

Gwen couldn't watch it go because another snake was right behind the first. She slashed again and missed. The creature jerked to the left and brushed Rhiannon's leg.

Rhiannon screamed and released Gwen's arm. She stumbled in a wild panic past Aidan and Tristan.

"No, Rhiannon! Come back!" Gwen slashed at another snake, blade meeting flank in a spray of red blood, and kicked another aside in her pursuit of Rhiannon. The other girl was swift and nimble, but even she couldn't avoid roots she couldn't see. Before long, she tripped headfirst, sprawled on her front along the path. Within seconds, two snakes slid onto her legs.

Rhiannon screamed again and tried to crawl. Gwen sprinted to her side but before she could fend off the creatures, blood spurted from where fangs met calf. Gwen sliced at the serpents. Distracted as they were by Rhiannon's blood, neither were difficult to dispatch, and Gwen kicked away the limp carcasses in disgust.

"Rhiannon! Are you okay?" Gwen dropped to her knees beside Rhiannon. No other snakes came their way and the hisses of the rest faded into the distance, hastened by Aidan's yells of triumph. Rhiannon's tear-streaked face turned to Gwen and looked her straight in the eye.

"I can see now," she said hoarsely. She glanced down at her legs and swallowed. Gwen's eyes followed and she gasped.

The backs of Rhiannon's calves were a mess of blood and ripped flesh. There was far more damage than any natural snake should have been able to inflict. The snakes had focused on immobilizing their prey. There was no way Rhiannon could walk. Gwen wondered if she would ever walk again.

The others ran up and Tristan skidded to his knees at Rhiannon's side.

"No!" He stared in horror at her mangled legs.

Aidan went straight to work. He cut the sleeves off of his shirt with the dagger and threaded them under Rhiannon's shins to wrap around the bleeding flesh.

"This should keep everything together, at least. Tristan, do you know any healing spells? Mine are fairly rudimentary."

"I don't know much."

"At least something to stop the bleeding?"

"Yes, I can do that." Tristan visibly collected himself and held a hand over each leg. "Hold on, Rhiannon—this might sting."

Rhiannon let out a gasp that might have been an attempt at a laugh. Her face was pale and her forehead glistened with sweat. She clenched her teeth together and Tristan closed his eyes. Gwen held her hand, unsure what else she could do.

"You're doing great," she said.

"It's done," Tristan said a moment later. He sat back on his heels. "There's not much else I can do. We'll have to carry her."

219

"Don't be ridiculous," Rhiannon said faintly. "You're not carrying me anywhere."

"There's no way you can walk. I'm sorry, but it's the truth."

"Yes, I'm not an idiot. I know what happened. I won't come with you the rest of the way. Find me a bush to hide in, and keep going. Or did you forget we're on a timeline?" She looked pointedly at Gwen's wrist, where the bracelet hung innocently. Gwen glanced at the tracker ring, insubstantial on her thumb.

"We're not leaving you," Tristan said at once.

"Yes, you are," Rhiannon said. Her voice was thin, edged with pain and irritation. "Finish this thing. It's my fault I'm hurt."

"What? Don't blame yourself for this."

"I should have trusted Gwen. That was the whole point of this obstacle, and I failed." She shrugged, and grimaced when the motion shifted her injured body. She smiled wryly at Gwen. "Nice dagger work, by the way."

"I'll stay with you, then," Tristan said.

"No. We've made it this far, you have to see the quest through to the end. Find the spell and make this all worthwhile. Don't you dare quit on me."

Tristan hesitated, then nodded. He slid his hands under her body and lifted her up.

"All right. Let's find a tree to stash you in."

Gwen ran ahead to scout for a safe place to leave Rhiannon, heedless of potential dangers. Rhiannon was top priority, now. Over a small hillock, Gwen came across a tiny stream that burbled with fresh spring water.

"Perfect," Gwen said aloud, and followed the water to her left. Thick bushes surrounded the stream, but opened

220

up enough for a small, welcoming patch of soft moss to grow.

Gwen ran back to the others. Tristan labored with Rhiannon in his arms, who was white-faced and clung desperately to her brother. Aidan carried the satchel, his brow creased with worry.

"Why don't you levitate her?" Aidan said.

"We might need all the magic I can muster. Who knows what's up ahead? I have plenty of physical strength, but there's only so much magic I can manage at once. Don't forget Bran's fate."

"This way," Gwen called out. "I found a good spot." She led them to the mossy bank and held branches aside so Tristan could lay his burden down gently. Rhiannon hissed in pain, then pressed her lips together as if determined not to show any more signs of discomfort.

"There's water from the stream, and food in the bag," Gwen said. Aidan passed Rhiannon the satchel. "We'll be as quick as we can."

"You don't have much time left, in any event. I'll be fine. Go, and good luck."

Gwen nodded and turned to go. Behind her, Tristan said, "Are you sure you'll be all right?"

"Go, brother. Don't make me angry." There was a smile in her voice as she said, "You know what I'm like when I'm angry."

Tristan joined them on the path, his face grim.

"Come on, let's find this spell and be done."

"Can she be healed?" Aidan said. "When we get back?"

"I don't know. Her tendons are completely ripped apart. Her skin can be healed, but who knows if she'll ever walk properly again." He swallowed hard, and strode down the path. Gwen bit her lip at Aidan's stricken face.

"Come on," she said. "Let's finish this."

The trees thinned as they progressed. The sullen sky that hid the sinking sun shone a dull light through the canopy of rustling autumn foliage. Wind whipped dead leaves up from the forest floor to dance around their calves.

Between the thinning trees, low bushes of gorse and buckthorn appeared with greater and greater frequency. They were too well-placed, too perfectly maintained, to be entirely natural. A twist and curl of one plant stirred something in Gwen's memory, and she trotted forward to join Tristan.

"Do these bushes say anything? I thought I recognized—well, something. I don't know."

"Good eye. The motif of Lady Maeve is repeated over and over. It's pretty common on the approach to a grand estate. Marking territory. Unless someone still lives here, which is doubtful, the plants must be maintained by magic."

"Isn't that a very long-lasting spell?" Aidan caught up to them on the widening path. "Most spells I do tend to have a time limit."

"It's a very long time. Even strong magic rarely lasts past the death of its maker. The legends say Lady Maeve was powerful—looks like they were right."

The forest brightened, and the trees ended in a wall of tall grasses. Gwen blinked in the unfiltered light. Before them, a rolling meadowland covered the entire promontory. The island's edges fell away to steep cliffs where crying seabirds circled and thunderous waves crashed far below. Grasses in the meadow waved and rustled their dry stalks together. The wind flowed visibly across the land, below clouds of a threatening black. To their left lay the crumbling remains of a stone castle. Once upon a time a magnificent mansion must have stood proudly on the hillside, overlooking the stormy sea, but time had not been kind. The crumbled structure on the edge of the desolate cliff surrounded by dying grasses had an air of majestic melancholy.

The real focus of the vista, however, was located directly in the center of the meadow. Gwen's eyes were drawn to it, and her body inadvertently shifted to face its direction. It was a garden, encircled by an ancient tall stone wall. The wall was topped with blousy tufts of late-summer roses in pinks and whites. Only hints of the garden appeared within, but it seemed well-maintained and alive. The contrast with the ruins beyond was staggering.

"Which way do we go?" she said quietly to the others.

"Only one real choice, isn't there?" Tristan's body was also aligned to face the garden. "The garden is the only thing maintained here, by magic for certain. Can't you feel its pull?"

"And the castle looks like it should be condemned," Aidan said. "I doubt anything is left in there."

Without another word they walked down the hillside toward the garden. Seed heads on the ends of long stalks tickled Gwen's hands during their passage, and the wind blew her ponytail against her neck. The garden grew larger upon their approach, and a small clearing in the grass opened up to a curved archway in the high stone wall, which supported vast expanses of frothy roses. Gwen wondered how such an ancient-looking wall, the gaps between stones stuffed with yellowed moss, could support

223

such a display. The garden's pull was even stronger here, and Gwen could hardly help putting one foot in front of the other.

"Do you feel the pull?" she asked Aidan.

"Makes a nice change from the obstacles, I thought." He grinned in reassurance, and she felt better. Loss of control was unnerving, but this is where they wanted to go. And she was sure that she could leave if she really wanted to—the pull was strong, but not all-encompassing. It was a strong suggestion rather than a compulsion.

They reached the clearing and stopped. Tristan looked to the top of the archway and Gwen followed his gaze. Even to her eyes, the flowers and vines appeared more purposeful there. Directly above the keystone, a flower surrounded by a curling vine with three leaves looked very familiar to Gwen. She'd seen a motif like that before, at the Garden of Love Made Visible, back on the beach.

"Does that say garden?"

Aidan looked impressed, and Tristan nodded slowly.

"Among other things. It says, 'Garden of Unity.'"

They all looked at each other. Gwen's own uncertainty was mirrored in the others' eyes. This was it, the end of the road, the place where magic hummed so loudly along Gwen's spine that she trembled. They were close, so close to achieving the impossible, to saving Bran and Isolde and her own life. She glanced at her hand. The bracelet twitched and buzzed on her arm and her thumb was visible through Bran's ring.

Aidan wrapped his hand around the bracelet and she looked up.

"We're almost there," he said, his eyes sure and his voice calm. "We made it this far, against the odds. Let's get this spell and go home."

Gwen nodded, comforted by his show of certainty.

"And Rhiannon's waiting. We shouldn't hang around," she said.

Tristan started forward when she mentioned Rhiannon, and they followed him into the garden.

Chapter 13

The perfume of a thousand flowers infused the air. A wilderness of plants greeted Gwen's eyes—towering rhododendrons, opulent roses, sweeping clematis, carpets of bluebells, all seasons of flowers blooming together. It was full and wild, yet there was a certain order to the chaos, a pleasing arrangement to the disorder. A calm quiet fell on her ears—it was a living, breathing silence, full and lush. A path followed the curve of the garden's wall and traced outward from their vantage point to disappear beyond the voluminous foliage. A central path lay directly ahead, but its winding way didn't allow for long views.

The magic's pull took them toward the center without discussion. There was only one choice, one way to go. Gwen passed Tristan and took the lead. Her bracelet buzzed uncontrollably, and disrupted the serenity of the garden for her. Their quest came first. Aidan followed close at her heels.

"There are directions for spells everywhere." Tristan's hushed voice broke the silence. "Absolutely everywhere.

Look, this one tells you how to build a sturdy wall, and here's one for changing the color of your horse's mane." He snorted, then looked closer. "They all need two people to work the spell, though. Only one magic-user, but two people present and willing. Strange—I've never seen spells like them."

"Keep your eyes open for our restoration spell," Gwen said. Her heart sank. Would Tristan have to search the whole garden? She and Aidan couldn't read the spells to find the correct one. How long did they have? The bracelet jumped on her wrist uncomfortably.

"Oh, a spell that powerful? It's probably the one that's pulling us. The magic is so strong that we're drawn to it. I doubt it will be hidden."

Relieved, Gwen continued forward with Aidan. Tristan exclaimed now and then behind them at the spells he read. They turned and twisted down the path, unable to see farther than a few paces for the glorious profusion of plants. There were far too many flowers for this late in the summer.

"I'm sure that's an iris. They should be blooming in the spring, not now," Gwen said.

"It's like magic," Aidan said, and they grinned at each other.

A magnificent cluster of lilacs marked the entry to a central clearing. It appeared as a small green room. Verdant foliage loomed on all sides and the air was heavy with the scent of honeysuckle. Crushed oyster shells on the ground surrounded a circle of bare soil below a pedestal.

The pedestal was cut from gray granite, carved with designs so ancient and weathered that Gwen could hardly make them out. The top was large and flat, pitted with small divots worn away over the centuries.

Gwen and Aidan walked slowly toward the pedestal. Gwen knew that here lay the restoration spell. Her whole body practically vibrated with the magic that emanated from the pedestal.

The blank surface of the pedestal shifted and shimmered, in a way that stone had no business doing. Slowly, an inscription in English appeared chiseled into the top. Gwen held her breath until the words settled into the stone as if they had always been there. She and Aidan leaned forward as one to read the inscription.

Only those of pure intent
Can death and destruction prevent.
Power of creation must preside
But magic will also provide.
Write the spell in living motif
From a plant that brings relief.
A connection must be made
Between growth and those receiving aid.
Bind it all with powers outpoured
Only then will health be restored.

Gwen stood upright and puzzled over the words. Aidan looked at her.

"Typical. Another cryptic message. Why do the Breenan never say what they mean?"

"Luckily it's in English. I wonder if the spell somehow sensed who we are, so it could write in language we understood."

A strangled yell erupted from behind them. Gwen whirled around. Tristan's boot thrashed on the path from behind the lilac.

They ran back to him, and Gwen gasped. Tristan's arms

228

were encircled by bright green vines, and another thick vine snaked around his chest. Tristan's eyes were open wide with fear.

"Help me!"

"Hold on!" Gwen dove toward him with her arms outstretched, intent on ripping away the strangling vines. Her body slammed into an invisible wall and she fell back on her bottom. Aidan reached out to the struggling Tristan, and met the same resistance.

"There's a barrier here." He patted his hands over the invisible surface, and then ran sideways to feel the extent of the barricade. There was no way around.

"What happened?" Gwen said. "I thought you were right behind us." She raked the wall with her fingernails, but the empty air was as smooth as glass. "Can you tear away the vines?"

"No, I'm stuck." Tristan wriggled and kicked his legs, then gasped when the vines drew tighter around his chest. "I tried to use a spell, and the plant attacked."

"What spell? We need to do the restoration one!" How could Tristan have forgotten their quest so easily?

"I know. But this spell said it would heal any flesh wound." Tristan closed his eyes briefly, his face woebegone. "I was trying to help Rhiannon. But the spell needed two people to work."

"Dammit," Gwen said. She looked helplessly at Aidan, who shook his head. "Just—don't struggle, okay? We'll figure out this spell and fix you, Rhiannon, everyone."

"Please hurry." Tristan's voice wheezed hoarsely, his chest movements constricted. "It's getting tighter."

Gwen ran to the pedestal, Aidan right behind her. She read the inscription again.

"Gwen, is it your bracelet making that buzzing sound?"

"Yeah." She scanned the inscription. Her eyes flicked back and forth frantically, without comprehension. "I don't understand this. What do they want us to do?"

Aidan looked up at the tracker ring on Gwen's thumb. It flickered feebly. Thunder rumbled in the distance.

"Bloody hell. Bran must be almost gone."

At this, Gwen tore her eyes away from the pedestal and looked at Aidan. Panic licked the edges of her mind. The restoration spell was hidden behind cryptic instructions. They had failed at their quest. She would die, along with Bran and Isolde, and now Tristan. Aidan would be left to drag Rhiannon's injured body back to the mainland, where they would be vulnerable to any ill-fortune. Gwen's father would never see her again, would never know what had happened to his only daughter.

This was it. She reached out and took Aidan's hand.

"Don't leave me alone," she whispered. "Stay with me until the end."

"You won't die," he said, his voice fierce. "We will figure out this stupid inscription, now, together. And we will survive. Both of us. Don't you dare give up."

Gwen closed her eyes and took a deep breath.

"Okay." There was nothing to lose by trying. "Let's work it out."

"Line by line. First one, 'Only those of pure intent.' Well, I'd say we're being pretty damn selfless. If this doesn't count, I don't know what does. 'Can death and destruction prevent,' fine, that's what the spell does."

"'Powers of creation must preside, but magic will also provide.' Okay, so we've got to be creative about this spell."

230

"Well, we have a leg up on any Breenan, being part-human and not so dense about thinking outside the box."

"But we also need magic," Gwen said. "This sounds like a human-Breenan combo to me. Which makes sense, given the queens who made up the spell. Every obstacle we've encountered so far has needed creativity and magic together, or at least people from both worlds to read instructions."

"And someone skilled in knife work to slice up sea monsters."

"That too. The queens didn't want either humans or Breenan to get the upper hand over the other."

"Looks like we're the right people for the job," Aidan said. He squeezed her hand. "Now what? 'Write the spell in living motif, from a plant that brings relief.'"

"Plant writing, that's pretty clear. Just like all the spells in this garden. I don't know how we'll manage that. And what kind of plant brings relief?"

"Let's come back to that. 'A connection must be made, between growth and those receiving aid.' How do we connect the plant to those we want to heal? No one is here in person."

Gwen's mind whirled frantically.

"A connection, not their presence," she said slowly. "Something that belongs to them, maybe. How about Bran's tracker ring?"

"Yes! Perfect. And Rhiannon?"

"Maybe we can run back and get something from her. She might have an idea. But what about Isolde and the realm? That's kind of abstract."

Aidan's brow furrowed in thought.

"The locket," he said finally. "Isolde wore it for years,

and it has her picture in it. And it was how she kept the realm functioning, so in a way it's a connection to the entire place."

"Not a bad thought. I don't have anything better, so let's go with that." Gwen looked to the last two lines of the inscription. "'Bind it all with powers outpoured, only then will health be restored.' Powers outpoured—that just sounds like a lot of magic all at once. I think maybe we can do this. If we do it together."

"Always," he whispered, and brushed her cheek. He straightened. "So, we need a plant, and tokens from Rhiannon. Let's talk to Tristan, then I'll run to Rhiannon while you set everything up."

Tristan lay as still as if he were asleep, but opened his eyes when Gwen and Aidan approached. His pale face shone with sweat.

"What's happening?" he whispered, his voice a wheeze. "Did you do the spell?"

"Not yet," Aidan said. "We need something that belongs to Rhiannon, something that will make a magical connection. Any ideas?"

"Find Rhiannon. Take some of her hair." Tristan closed his eyes, the energy of talking clearly too much.

"I'll be back as soon as I can," Aidan said to Gwen. He squeezed her hand and let go. "Ask about the plant."

Gwen nodded and Aidan ran up the path. His long legs pounded on the crunching oyster shells.

"Tristan, I need your help. I'm looking for a plant 'that brings relief.' Maybe something that has healing properties?"

Tristan's eyes remained closed for so long that Gwen wondered if he had passed out.

"Relief," he said quietly. "Find some meadowsweet. It's a pain reliever. One of the best, when augmented by magic."

"Perfect." Gwen nodded and turned to go, then paused. "What does meadowsweet look like?"

"As high as your waist, frothy clusters of cream-colored flowers in season. It has dark green leaves with three points."

"Hold on." Gwen ran up the path and glanced wildly around for a plant matching Tristan's description. There were so many plants, growing in such profusion, layers and layers of flowers and leaves and branches. How would she spot a plant with dark green leaves that may or may not have flowers blooming among all of this?

Pinks and purples and oranges flew by her searching eyes, but none matched Tristan's description. Once, she saw creamy white and her heart leaped, but the flowers were huge trumpets peeking out from glossy green foliage. Thunder punctuated her pounding footsteps. At the archway, she turned right at random to run along the wall and looked carefully into the garden. The bracelet vibrated with such a frequency that her wrist grew red and sore.

A quarter of the way around the circular garden wall, soft white emerged from deep in the garden. Gwen stopped. Small flower clusters, three-pointed leaves—this was the plant she needed. She dove into the garden, heedless of other plants, and reached the meadowsweet with broken branches clinging to her clothes.

"Now what?" she said aloud. Did she have to dig up the whole plant and cart it back with her? It was awfully big, she had no shovel, and the bracelet jumped on her wrist. She snapped off a large branch, deciding to rely on magic to grow the plant if needed.

She ran back to Tristan.

"Any sign of Aidan yet?" she said, her breath coming in gasps. Tristan shook his head slightly. Gwen turned to run to the pedestal, but paused when a thought struck her.

"Tristan, how would I spell out something with this plant? Specifically, I want to say 'bring healing to those connected,' or something to that effect."

He frowned in thought.

"Grow two flower clusters close together, wrap a six-leafed branch around them in a figure-eight. Just below, grow a cluster of leaves in an upward spray. No more than nine, no less than seven."

"Huh. That's—actually doable." Gwen had expected Tristan to say that it wasn't possible to tell her how without showing her. "I might be able to do that."

She flew to the pedestal, which stood as still and timeless as when she had first seen it. The bare patch of dirt at the base of the pedestal beckoned. She knelt down and shoved the end of the meadowsweet into the soil so it stuck upright, waving from the motion.

Now, how to make the plant grow? Gwen scrambled in her mind for a spell that might work. Her repertoire was so limited, limited to a few silly spells that she and Ellie had made up themselves. She wished Aidan would hurry up. Then she thought of the lifting spell they used on Bran. Could that work, modified by her own core's vitality and the heavy scent of growing magic already present in the garden?

Gwen squeezed the plant's stem firmly between finger and thumb, and reached into her magical core. Her center burned bright and hot, ready and eager to be released, fully recovered from her exertions on their journey with Bran. She let it leap through her arm and into her hand, infusing the stem with her magic while she concentrated on the spell. Before her eyes, the plant began to sprout. The stem grew thicker, woodier, and the wrinkled leaves with their grayish undersides multiplied over and over. Newly-formed branches spread and reached up to the sky. A faint scent of wintergreen perfumed the air.

Gwen's mouth broadened in a triumphant smile, but she kept her concentration focused. Now was the difficult part—she had to encourage the plant to grow in a certain configuration. When the meadowsweet reached the top of the pedestal, Gwen poured her magic into the plant. The tips of the branches folded sideways and twisted around the circumference of the pedestal. She stared intently at the foliage, willing it to grow in the formation that Tristan had specified. Slowly, the branches writhed and curled. Two flower clusters blossomed between a figure-eight branch, and a mass of leaves sprouted below.

Satisfied, Gwen pulled her magic back into herself and let go of the meadowsweet. It stopped growing at once and its fullness surrounded the pedestal like a green scarf. The message seemed clear enough to Gwen, and stood out now that she knew what to look for. She hoped she hadn't spelled out anything unintended in the rest of the meadowsweet.

She unclasped the locket from around her neck, slipped Bran's pale ring off of her thumb, and set them both down in the center of the pedestal. Her part was done. But where was Aidan? The bracelet thrummed uncomfortably on her wrist. It was louder now, and Gwen glanced up at the gray clouds, sullen and dark once more. She couldn't tell what time it was under the gray cloud cover—when would the bracelet detonate? Maybe she should try out the spell first, make sure Bran was healed, and then they could heal Rhiannon later.

***

Aidan flew through the meadow where the overlong grass whipped his calves. Rhiannon's stream wasn't far, but far enough to necessitate sprinting. Aidan's breath came in short, sharp pants as he labored up the slope toward the forest. The brooding trees loomed ahead, their fiery reds and yellows adding an air of vibrant menace to the ominous sky.

Once within the trees, Aidan leaped forward until the sound of running water directed his feet to the right. Ten paces in, he burst through the bushes and skidded to a stop, a dagger pointed at his thigh.

"Oh, it's you," Rhiannon said. She sheathed her dagger with a trembling hand. "You might have warned me. I almost skewered you."

"Sorry. We found the spell, but I need something of yours. Hair or something. We're going to heal you too."

Rhiannon's usually emotionless face melted into an expression of hope, before she masked it again.

"Do you think it will work?"

"We have to try. Cut me a piece, will you?"

Rhiannon slid her dagger out again and deftly sliced the end of her long blond braid. Aidan shoved it into his pocket.

"Wait. Where are the others?"

"Gwen is preparing the rest of the spell—"

"Really? She's the one doing the magic? Where's Tristan? He's much more practiced, with more power."

"Tristan is trapped in some vines that are squeezing him. I don't know how long we have. We were hoping that once you were healed, you could release him from the spell."

Rhiannon stared at him for a long moment, then slid a ring off the smallest finger of her right hand.

"Here, take this. It's a tracker ring of Tristan's. We use it while we're hunting, in case one of us gets lost. It's usually him." A flash of fear crossed her face. "Include him in the restoration spell. If he's being held by the magic of Lady Maeve, I don't know if there is much I can do to help."

"Good," Aidan said. He put the ring into his pocket with Rhiannon's hair. "I have to go. There's not much time—Gwen's bracelet will activate soon."

"Wait, one more thing. You and Gwen both have magic, but it's not as strong as a full-blooded Breenan."

"What makes you say that?"

"That's what the old stories always say about half-bloods. If you're to pull off a spell of this magnitude, and Tristan can't help you, I expect you and Gwen will have to do it together. Combine powers."

"All right, fine." Aidan shuffled his feet back and forth with impatience.

"You don't understand. Joining powers is, well, you don't do that with just anyone. You need to be close. Emotionally close."

Aidan stopped and looked at her.

"That should be fine," he said slowly. Rhiannon shrugged.

237

"Gwen has some issues about you. She talked to me the other night, about how she feels guilty for making you come to her land, about her fears if you and she aren't a good match. It might be difficult for her to let go enough to join fully." Rhiannon smiled wryly. "It'll be up to you to convince her."

"Right." Aidan looked worried. "I don't know what more I can say."

"Find the right words. We're counting on you."

Aidan turned and ran back to the path. Rhiannon lay back with a grimace of pain to stare up at the shifting leaves.

***

A strangled yell from behind Gwen made her twirl on the spot. She ran back to Tristan and stopped, her hands clenched in tight fists. Tristan's face was red and he gasped for air. The vine around his chest squeezed so tightly that it cut into his skin, and blood stained his shirt along the line.

"Tristan!" Gwen shouted. She ran her hands along the invisible wall, punching and kicking it, but only ended up with sore toes for her efforts. Tristan stared wildly at her.

Gwen stood still and pressed her hands against the wall. If physical force wouldn't work, maybe magic would. She dug into her core and pulled out a sizeable chunk of the viscous warmth within. It passed down her arms and out her palms, which glowed with a pure white light.

Moments later, the light flickered and died. Puzzled, Gwen drew out more of her magic. Her palms only glowed for seconds.

"Stop," Tristan gasped. He wheezed for a moment. "Waste—magic—won't work."

"Dammit!" Gwen slammed her fist against the wall. "Where's Aidan? We need Rhiannon's help."

"I'm here!" Aidan crashed into view. He stopped with his hands on his knees, gasping. "Oh, no. What's happening to Tristan?"

"Give me the hair!" Gwen held out her hand and Aidan dug into his pocket to find Rhiannon's braid. He put a ring in Gwen's palm and she looked at him with a silent question.

"It's Tristan's, to release him from his spell."

Gwen nodded and ran to the pedestal. They had all the pieces now, everything they needed. It was time to pour out her magic.

Where should she put her hands? Did it matter? Gwen quailed under the responsibility. So much was at stake, so many people counted on her to do this and do it right. She knew so little magic. All she could do was to pour out her core and hope for the best. She threaded her hands through the prolific branches of the meadowsweet to grasp the edges of the pedestal. Her core simmered within her chest, and she took a large piece of it and thrust it out through her hands.

Her fingers fizzled and sparked, and then—nothing. She turned to Aidan, who looked at her with concern in his eyes. Concern, and something else.

"It won't work with only one of us." Aidan stepped up to the opposite side of the pedestal. "Rhiannon said that since we're only half-Breenan, we don't have enough power to activate the spell."

"What? So much for the queens' unity and cooperation

thing. I thought a half-breed would be exactly what they wanted."

"I doubt they considered a half-breed. I reckon they wanted Breenan and human to work together, but they expected a full-Breenan to perform the magic, and a full-human to understand the inscription. Rhiannon said it's possible for us to do the spell, but we have to work together."

"Fine." The bracelet throbbed insistently. "Let's do this."

"She said that we have to open up fully to each other. She said there mustn't be any issues between us. So, if there's something you want to say to me, you should say it now." He looked at her expectantly. Gwen wasn't sure what he was trying to say.

"Everything's fine. Come on, let's give it a try. Time is ticking."

Aidan sighed, but held out his hands on either side of the pedestal. She grasped them firmly in her own above the tokens.

"Okay, pour your magic into the tokens with 'pure intent,'" Gwen said. "And try to join our magic together, I guess. Somehow. Ready?"

"One, two, three," Aidan said, and Gwen stared at their hands intently while she drew out some of her core.

White light from her hands welled out to meet blue light from Aidan's. The blue light, fluid and agile, flowed gently around and beside the white light, which was a solid, unyielding lump around Gwen's fingers. Nothing happened for a few seconds, then both lights faded. Aidan took his hands away.

"What's blocking you?"

"Nothing. I don't know. I don't know how to mingle magic." Gwen's heart hammered in her chest to the pulse of the throbbing bracelet.

"There's something bothering you. Something about us. What is it?"

"We don't have time for this." Gwen's nails clenched into her palms. The inscription on the pedestal was too clearly visible through Bran's translucent ring. "We need to figure out this spell. Then we can talk all you want."

"That's the problem. We can't do the spell unless you tell me what's worrying you. Otherwise, we can't do a thing." Aidan grabbed the edges of the pedestal with white knuckles. "Please, Gwen, talk to me. Tell me what's wrong."

Gwen stared into Aidan's green eyes, wide and determined. Was this really the only way? What did she want to say? How could she say it? It had seemed clear, talking to Rhiannon, but now... She paused, trying to formulate her thoughts.

"I've been worried lately." She swallowed through the thickness in her throat from fear. "I've been worried about you moving to Vancouver." She looked away, but felt his eyes on her face. "You're coming there for me, mainly, and what if it doesn't work out? Not that things aren't great now—because they are—but we haven't known each other for very long, and if we fall apart, then I've dragged you halfway around the world for nothing—"

Aidan reached out to hold her chin in his fingers and turn her face his way. His eyes were serious.

"You aren't dragging me anywhere. It's my own choice. I truly believe that we have something special, but let's say for argument's sake that it all goes south. Then,

241

so what? I finish my year of school, and then decide if I want to stay in Vancouver or transfer elsewhere. It will be an incredible experience living in a new country, whether or not you're a part of it. I reckon we really have something, and the more I know you, the more I want to know you. But I do understand the consequences."

Gwen gazed into his earnest eyes, at the face that had followed her into the portal and through the wilderness of the Otherworld. He was still helping her and supporting her—he was there for her. Then she thought of herself, and the times she had comforted him—when they had found out their heritage, when he met his father... Maybe she couldn't know the future. But if all she had to go on was this, it was a good start.

Gwen let out a breath she hadn't realized she had been holding. Her shoulders felt lighter, somehow, the weight of guilt lifted off them. She wondered why she had been fussing about this for so long, why she hadn't talked to Aidan before. She reached up and placed her hand alongside his face.

"Let's do this. Now, before there's nothing left to restore."

Aidan searched her face. He must have seen something encouraging, because he smiled and took her hands to place them above the tokens.

"Ready?" he said.

"Ready," she whispered. She kept her eyes fixed on his, and reached into her core.

Once again, white light the color of moonlight welled up between her fingers, and a glow the blue of a summer sky poured out of Aidan's. But this time, Gwen's light was fluid and moved like water over her knuckles and onto the pedestal. She didn't watch the light, but stared into Aidan's eyes, connected with him. When their lights joined she felt it—her core grew warmer, and a flow of magic from her center to her hands connected her with the outside world. Aidan was at the end of that link, and her magic traveled from her core through her hands straight to him. Tendrils of white and blue light twined around each other. When the first two tendrils joined in a glistening spark of pale blue, Gwen gasped. Aidan was there, right there, so close. She almost shied away from the contact, but his steady green eyes reassured her and she allowed the link to remain. More and more tendrils connected in bursts of pale sparks and left behind a hemisphere of light that covered their joined hands.

Gwen's mouth opened in an irrepressible smile when their hands stopped sparking and the connection was fully complete. Aidan's face mirrored hers. Vaguely, Gwen sensed movement around them. It was hard to care, really—all she could think about was the joy of being with Aidan. But when Aidan looked to the side with an expression of amazement, she followed his gaze.

The garden around them was alive. Every single plant in every bed was growing, twisting and reaching for the sky, blossoms bursting forth in a dazzling display of colors from every season. Brilliant reds and rich violets mingled with sprays of frothy yellows and delicate whites. Vines twisted and curled over every surface, and roses on the high stone wall bloomed with a profusion of pale pink flowers just visible through the foliage. The light surrounding their hands glowed brightly.

"I think it's working," Aidan said. He turned back to Gwen. "It's really working."

Gwen laughed then, for sheer joy and relief.

"Yes, I think it is."

The quality of light above their clasped hands changed, and images began to appear within the translucency of their magic. A moving picture of Tristan appeared first. Gwen watched him sit up and rip limp vines off his torso, which healed before her eyes. The magic rippled, and Rhiannon appeared. The blond girl looked at her legs in astonishment as the torn edges of her flesh knit themselves together. She wiggled her ankles, then jumped to her feet, laughing. The next picture showed a pale Bran in a circular room lined with carved wood, his face flooded with color. He sat up on the table next to his kneeling father, whose astonishment was no less than his joy.

The last image rippled to show Isolde on her throne. A ringed hand swept away cobwebs from a face filled with fullness and life. Isolde stood up, unwavering, and held out her hands. The fires behind her instantly died and she gave a triumphant smile.

The images faded into the milky blue of their combined magic.

"It's done." Aidan looked at Gwen. "We did it."

"Does this mean we have to stop?"

Aidan smiled.

"For now."

With regret, Gwen pulled the magic back to her core. It felt lonely without Aidan's connection, and the living, growing world around them slowed to a stop. Huge bushes towered above them and crowded into the clearing around the pedestal. The spell was complete.

"I can't believe we did it," Gwen said. She released Aidan's hands and stepped back from the pedestal. "That's incredible."

"Mission impossible, completely possible." Aidan stepped around the pedestal until he stood before her. His eyes were alive with the same joyous light Gwen felt in her own. She didn't want to be apart from him for one more moment, and flung her arms around his neck. Her lips pressed into his with fervent abandon.

They stayed entwined until a voice interrupted them.

"All right, that's enough, lovebirds. You can do that sort of nonsense when you get home."

"Tristan!" Gwen broke away from Aidan to look at a grinning Tristan. "You're free! Feeling better?"

"All healed." He lifted his torn and bloody shirt. Only one faint red line on his torso indicated where the strangling vine had wrapped around him. "Still a little dizzy. There wasn't a lot of air there for a while."

Aidan strode up to Tristan.

"I'm glad you're all right." Aidan wavered for a moment while Tristan looked at him curiously, then he hugged him briefly. Tristan grinned and returned the embrace.

"It's good to see you too, brother."

"Oh, come here," Gwen said, and she threw her arms around Tristan, who squeezed her back. When they parted, he grabbed her wrist with a frown.

"Why hasn't the bracelet stopped?"

Gwen looked down at the deadly bracelet. She had forgotten about it in the excitement and jubilation of their triumph. Now, however, it was all too clear that the bracelet had not given up on its quest to kill her. It thrummed and buzzed on her wrist. She looked at Aidan, her gut writhing, and he stared at her in dismay.

"No," Gwen whispered. "No, no, no."

"Faolan must not have deactivated it yet," Aidan said, horror in his voice. He whirled on Tristan. "What can we do? Is there anything we can do?"

Tristan shook his head.

"Faolan's magic is too strong. Anything I try will almost certainly backfire." His eyes were grief-stricken. "I'm sorry, Gwen."

Gwen stared at the bracelet. After all this—travels through her mother's tortured realm, the long journey to the sea, monsters and birds and everything they had to do to get to this point, even after completing the restoration spell—Gwen would still die. A pulse of hatred for Faolan coursed through her. She had given him back his son— was it too much to spare her life? Anger quickly fizzled out in the wake of her overwhelming fear.

"I'm scared," she said to Aidan. She didn't want to die. She wanted to see her father again, laugh with Ellie again. She wanted to start another chapter in her life with Aidan and all the new experiences and adventures that it would bring. She didn't want her life to end here, on this island, all because of someone else's selfishness and incompetence.

She only caught a glimpse of Aidan's distraught face before he enveloped her in his arms.

"It's all right. I'm here. Everything will be all right."

She nestled into his shoulder, comforted despite the thrumming bracelet on her wrist. If she had to go, at least Aidan was here with her. She could think of worse ways. Aidan's tears dripped onto her forehead.

Buzzing from the bracelet grew louder, almost piercing. She buried her head deeper into Aidan's shirt and he squeezed her so tightly that she wouldn't have been able to breathe, if she hadn't already been holding her breath. They hung there, waiting, waiting for the end, the vibrations taking over Gwen's head until she couldn't hear or think of anything else.

Then, silence. The buzzing abruptly stopped, and into the vacuum the living sound of the garden gently filled Gwen's ears. Gwen shifted and raised her head.

"What happened?"

She broke away from Aidan and held up her wrist between them. The bracelet was quiet and still at last. Was this when the magic would leach out from the metal? How long would it take to overcome her? Would it hurt, dying?

"Look," Tristan said. "The bracelet—it's crumbling."

The fine filigree of the bracelet disintegrated before their eyes, crumbling as if made of sand. It blew away in the breeze and dissipated into thin air. Before long, Gwen's wrist was bare.

Gwen's heart hammered in her chest.

"Is that it? Is it—gone? Am I going to be okay?"

Tristan beamed at her.

"Faolan must have deactivated it in time. You'll be fine."

Gwen gasped for breath, her chest suddenly far too small for her lungs. Tears of relief sprang to her eyes. Aidan threw his arms around her again and she clung to him. They rocked together.

"Let's go home," Gwen said after some time had passed. Aidan gave a shaky laugh.

"Yes, please. We've had enough Breenan madness for one week."

Chapter 14

Gwen's feet felt lighter than air during their walk back, through the now-overgrown garden and up the waving grasses of the meadow. The storm was passing without incident—rumbles of thunder grew most distant and the western sky lightened with an afternoon sun. She kept her hand firmly in Aidan's while they walked. Tristan swung his arms in the air repeatedly.

"It feels so good to be free of that ridiculous plant. I can move again, breathe again."

"We had visions of everyone we healed, and Rhiannon was walking by the end of hers," Aidan said.

"That's good news. I don't know how she would have handled not being able to walk. She's used to taking care of herself. She likes being independent, Rhiannon does."

"Really? I hadn't noticed." Aidan grinned at Gwen and squeezed her hand.

Aidan led them through the forest to the burbling stream where they had left Rhiannon. She waited for them on the path, satchel on her back and her face serene.

"Rhiannon!" Tristan bounded to her side and gave her a

swift hug, which she returned with a calm smile.

"Hello, brother. Miss me?"

"You're standing."

"The spell worked." She waved at her legs, healed underneath her shredded leggings. "Thank you, you two."

"It's so good to see you healed." Gwen stepped up and hugged the other girl, who returned the hug stiffly but sincerely.

"Thanks for your advice," Aidan said to Rhiannon, who nodded with a knowing smile. "I needed it."

"What advice?" Gwen asked.

"Oh, Rhiannon had some insight—on the spell."

"Let's go, get off this island." Tristan rubbed Rhiannon's shoulder. "I'm so glad to see you on your feet."

"Worried about me, were you?"

"I was mostly worried about who my hunting partner would be in the future."

"Of course you were." Rhiannon rolled her eyes with a smile, and pushed Tristan's shoulder. "You'd never catch anything without me." She turned to Gwen and Aidan who walked on the path behind the two siblings. "So? Do you plan to ever tell me how you managed to finish the quest, alive?"

"Oh, a bit of magic, a bit of creative thinking." Gwen outlined the events leading to the moment of restoration— the inscription, the tokens, the meadowsweet and its growth, the combined magic, the dissolution of the bracelet. When she finished the tale, Rhiannon and Tristan exchanged a glance.

"I don't think in a million years we'd have figured out the inscription, even if we could have read it," Rhiannon said. "And coming up with the growth spell on your own, without a spell transfer? I'm impressed. This was definitely a job for you two."

"The queens knew what they were doing when they set up the spell," Gwen said. "There's no way just a Breenan or just a human could have managed."

"Clever, really." Aidan looked around. "I wonder what other interesting spells are on this island. You and I seem to have a free pass here."

Gwen shoved her shoulder into his playfully.

"No. We're going home. The island can keep its secrets."

The trail back to the beach was uneventful. Gwen was hesitant when they reached the region with the blinding fog, but the air remained clear and no creatures attacked. The rope bridge took some careful navigating, but since Gwen had done it before, she knew she could do it again. She breathed easier once she had crossed, though. Hanging that high above a chasm was still highly unnerving.

Once at the beach, Aidan poked at the sad shell of their coracle with his foot.

"Do you reckon it will hold water long enough to row to the mainland?"

Rhiannon examined the coracle with a knowledgeable eye.

"Now that we're not hampered by an attacking sea serpent, we can spend time shoring up the holes. The putty was only a temporary fix, but we can do better. Tristan, fetch me some of that seaweed."

Tristan brought an armful of slimy brown kelp fronds from the tideline and dumped them at Rhiannon's feet. She nodded briskly and began to lay a piece of frond over each hole in the coracle.

"Anyone up for a melding spell? These holes won't mend themselves."

"If someone shows me how," Gwen said.

Tristan walked around the boat and placed two fingers of each hand on her temples. Gwen had a fleeting vision of a very young Tristan holding two pieces of frayed rope. She felt the sensation of the magic needed, deep in her core, as she watched the boy push the ends of the rope together. They merged into one solid cord. Tristan removed his hands.

"Got it?"

"I think so," Gwen said. She wiggled her fingers. "Let's find out."

Tristan moved to Aidan, and Gwen knelt next to Rhiannon. She touched one hand to a slippery piece of seaweed, and the other to the coracle's hide. The warmth of her core pulsed, and she drew up a small piece for the melding spell. The seaweed wriggled before her eyes and the edges melted to form a seamless bond with the animal skin beneath.

"It worked!"

Rhiannon looked at Gwen's handiwork.

"A bit rumpled, but it should hold."

Gwen gave her an exasperated glance and Rhiannon laughed.

"Good work, half-blood. We'll bring out the Breenan in you yet."

The coracle had so many holes that Gwen wondered how they had managed to land on the island at all. But with the four of them patching the gashes, it wasn't long before Rhiannon declared the little vessel seaworthy.

"It will take us to the shore, at least."

"That's all we need." Aidan peered toward the mainland. "Oh, look. We have an audience."

Gwen followed his gaze. A small crowd had gathered on the opposite shore. It was difficult to tell from this distance, but Gwen thought she recognized the fisherman they had bartered the boat from yesterday.

"So, who wants to paddle with the experts watching?" Aidan held out the paddle.

"But you're so good at it now." Tristan slapped Aidan on the back. "I wouldn't want to deprive you of a chance to show off your skills."

"Come on, you three." Rhiannon dragged the coracle into the water. The waves lapped at her calves, and loose tendrils of her leggings floated in the foam. "Stop jabbering."

Aidan muttered under his breath, but maneuvered to the front of the coracle. Gwen followed carefully, still sure they would tip at any moment.

"What a ridiculous design," she said to Aidan. "It's way too small and tipsy."

"Would you like a sailboat instead, with a nice deep keel?"

"That would do. Or maybe a ferry. Or a cruise ship."

"Or we could get to the mainland and not worry about the water anymore."

Rhiannon pushed off the shore and leaped into the coracle with light feet. Gwen leaned over the side to peer into the water.

"Are we sure there was only one sea serpent?"

"Not to worry," Tristan said. "We're expert sea serpent tamers now."

Gwen shuddered.

"I'm never going swimming again, after this."

When they drew close to the beach, the fisherman they had met yesterday called out to them.

"Welcome, travelers, serpent conquerors."

"I like the sound of that," Aidan said to Gwen. "I might have that printed on my business card."

Aidan paddled them to the beach, where the coracle scraped over rocky pebbles. Rhiannon leaped out and pulled the coracle ashore. The fisherman stepped up to speak with them, and his fellow villagers stared avidly.

"Never in my lifetime have I seen anyone conquer the serpent. The last time was in my father's grandfather's day. You fought bravely—we were watching."

"Everyone loves a train wreck," Aidan whispered to Gwen.

"Thank you for your kind words," Tristan said formally. "I hope that you may now travel these waters with greater safety than before."

The fisherman shook his head.

"I see you do not know the ways of a sea serpent. This one has undoubtedly laid an egg deep in the bay. When the blood of the mother sinks to touch the egg, it will hatch. Within a week, we will have to be wary once more. No matter. The serpent is contained between the rocks, and we stay out of its way."

He turned and beckoned to a villager who came forward with a bundle of fish wrapped in fresh green seaweed.

"A token of our respect, to help you enjoy your success tonight."

"We thank you," Rhiannon said. She gestured to the

coracle. "She's in poor condition, but I know you have the skill to fix her. May we leave her with you, with our thanks? We have no need of a boat where we're going."

The fisherman's eyes raked over the coracle appraisingly, and he nodded.

"It would be our pleasure."

The villagers watched them walk up the beach. Gwen looked back and caught the eye of a small child, who waved tentatively at her. She grinned and waved back.

"It's kind of fun being a minor celebrity," she said to Aidan.

"Mmm, especially when they provide dinner." Aidan looked longingly at the fishy bundle under Tristan's arm. "I'm starving."

Tristan turned back to them with amusement.

"We'll camp on the beach and leave in the morning. The fish will be ready as soon as you collect enough firewood."

"And what will you be doing, might I ask?"

"Watching you work, as befits the eldest."

"You're taking your brotherly duties a little too seriously," Aidan said. Tristan laughed and turned around. Quicker than blinking, Aidan snapped his fingers and flicked a ball of blue light forward. It hit the back of Tristan's head with a loud pop and a flurry of sparks. Tristan yelped and Rhiannon burst out laughing.

"He's definitely one of us."

***

After a meal of fresh fish steamed over coals in blankets of seaweed, beside the fire's glow in the darkening twilight, Gwen barely lay down next to Aidan before she fell asleep. She awoke to the sound of huffing and stamping.

"What's going on?" She squinted in the morning light. Large brown eyes looked down at her from above a long hairy nose. She blinked in surprise. "Where did the horses come from?"

"I called them back." Rhiannon attached the last of the saddlebags to the nearest horse. She tossed a piece of hard bread to Gwen, who caught it in fumbling hands. "Eat up. If we make good time, we can be at the Wintertree palace by late afternoon."

Aidan sat up next to her, his mouth open in a huge yawn. Gwen broke her bread and tucked half into his hand.

"The sergeant says to eat on the run. Come on, sleepy. Let's get on these infernal horses."

Aidan groaned.

"I forgot about the horses. Suddenly, I'm longing for the coracle, sea monster or no sea monster."

It only took an hour of riding before Gwen's bottom was as sore as her first ride, but she found she hardly minded. Her exhilaration over their triumph overshadowed the discomfort. They rode all morning, stopping only for a brief lunch of bread and fish under the sweeping awning of a riverside willow.

They crossed the border from the Longshore to the Wintertree realm early in the morning, and by midafternoon the town surrounding Faolan's castle appeared on the horizon. Gwen's teeth clenched at the sight.

"Do we have to go in?" she said to Aidan. "I don't have fond memories of our previous visit, and Faolan is the last person I want to see." She shivered with anger at the thought of Faolan's impassive face.

"It'll be different this time, I expect. We saved Bran's life. And don't forget, you'll want to see Bran."

"That's true, but I wish we didn't have to see his father as well."

The last hour passed by very slowly. Gwen's legs screamed at her, and her happiness at their success was tarnished by apprehension of the upcoming meeting with Faolan. Rhiannon was unperturbed as usual, and Tristan was effusive in his anticipation.

"I cannot wait for dinner. Faolan has the best cooks. Remember, Rhiannon, when we visited a few years ago and they served roast swan? That was incredible."

"Oh, stop it, Tristan," Aidan said. "I'm too hungry to hear about food."

A guard stopped them at the gate.

"Your name and business here?"

"Tristan, Rhiannon, and Aidan, children of Declan, and Gwendolyn, daughter of Isolde. We're here to speak to the king."

The guard nodded.

"You are expected. Please, follow me."

The guard led them through the town, a process Gwen found much less disturbing than the first time they had been dragged through. The townsfolk hardly looked at them this time, except to glance at Rhiannon's ragged leggings.

At the massive doors of the wooden palace, the guard passed them off to a servant. Gwen stepped into the dim cool of the grand entrance. Before she could adjust to the change in light, a shout made her jump.

"Gwen! Aidan!"

Copper hair and a beaming face enveloped her in a crushing hug before Bran moved to clap Aidan on the back.

"You're here! You made it. Hello, Tristan, Rhiannon." Bran looked around at them, his smile so wide that Gwen feared his face would split in two. "You saved me. I can't thank you enough. And now you're here! This will be the best night ever."

Bran's cheer was infectious. Gwen found herself grinning in response, and even Rhiannon cracked a smile.

"Come on, everyone. I'll take you to your rooms for the night." A servant trotted up and Bran waved him away impatiently. "No, I'll do it. I feel fine now." He said to them, "Father insists on having me watched to make sure I'm well again. But I feel wonderful. I don't know what was in that spell, but it worked." He jumped to Gwen's side and grabbed her hand with an uncharacteristically earnest look in his eye. "Gwen, I'm so sorry that Father put that bracelet on you. If I had had any say…"

"It's okay, Bran." Gwen patted his hand on hers. "You were out of it."

"I know, but to think—" Bran scowled. "Trust me, I had words with him when I found out."

Gwen laughed at the thought of anyone "having words" with Faolan. "You must be the favorite. I can't imagine many brave enough to stand up to your father."

Bran grinned, then ran ahead to a sweeping staircase to his right. A line of stuffed animal heads followed the curve of the stairs.

"Come on, I made sure that you four had the best rooms."

They followed Bran up the gleaming wooden steps and emerged on the second floor. A corridor ran the length of the building, where numerous doors interrupted the hall's paneling. The overwhelming timber of Faolan's mansion during Gwen's first visit had felt oppressive, but now struck her as warm and natural, like a mountain hunting lodge.

Bran opened the second door on his left with a flourish.

"Here, Gwen. You'll be in this room." He darted in before Gwen. She followed and stopped to blink.

The hunting lodge theme continued in this room, but it had a decidedly feminine slant. The wood paneling on the walls was of pale maple, with window frames and door lintel carved with a motif of roses. A huge bed stood foremost in the spacious room, spread with a coverlet of soft white furs that Gwen longed to touch. A chaise longue of soft almond suede, an imposing wardrobe, and a screen painted with a scene of four graceful deer completed the furnishings.

"Have a look," Bran said. He bounded to the wardrobe and threw open the doors. "You can wear this tonight, if you like it—we can find something different if you don't."

In the wardrobe hung a floor-length dress, sewn from a lightweight fabric whose color shimmered between warm silver and sandy brown. Its long sleeves flowed from a fitted bodice of tan leather with a flattering neckline lined by a thin strip of rich chestnut-colored fur. Gwen gaped.

"Wow, Bran. Is everyone else going to wearing the same sort of thing?"

"Oh, for sure. Don't you like it? We can find another one."

"No, no, it's beautiful." It was lovely, but Gwen was

258

sure she would feel out of place in the opulent gown. She sighed, then squared her shoulders and chided herself for her ingratitude. "Thanks, Bran."

"Perfect!" Bran moved to the door and motioned the others to follow. He turned and waved at the screen. "Oh, there's a bath back there. Someone will be by later to do your hair and take you to the feast. See you there."

Gwen waved at Aidan as he followed Bran with an air of bemusement. Once alone, she dropped her satchel on the chaise longue with a sigh of relief. A bath after their travels and trials? That was a task she would gladly complete.

***

Gwen had started to wonder whether she should leave her room to find Aidan when a knock on the door interrupted her thoughts. She swished over to open the ornate doorknob. A servant dressed in the livery of Faolan's house bowed to her.

"I am here to direct you to dinner, my lady."

"Thank you." The servant moved down the hall and Gwen noticed Aidan behind him. Aidan's eyes took her in.

"You look incredible. You wear Breenan styles as if you were born to it."

"You don't clean up so bad yourself." She took his offered arm and they followed the servant down the hall. Aidan wore suede pants and a loose shirt under a vest trimmed with velvety black fur. Gwen's heartbeat quickened at his warm herbal scent and the solid heat of his arm under hers.

"What did you do with the locket?" Aidan said. "You

259

know Bran will want to snitch it again."

"Oh, I know. That's why I left it in my bag."

They glided down the stairs and Gwen's dress swept elegantly behind them. This, more than anything, felt like she was in a true fairy tale. The quest, the obstacles, the sea monster—that was all too real. But waltzing down a palatial staircase in a faerie castle, dressed in a ball gown, on the arm of a handsome man? This was the dream that she would wake up from at any moment.

Servants stationed at a pair of massive double doors bowed and pushed them open wide to reveal the feast room.

"Pinch me," she whispered to Aidan. He laughed.

"Haven't you had enough trauma to last you a while? If this is a dream, then let's not wake up." He sniffed the air. "Not until we've eaten, at any rate."

The hall in which they had first encountered Faolan had been transformed. Night darkened the immense windows, but thousands and thousands of dancing white lights glowed through the translucent glass like stars. They lent the scene below an ethereal air, somehow not at odds with the gleaming wood floors. Long tables were decorated with huge displays of autumnal foliage, bright gourds, and tapered candles with warm golden flames. The people of the court sported rich furs and sumptuous leathers, topped with shifting veils of fabric in burnt orange and fiery red to match the displays. Leaves drifted magically from the ceiling to give the impression of the feast taking place in a twilit autumn forest.

Faolan stood at the far end of the room, behind a long table dotted with elaborate candelabras and swags of glossy green ivy. He beckoned to Gwen and Aidan, and walked around to stand in front of the table. Gwen gulped and Aidan squeezed her arm against his side.

"Looks like we've been summoned."

"I don't think I'm brave or foolish enough to decline." Gwen raised her chin. "Come on, let's run this gauntlet."

They stepped forward. Chatter in the hall quieted as they passed, and dozens of eyes burned into Gwen's back. She kept her eyes to the front. Not at Faolan, but at the swirling lights in the window beyond him. She was still angry at Faolan and didn't wish for any more interaction with him than was strictly necessary.

When they stopped ten paces away from Faolan and Gwen finally looked at him, he spoke.

"Aidan, son of Declan, and Gwendolyn, daughter of Isolde. You are most welcome here. You are honored guests at this banquet, the celebration of my son's recovery from his terrible malady. As the architects of his recovery, I cannot thank you enough." He gestured with his hand and two servants glided to him from the side of the room. Each held an angular object wrapped in a covering of soft leather. "Nevertheless, I hope you will accept these tokens of my gratitude for your part in Prince Bran's healing. For you, Aidan, I present this instrument." He unfolded the leather from one of the objects. Nestled inside was a flute of a strange, antique style, fashioned from dark wood with burnished golden keys. "It was my son's idea—he mentioned your way with music."

Aidan's jaw dropped. He held out his hands when Faolan offered him the flute, and wrapped his fingers around it reverentially.

"It's beautiful."

"It was brought to this realm many centuries ago by a

half-blood famed in the human world for his music. It has been kept in the treasury since then, but an instrument unplayed is an instrument wasted. May it sound sweet melodies for you."

"Thank you. Thank you so much." Aidan stepped back and ran his fingers up and down the length of the flute. Gwen could tell he itched to try it out.

"And for you, Gwendolyn." Faolan unwrapped the second bundle. "A gift worthy of your mother's daughter."

Candlelight fell upon the object within the leather, which sparkled with a hundred refracted lights. A rose gold tiara shone, its front crowned by a glittering pendant of cut emeralds and blue sapphires that gave the appearance of delicate blue flowers surrounded by deep green leaves. Gwen gasped.

"That's for me?"

"Indeed." Faolan tilted his head as if evaluating her reaction. "You may have need of it one day." Before Gwen could ask what he meant, Faolan held the tiara out to her.

"You have saved my son's life, and brought peace to the Velvet Woods and the Nine Realms. Please accept this gift."

She traced the precious stones with her finger, marveling. Then she frowned.

"Thank you very much. I'm grateful. But I still think it was unjust of you to put the bracelet on me."

Aidan stiffened beside her, but Gwen was undeterred. It needed to be said. She had a feeling that Faolan wouldn't do anything to them, not with Bran watching.

Faolan's expression did not change, but he said, "It was the action of a distraught father, in fear for his son's life. It was not just, but we are all fortunate that you have a strength in you to prevail against all odds." He spread his left arm toward a nearby table. "Please, sit and enjoy the feast."

Gwen nodded and they turned to the table. That was as close to an apology as she was likely to get from Faolan. She fingered the tiara in its leather, wondering. It was beautiful, and probably worth more than she could imagine, but what would she do with it? And why might she need it some day?

She put her questions aside when she spotted Tristan, Rhiannon, and Bran seated at a small table below the head table. Bran waved them over.

"Father wanted us at the head table, but it's far too stuffy up there. I thought it'd be more fun if we had our own table."

"I'm starting to get the feeling that whatever Bran wants, Bran gets," Gwen said. Bran laughed.

"It's hard being me sometimes, but I manage."

Bran was in high form. He entertained them with stories of recent exploits and pranks played on his elder brothers, and kept them laughing throughout course after course of exotic dishes with spices Gwen had never tasted before. Even Rhiannon sputtered out her soup laughing at one of Bran's tales.

Eventually the talk came around to Bran's mishap in the human world.

"I had no idea you were so far away, Gwen." Bran picked a fig up from a platter of dried fruits and popped it in his mouth. Through his chewing he said, "Is the human world larger than this one?"

"Don't be silly, Bran," Rhiannon said. "No one here

has traveled far enough into the western ocean, that's all."

"Well, the human world was fun while I was there." Bran gazed reflectively into his goblet. "Whatever happened to the locket, Gwen?"

Gwen shot a half-glance at Aidan, who raised an eyebrow. She said, "I used it as a token to heal Isolde's realm in the restoration spell. It was destroyed by the magic."

Rhiannon looked surprised, but said nothing. Gwen had handed back Tristan's intact tracker ring as soon as they had met up with her on the island. Tristan, eyeing a pretty Breenan girl at the next table, didn't appear to hear.

Gwen figured it would be safer for Bran if he didn't try to steal the locket from her again. She didn't want to go through another deadly obstacle course the next time he tried his luck in her world.

"Pity," Bran said with a sigh. "There was so much I hadn't yet explored."

Chapter 15

Gwen had a hard time waking up in the morning. They had gone to bed just before the full moon set below the horizon, surrounded by dancing lights in the hall's windows. The late morning sun poured in through her open curtains, highlighting rich ambers and chestnuts of furs strewn across her floor.

Eventually, she made herself roll out of bed and get dressed. She tucked her new treasure in its leather envelope into her satchel after peeking inside to make sure it was still real. An emerald gleam convinced her it was.

She peered her head out the door, wondering where to go. A passing servant immediately came to her aid.

"You will find your party at the stable entrance, my lady. Down the stairs and to your right."

Was everyone waiting for her? Gwen ran down the steps. A narrow hallway to her right led to an open door, through which jangling of reins and huffing of horses filtered. Gwen burst through into a vast, cavernous stable, with at least fifty stalls for horses on either side of a wide corridor that led to an outside door. The dusty scent of hay and warm horse drifted past her nostrils.

Tristan and Rhiannon saddled horses in front of her while Bran attached full saddlebags. Aidan leaned against the nearest wall and crunched an apple. A nearby horse watched him enviously.

"Good morning, sleeping beauty." He offered her an apple. "Hungry?"

"I never thought I'd be hungry again after that meal, but yeah, actually, I am." She bit into the green skin. "Thanks."

Tristan patted his horse's flank.

"Since we're all here and accounted for, finally," he winked at Gwen. "We might as well push off. Good to see you, Bran. Don't be a stranger."

"Oh, I won't. Father wants me to start border patrols. It will probably be a bore, but I'll pass your way soon, I don't doubt." He swung around to face Gwen and Aidan. "As for you two, you had better visit. Especially since I can't come say hello to you anymore." He looked so abnormally woeful that Gwen couldn't help but laugh.

"How could I refuse that face? We will try to visit again someday." She hugged him, and Aidan and Bran exchanged a Breenan farewell, with hands clasped to each other's heads and foreheads touching.

"I'll see you soon, cousin," Bran said to Aidan. "Make sure of it."

"We'll make it happen," Aidan said. He turned to look at his horse, and sighed. "Back in the saddle. I'll never complain about the bus again."

Whether from good company, or a short journey, Gwen was surprised when Declan's cottage came into view across a meadow. Dry grasses waved in the warm breeze of the hot noon sun. A child playing outside noticed them first, and shouted into the house before he ran through the grass to them. Tristan bent down and swung the boy up to sit in front of him. The child shrieked and giggled.

More children poured out from the open doorway and from behind the cottage. Declan appeared from inside and shaded his eyes. Once satisfied of their identity, he strode forward with open arms.

"Welcome back! Prince Crevan sent word when you set off to Isle Caengal, telling us of your quest." Tristan and Rhiannon leaped off their horses and Declan hugged them swiftly. Aidan slid off his saddle more slowly and stayed by his horse, fidgeting.

"You prevailed," Declan said. "You must tell me everything."

"Well, we helped," Tristan said. "But Aidan and Gwen really saved the day. Without their human skills—"

"And Breenan magic," Rhiannon said.

"And magic, we wouldn't be standing here today, and Bran would be dead for certain."

"It was a team effort," Gwen said with a smile. "That was the point of the island, after all."

Declan looked at Aidan with pride. Aidan flushed.

"I'm not surprised at your triumph. Congratulations, Aidan, Gwen." He pointed to the cottage. "Please, come in and make yourselves at home."

Aidan glanced at Gwen, and she tried to say with her eyes that it was his decision.

"Thank you, but we should be getting back. We've already been away longer than we meant to. Mum will be worrying."

Declan looked disappointed, but tried to hide it.

"Of course, I understand. I wouldn't want you to keep Deirdre waiting. But you know you are welcome at any time? My home is your home, whenever you desire it."

Aidan finally looked at Declan and smiled at him for the first time.

"Thanks. If we ever come back, I might take you up on that."

"You'd better," Tristan said. "It's not every day I find a new brother who isn't knee-high. You make sure you come back and visit your family. We'll be here."

Rhiannon stepped forward and gave Aidan, then Gwen, a hug.

"Good luck with your new adventures," she whispered in Gwen's ear. "It will work out."

"Thanks, Rhiannon." Gwen hugged her back fiercely, then embraced Tristan. She was surprised at how attached she had grown to these two. It was a shock to realize that she wouldn't see them again for a long while, if ever.

"Please, take the horses," Declan said. "You will travel far more swiftly with them."

"We can't do that," Aidan said at once. "What would we do with them when we leave?"

Declan laughed.

"They know their way home. Set them loose. They will come back eventually."

Gwen and Aidan rode away from an enthusiastic farewell party. Children waved and called out, and Declan watched them until they rounded the top of a hill and the cottage was lost to sight.

Aidan sighed.

"Is it strange, leaving?" Gwen asked him. "Now that you know your father, and all your siblings?"

"I suppose. I'll miss Tristan and Rhiannon, but I'm not sure how I feel about Declan. It's hard to let go of years of resentment. But I'm still glad I met him. And I know where he is, where they all are, if I ever want to be surrounded by more family than I know what to do with."

Gwen chuckled.

"Can you imagine if they celebrated Christmas here? What mayhem."

***

They made much better time heading southwest, on horseback and without the burden of Bran. At Gwen's insistence, they skirted Leafly and other towns on the way. Bran had made sure their bags were packed with far more food and drink than they needed, and the fewer interactions with Breenan, the safer Gwen felt. By early evening, they reached the borders of the Velvet Woods, a journey which had taken them a full day on foot previously.

Aidan shifted in his saddle with a groan and peered into the woods.

"I don't see any mist. What a concept—a forest that isn't inherently eerie."

"I guess the defenses and spells are back up, now that the realm is restored." Gwen nudged her horse forward, eager to see Isolde's recovery with her own eyes. And then back to the human world, back to normal life. She looked forward to it. "I forgot how pretty the forest is with the spells on. Hey, look, a butterfly."

"Is that a deer?" Aidan pointed to his left. In dappled light from the slanted evening sun, a deer watched them

269

placidly. Another stepped forward to join it, and together they trod with silent hooves into the undergrowth.

"That's a good sign," Gwen said. "Now the villagers can feed themselves."

"What's the plan? Do you want to see Isolde before we go home?"

"Yeah, I think so. Just to see with my own eyes that she's okay. Not that I'm expecting a warm welcome, but it would be nice to know my way into the Otherworld is still alive and kicking."

Aidan nudged his horse beside hers, and held out his hand. She grasped it, grateful for the connection.

"Do you think she'll give you some jewelry to go with that tiara of yours?"

"Ha, I doubt it. The last time she gave me a necklace, the realm fell apart. And what am I going to do with the tiara, anyway? It's gorgeous, and definitely worth more than anything I've ever owned, but really."

"Keepsake, I suppose. Fancy dress party?"

"Right. The next time I'm invited to a ball, I'll wear it. Because that happens so often in Vancouver."

"Really?"

Gwen rolled her eyes at Aidan and he grinned.

"I'll leave my three-piece suit at home, then."

***

The path, now that it was cleared and widened by magic, led them straight to Isolde's castle. Pennants flew from crenellated towers, and the open doors spilled music into the surrounding forest.

"This looks a little too familiar," Gwen said.

270

"I know. I'm getting traumatic flashbacks. Come on, let's say hello to your dear mama."

Gwen climbed the steps with trepidation. She knew everything was different this time, but memories of their visit here in the spring kept intruding. Fear was the primary ingredient in her recollections.

Inside the ballroom, nothing was different from the first time Gwen had seen it. The same tapestries lined the stone walls, miraculously restored from their moth-eaten state of a week ago. The same company danced in splendid gowns and suits of colorful feathers and jewels. An orchestra of Breenan musicians played a waltz in the corner. Gwen frowned.

"I thought they wouldn't dance anymore. How is Isolde getting new musical talent without the locket?"

"Thanks to you, dear Gwendolyn, the restoration spell now powers the realm." Isolde's rich voice spoke beside them, and Gwen whirled around. Isolde stood smiling at her in an opulent ball gown of deep plum with large garnet earrings. Her dark hair was glossy, and the white stripe at her temple gleamed brightly. She waved at the dancers. "This is perhaps unnecessary, but I do love dancing."

She glided forward and picked up Gwen's hands in both her own. Gwen stiffened.

"You saved the realm, Gwendolyn. You are truly a daughter any mother would be proud to have."

Gwen sighed. Isolde's affection could only be earned, never freely given. Gwen didn't expect anything better, but it was disheartening all the same.

"I wanted to make sure you were okay." Gwen looked around the room. "Looks like everything is in order."

"For now." Corann stepped forward from behind

271

Isolde. He looked Gwen up and down with his mouth twisted, as if a bitter taste lingered on his tongue. "The spell won't last forever. There is no basis for our defenses beyond it."

"Oh, Corann. So gloomy." Isolde laughed lightly and touched his elbow. "Rejoice, and enjoy what we have. You should be grateful to Gwendolyn for repelling enemies on our borders and for bringing me back to health. This is a happy day."

Corann bowed stiffly.

"Today is a happy day, but what of tomorrow? Excuse me, my lady, but I cannot celebrate when our happiness is only an illusion." He turned on his heel and strode away into the crowd.

Gwen glanced at Aidan, who shrugged. Isolde brushed off Corann's words with a wave of her hand.

"Don't mind him. I am very grateful for what you've done for us. Is there anything I can do?"

"No, thanks." Gwen backed away. She didn't want anything from Isolde. Taking the locket had resulted in their most recent trials. There was nothing she needed from her, and she didn't want to risk a repeat of recent history. "We'll go now. Take care of yourself, Isolde."

"You too, my daughter." Isolde smiled graciously at her as they backed through the door. "Safe travels."

"That was odd," Aidan said once they had walked down the steps.

"Did you expect anything better?"

"No, I meant about Corann. I wonder how long the restoration spell will last. Isolde didn't seem that fussed."

Gwen shrugged.

"We've done what we can. They have to figure it out

now. They have a fighting chance."

"That's the spirit," Aidan said with approval. "See? You don't have to take on the weight of the world, at least not every day." Aidan unstrapped his backpack from his horse, who nibbled nonchalantly at the grass. Gwen did the same and they watched the horses for a minute.

"Do you think they'll make it back?" Gwen said.

"Hopefully. Eventually." Aidan looked uncertain, then shook his head. "This is what Declan told us to do. Not our worry, right?"

"Right. Okay, I guess it's portal time. Are you ready?"

"More than ready. After you, my lady."

"One moment, if you will." A familiar voice spoke from behind them. Gwen peered into the trees in the dim evening light.

"Loniel?"

"Hello, little birds," Loniel said. The wild man from their first visit stood before them in the shadows. His mouth opened in a wide smile that was somehow not reassuring. A patchwork cape of uncountable shades of green over an open-necked shirt exposed the multitude of tattoos that Gwen knew covered his entire torso. They had first met Loniel on their previous visit to the Otherworld when he had rescued them from Isolde's forest and brought them to his bonfire. Loniel had then contrived for Gwen and Aidan to receive their Breenan marks. His tawny eyes examined them. "I heard of your exploits, and watched carefully as this realm faded and then bloomed once again. You did a brave and wonderful thing, and the people of this realm are happier for it. For now."

"That's what Corann said. What's going to happen? Why won't the spell work for long?" An unpleasant thought occurred to Gwen. "Wait, will our friends stay healed?"

"Restoration of a body, from broken to whole, is a relatively simple matter for magic that powerful. But restoration of an entire realm, and maintenance of everything that the realm relies on magic to provide, well, that is no small feat. The Velvet Woods has been given a reprieve, but it will not be long before a new regime is needed. And, I fear, Isolde is not the woman to usher in that new regime."

"What do you mean? Who else would?"

Loniel half-closed his eyes and gazed at her in consideration.

"Some would say that you are a natural choice for the succession. The queen has no other children, no other family."

Gwen let out a laugh of shock.

"You've got to be kidding. Me?" She glanced at Aidan, who looked bewildered, then back to Loniel, who hadn't reacted to her outburst. "But I'm half-human. I don't belong here."

Loniel gave her a sad smile that didn't reach his eyes.

"You can belong wherever you want to belong." He pierced her with his golden eyes, and Gwen remembered that Loniel had been banished from his father's world, and had had to live here in the Otherworld forevermore. She swallowed.

"I don't want to be here." She grabbed Aidan's hand and held on firmly. "I want to be in the human world."

"That is a different reason, and an understandable one. But Isolde will not last forever on a throne that is now supported by little more than air and illusion. I wished to warn you, and give you the choice you are entitled to." His breath caught, and an arrested look passed over his face. "The locket, little bird. Do you have it still? May I see it?"

Gwen silently dug the golden necklace out of her pocket and held it out on her palm. Loniel did not take it, but touched the dried blood encrusted between the patterns of vines, blood spilled deliberately by Isolde many months ago. He backed away and smiled a secret smile. "Farewell. I am sure we will meet again one day."

One moment Loniel was there. The next, only tranquil undergrowth lay before their gaze. Gwen shivered.

"Can we go home now?" she said to Aidan.

"Please."

She pulled out magic from her warm core, thought of her father, and ripped open a portal. The welcome sight of a paved road greeted them.

"Britain, there you are," Aidan said with feeling, and they stepped through the portal and back into their world.

Chapter 16

It was less than a mile's walk to Amberlaine from the small village they had arrived in. Gwen relished the cool evening air and Aidan's warm hand as they walked.

"Do you reckon Faolan knew?" Aidan said after a car rumbled past.

"Knew what?"

"About the spell not working for long, for Isolde's realm. Perhaps that's why he gave you the tiara."

"That would make sense. Breenan never say what they mean, do they? Honestly, Loniel's warning was the most straightforward I've ever heard him speak. But what does he expect me to do? Give up my life here and move to the Velvet Woods, and wear a ball gown and tiara for the rest of my life? The idea is so ridiculous, it's laughable."

"I agree. I don't see why anyone should expect you to take over Isolde's throne. I'm sure there is someone who would rather do it. Besides, hereditary monarchies are overrated. Perhaps they should try democracy for a change."

Gwen laughed. Loniel's words had shaken her, but

Aidan's common sense brought her back to reality.

"Could you imagine Isolde's face if we tried to describe how voting works?"

***

The stars had begun to wink into existence above them when they approached Deirdre's house. Gwen was apprehensive, and she looked down at her clothes.

"What are you going to say to your mum? I don't even remember where my backpack went. My sleeping bag is still in my satchel, here, but that's about it."

"She doesn't use it. It'll be fine, don't worry. We won't give her time to notice." He knocked on the door and opened it to peek his head in. "Mum?"

"Aidan!" Deirdre bustled into view. "You're back. How was camping?"

"Oh, it was good fun."

"What are you wearing?"

"Ah, something new." He hurriedly pecked Deirdre on the cheek. "Mum, could I borrow your car to drop Gwen off at her aunt's?"

"Oh. Yes, of course." She rummaged on a side table by the door. Before she handed the keys over, she asked, "And where does Gwen's aunt live, exactly?"

"She's in Cambridge. Not far at all," Gwen reassured her.

"All right. Mind yourself with the car, and I'm looking forward to hearing about your trip, Aidan." She looked at her son with a hopeful expression.

"I'll be right back, Mum. I promise."

***

On the drive to Cambridge, Gwen turned to Aidan.

"Promise me you'll spend some time with your mum before you fly out, okay?"

"Sure," he said. He looked a little confused.

"I don't need another reason to feel bad that you're coming to Vancouver, that's all."

"Oh, Gwen. I thought we'd figured this out."

"Just spend some time with her. She'll like it."

"I'd planned to, but thanks for the reminder. It'll be strange when I'm gone—I usually have dinner with her a few times a week. And now I won't see her until Christmas." He looked pensive. "She'll be all right, though. My aunt lives nearby. It'll be fine."

Gwen reached out to stroke his hair.

"Just leave on good terms, and don't forget to call her lots. I promised her you would."

Aidan looked at her askance.

"Teaming up on me already, are you?"

"Girl talk. Nothing you need to worry about." She leaned back in the seat. "One more week, and you'll be in Vancouver."

"Yes, I will." He pulled over in front of her aunt's house. "A new chapter. A new life." He put a tentative hand on her knee and she shivered pleasantly. Their eyes met. "And new kisses?"

"Those never get old," she said, and leaned forward to put her lips to his.

Dear reader,

I hope you enjoyed reading *Garden of Last Hope* as much as I enjoyed writing it. Gwen and her friends had only just started their adventures in *Mark of the Breenan*, and I was keen to get them back to the Otherworld.

I have a favor to ask of you. If you're so inclined, I'd love a review of *Garden of Last Hope*. If you loved it, if you hated it, if you're somewhere in the middle—I want to know what you think. I write because Gwen and her friends won't leave me alone, but I also write for you, dear reader. Reviews are difficult to come by, and you have the power to make or break a book. You can find my book list if you search for my name on Amazon and on Goodreads.

If you enjoyed Gwen's adventures in the Otherworld, keep your eye on my webpage or sign up for my newsletter at emmashelford.com where you can receive news of upcoming releases and sneak peeks.

Happy reading!
Emma Shelford

Titles by Emma Shelford

Breenan Series
> *Mark of the Breenan*
> *Garden of Last Hope*

Musings of Merlin Series
> *Ignition*
> *Winded* (due 2017)

Acknowledgements

As always, my editors deserve a big thank you: Gillian Brownlee, Wendy and Chris Callendar, Jude Powell, and Lynda Powell. Christien Gilston worked his magic on the book cover. My husband, Steven Shelford, always deserves thanks for his support. And last but not least, I thank Oliver Shelford for being such a good napper and giving me time to write.

About the Author

Emma Shelford is the author of *Mark of the Breenan* of the Breenan Series, and *Ignition* of the Musings of Merlin Series. She adores fantasy and history, which makes writing these series such a joy. She lives in Victoria, BC with her husband and young son.

44389490R00172

Made in the USA
Middletown, DE
05 June 2017